ON THE RIGHT PATH

HOME TO HEATHER CREEK

On the RIGHT PATH

Diann Hunt

Guideposts
NEW YORK, NEW YORK

Home to Heather Creek is a trademark of Guideposts.

Guidepost.org
(800) 932-2145
Guideposts Books & Inspirational Media

Cover by Lookout Design, Inc.
Interior design by Cindy LaBreacht
Typeset by Nancy Tardi
Printed in the United States of America
10 9 8 7 6 5 4 3

Acknowledgments

Special thanks to Beth Adams and Fiona Serpa for their ability to blow away the debris and find the gold. You both are amazing and I am blessed to be on your team! Thanks also to my critique partner, Colleen Coble, for her keen insight and constant encouragement. My world is a better place because of you. And finally, a huge, heartfelt thanks to you, the readers, who graciously give of your time to take this journey with me. Hope you enjoy it!

And thanks to my Monday Mentors, who truly have taught me that we can make a difference in the daily things of life. I am blessed to call you friends!

—Diann Hunt

Home to Heather Creek

Before the Dawn

Sweet September

Circle of Grace

Homespun Harvest

A Patchwork Christmas

An Abundance of Blessings

Every Sunrise

Promise of Spring

April's Hope

Seeds of Faith

On the Right Path

ON THE RIGHT PATH

Chapter One

Please don't bang the—" The metal screen slammed against the wooden frame. "Door." Charlotte Stevenson shook her head.

The sweet scent of early summer wafted in along with her tall, leggy granddaughter.

"Sorry about the door, Grandma. Can Ashley come over?" Emily Slater's quick words crowded together like corn on a cob. She paused to take in a deep breath.

Oh, to have such energy. Though Charlotte couldn't complain. For someone in her sixties, she did all right. Charlotte put down her cup of coffee and stared at her blossoming granddaughter, who wanted desperately to be older than her fifteen years. "Ashley may come over once you get your chores finished."

"But—" One look at Charlotte and Emily clamped her mouth shut. She simply rolled her eyes and stomped away.

Hannah Carter, Charlotte's neighbor and dear friend, dropped her hand from her mouth, revealing a smile. "For a twig of a thing, you've sure got a good bark."

"Twig? Bark?" Charlotte groaned.

Hannah laughed at herself.

"Besides, I didn't bark. I merely told her she had to finish her chores." Charlotte didn't think she'd barked. She hadn't raised her voice, after all, but merely kept it firm. "As I was saying about that recipe—"

"Grandma, would you tell Sam it's my turn to watch what I want on TV?" Her grandson Christopher didn't have much to say, but when he did, it was time to listen.

Charlotte frowned. "Sam is still watching TV?"

Christopher gave a reluctant nod, looking as though he wondered if he should have told on his brother after all.

"We'll see about that," Charlotte said, scooting out from her chair. "I'll be right back, Hannah." She imagined herself in a military uniform. Not the look she was going for. She hated being a disciplinarian, and didn't appreciate the kids forcing her into that role.

Hands on hips, she faced him down. "Sam?"

He didn't so much as flinch.

"Sam." Her voice was stronger this time. He looked up.

"Yeah?" Dressed in jeans, a T-shirt, and a ball cap, Sam stretched out his long legs and leaned back in the chair. Throw him some junk food and he was set to roost for the summer.

Charlotte picked up the remote and clicked off the television. She measured her words and gently said, "We told you kids you had to find something constructive to do with your time this summer. That doesn't include a lot of TV." She put down the remote. "Are your chores done?"

Wearing a scowl, he nodded.

"Remember our talk about getting a job this summer? Monday is as good a day as any to go out and look for something." This time her words were crisper than she had intended, but the time had come for a responsibility check.

"Come on, Grandma, there's nothing out there."

"How do you know? Have you tried applying anywhere?" Just because he'd lost his last job didn't give him the right to lie around all summer. "Sometimes you just have to push yourself, Sam. At the very least, you could go out and see if your Uncle Pete needs help."

With obvious reluctance, he heaved himself out of the wide-seated chair with a grunt. Charlotte had seen sick cows with more energy than that boy was showing. He mumbled his way out the back door.

She turned to Christopher. His eyes grew wide, reminding Charlotte of their milk cow, Trudy. "The horses are in the corral. I'd better go check on them." His sneakers practically burned rubber as he made a hasty exit. It was all she could do not to laugh.

"You handled that very well," Hannah said, tucking a loose strand into her gray-tinged blonde hair.

Charlotte watched after Christopher, dropped her hands from her hips, and sighed. "I don't know what I will do to occupy those children all summer."

"It sounds as though you're on the right track. They'll find something. Kids always do." Hannah placed her hand on Charlotte's shoulder. "Denise would be proud of you."

Charlotte sighed. "I don't know." She wondered if her deceased daughter would be happy with the job she and Bob were doing with the kids.

"It's plenty to deal with, losing a parent. Those children are blessed to have you for grandparents. At least they get to stay with family," Hannah said.

"Yeah, family they hardly know. We should have made more trips to California."

"I've never been a whiz at geography, but if I'm not mistaken, Nebraska isn't exactly next-door neighbors with California. And everyone knows farming requires a lot of time."

"Thanks, Hannah. You always make me feel better."

Hannah glanced at her watch. "Oh, I need to go. I promised Lydia Middleton I would come over and do her laundry for her."

"Is she all right?"

"Well," Hannah laughed, "considering that she's eighty-eight, she's doing just fine. Up till now she'd been doing her own cleaning around the house. Now it's getting to her. She's decided to hire someone to come in a couple of days a week to clean for her, but she can't seem to find anyone." Hannah shrugged. "I figured I could go help out once in a while."

Charlotte thought on that, wondering how she could help. With all the work at the farm and watching over the kids, she had her hands full these days.

"Do you suppose Miss Middleton would let the girls help her out? You know, Emily and Ashley?"

Hannah brightened. "I think that's a great idea. Teenagers could always use some money, and it would help her out at the same time."

Charlotte nodded. "I think you're right. I'll give her a call."

"See you later," Hannah said with a wave.

Hannah had no sooner disappeared through the front door than Emily sailed down the stairs and announced, "Ashley will be here any minute. I'll wait for her outside, and she'll help me finish the chores."

"But—" The back door slammed again.

Charlotte turned to their dog, Toby. "Something tells me this is going to be a long summer."

"THAT WAS A GOOD SUPPER, CHAR," Bob said, patting his belly. "It's been awhile since we've had pork chops. Mighty tasty."

"Thank you," Charlotte said pleasantly.

"Too bad Emily didn't save me more vegetables." He frowned and Charlotte laughed.

"She has to make up for not eating the meat, I guess."

"I guess," he said with a grunt. "Imagine, living on a farm and not eating meat." He shook his head. "Kids today."

After all these years, her heart still warmed to her husband. The sleeve of his T-shirt had slid up his arm a bit, revealing the tan line of a new farming season. Though it was only June, the sun had started working on Bob Stevenson in early spring, its golden rays deepening his skin tone throughout the summer. The recliner footrest held his long legs in midair while he clicked the TV remote and peered over his bifocals at the screen.

The soft glow of lamplight shone on Charlotte's small

embroidery stitches. The smell of fresh linen lifted from a nearby candle. If there was one thing a farmhouse could use it was candles. Nice fragrances wafting throughout the rooms were always welcome.

"Aren't you going walking with Hannah tonight?" Bob asked.

"No, she and Frank had a meeting for the church food pantry." Charlotte was actually thankful for the reprieve. She had baked several pies that afternoon for a couple of shut-ins from their church and had hung some laundry on the line to dry. With her aching back and tired feet, she was more than ready to sink back into the sofa and work on her embroidery.

"They sure do a good job keeping that pantry stocked," Bob said.

Charlotte nodded and worked her brown thread into the soft cotton. The kids had made quick work of kitchen duty. Sam and his friend Arielle had gone out for a soda; Emily and Ashley listened to the radio in her bedroom, and most likely talked about boys. She laid aside her stitching and walked over to the window to check on Christopher. She spotted him throwing a stick and Toby running after it. The scene made her smile. Christopher had really taken to Toby. Funny how animals could sometimes get people through their pain. She walked back to her chair.

The kids are accounted for, so why am I downcast, Lord? Is it merely because I'm tired? Are we too old to be raising teenagers? Please help us, Father. Grant us wisdom and strength.

I would ask you to help me with patience, but I'm afraid to pray for that one.

Just then tires crunched pebbles in the driveway and a car engine cut to silence. Bob and Charlotte exchanged a glance.

"Sam just left, so it shouldn't be him." Charlotte stuck the needle back into her embroidery piece, laid it on the table, and walked over to the door, where she spotted the silver Toyota sedan. "It's Bill, Anna, and the girls," she called back to Bob. As tired as she was, energy surged through her at the sight of them.

Charlotte slipped through the screen door to greet them. Seven-year-old Madison and five-year-old Jennifer tumbled out of the car and bounded up the stairs to meet their grandma. With arms open wide, Charlotte pulled them both into an enormous hug.

"Have you had your dinner?" she asked.

With eagerness shining in their eyes, they shook their heads vigorously. They knew what was coming next. This was a customary ritual they practiced each time they came to Grandma's house.

"Guess it's okay to open up the cookie jar, Anna?" Charlotte looked to Anna, who smiled and nodded but added, "Only a couple, girls."

The girls scurried to the kitchen as fast as their pudgy little legs could carry them.

"No decent grandma would be caught without cookies," Charlotte said with a laugh. She gave Anna and Bill a hug, and then they all made their way into the house.

The girls filled up on chocolate chip cookies, downed with chilled milk, and then dashed out to the barn to play with the cats and Christopher—most likely in that order.

Charlotte studied her daughter-in-law as she sat on the sofa beside her husband. Dark hair pulled up off her neck into an elegant twist on the back of her head, makeup applied to perfection as always, a navy pantsuit with stylish matching shoes and a beautiful diamond pendant adorning her graceful neck—she looked every inch a politician's wife. But something telling shone in her blue eyes tonight. Charlotte couldn't put her finger on it, but something . . .

"What brings you over on a Monday night? Did you have business in Bedford?" Guilt pricked Charlotte for pretending innocence when she knew good and well she was fishing for information.

Bill and Anna exchanged a glance.

She knew it. Something was up.

"Dad, would you mind turning off the TV a minute?"

Bob blinked, reluctantly picked up the remote and clicked off the TV.

Bill definitely had their attention now. Charlotte might have been concerned but for the glow on their faces. She had no idea what it could be. Maybe they had bought a new home, or Bill had decided to run for office again next term, or—

"We're going to have another baby," Anna said, threading her arm through Bill's and grinning from ear to ear.

Charlotte hadn't seen *that* one coming. She clapped her hands together and then stood up to hug them both. "That's wonderful news!"

"Great news, kids," Bob said. He reached for the remote control, but Charlotte shot him a look. He put it back down.

"We are thrilled," Anna said. "I'm due in late December," she smiled. "I've already scheduled a contractor to start renovations on the house."

"Oh?" Charlotte said. "Renovations?"

"Well, we hadn't planned on another little one, after all," Anna said flushing. "And we just don't have the room for another nursery."

Charlotte glanced at Bill, who wasn't saying much. His smile seemed to dip momentarily but then immediately bounced back into place.

"Couldn't you move the girls into one room and make a nursery out of the other?" Charlotte looked from Bill back to Anna.

Anna looked positively stricken. "Oh no. The girls need their own rooms."

"Oh, I see." But, of course, Charlotte didn't see at all. She had always been quite frugal, so the idea of the girls *having* to have their own rooms seemed foreign to her way of thinking. Nothing wrong with it, she supposed, as long as they had the means to afford such luxuries. Besides, she could hardly point a finger. They had been blessed to raise their children in this big old farmhouse with plenty of room for a growing family. Little had she known that one day she would need the room for her grandkids.

"Hey, everybody." Charlotte and Bob's younger son, Pete, walked into the family room with a cookie in hand.

"Where did you get that?" Charlotte asked.

He grinned. "Madison snuck a couple of them into the barn with her. I managed to finagle one from her." Pete slumped down at the other end of the sofa.

"So, what are you doing here on a Monday night, big brother?"

"Thought we'd drop in and tell Mom and Dad the news."

Pete turned to him. "Yeah? Did your goose lay another golden egg?"

Tension filled the moment. Charlotte regretted that her boys had a bit of competition between them—well, at least on Pete's part. Couldn't he understand that she and Bob loved both of them? What did he want Bill to do, apologize for becoming a lawyer and making a life for himself?

"Pete, don't you start," Charlotte warned.

"I'm just kidding him, Ma. He knows that." He took another bite from his cookie.

"I don't pay any attention to him," Bill said, which caused Pete to frown.

Anna hiked her nose a bit. "We came to tell the family that we're having another baby."

Pete nearly choked on the last bite of his cookie. "A baby? What on earth for?"

Anna gasped. "We love children," she said with great passion and a slightly defensive air.

Pete waved his hand. "Aw, I know you do, but you got a couple of rug rats already. Isn't that enough?"

Anna visibly bristled.

"Pete, go get another cookie," Charlotte said.

He shrugged and headed out to the kitchen.

"Anna, you know Pete. He doesn't mean any offense. He just has a knack for—"

"Being rude," Bill filled in.

Bob kicked the foot of his recliner in and headed toward the kitchen too. "Anyone else want a cookie?"

Anna and Charlotte stared at him as he disappeared through the door.

Charlotte, Bill, and Anna joined the others in the kitchen just as Sam stepped into view from the back porch. "What's everybody doing?" he asked, snatching a cookie from the jar just as Pete's hand went for it. He flashed a victorious grin at Pete, who frowned and dug for another treat. Charlotte would need to refill the cookie jar tomorrow.

"Bill and Anna are having another kid," Pete said, wiping a crumb from his face.

Charlotte glared at him.

"Well, they are."

Sam chewed on his cookie as he took in the news.

"What's going on?" Christopher asked when he, Madison, and Jennifer wandered in from the barn. They washed their hands at the sink and settled down for another glass of milk. Emily and Ashley sauntered into the room and joined them at the table.

"Can Ashley spend the night, Grandma?" Emily asked.

"Well?" Christopher persisted.

Finding just the right cookie and pulling it from the jar, Emily looked at everyone. "Did I miss something?"

"Bill and Anna are having another baby," Charlotte said.

Madison and Jennifer grinned from ear to ear.

Emily looked at them and then said, "That's great, I guess."

Charlotte almost chuckled out loud. She looked at the kids and decided that despite the different personalities and struggles of her family, she felt blessed beyond measure.

"Emily, Ashley may spend the night if her mother doesn't mind."

The girls smacked a high-five.

"And I need to talk to you girls in a little bit."

"Are we in trouble?" Emily asked, concern in her face.

"Yes, you're going to have to clean the chicken coop all by yourself for the next month," Pete said with a laugh that practically shook the kitchen cabinets.

Charlotte frowned at him. "No, honey, you're not in trouble. We'll talk about it later."

Emily stuck her tongue out at Pete, and he laughed again.

After the last cookie crumb had been cleaned from the jar, everyone gathered back in the family room.

"So have you struck it rich yet with that real estate deal?" Pete asked.

Charlotte wished the boys would discuss their differences in private.

Bill massaged the back of his neck. "Not yet."

Pete's eyebrows lifted. "Oh?"

"Just got to work through the details. No big deal." Bill shifted in his seat.

Pete shrugged and moved the conversation to the price of corn. Charlotte hoped Bill and Anna didn't get in over their heads with those house renovations.

After everyone left, Charlotte cleaned up the stray glasses in the kitchen and wiped off the table. Just as she finished, Emily and Ashley stepped into the kitchen.

"Did you girls want something else to eat?"

Emily shook her head. "We just wondered what you wanted to talk to us about."

"Oh, that." Charlotte squeezed the soap bubbles from the dishcloth, rinsed it out once more for good measure, and then draped it over the edge of the sink. She turned to the girls. "I know you like to have a little extra money now and then. I think I've found something you can do."

Emily looked skeptical. "What is it?"

"There's a woman at our church, Lydia Middleton. She's in her late eighties. She's not able to take care of things around her house like she used to, and she needs help a couple of times a week. I thought maybe you girls could go over and help her. I need to clear it first with her, of course. She's willing to pay you for your efforts. It may not be much, but it's better than nothing. Plus, you'd be helping out a dear woman."

"An old lady?" Emily wrinkled her nose. "I don't know."

Ashley elbowed her. "Come on, Em. This might be fun."

Charlotte held her breath. Emily didn't look so convinced. But if Charlotte could get this to work out, it would keep Emily out of trouble for the summer and give Charlotte some peace of mind.

Emily made a face but said nothing. Ashley's encouragement obviously had taken the fight out of her. Charlotte felt sure, however, that she hadn't heard the last of it from Emily.

Chapter Two

"Mmmm, smells good, Char." Bob went into the kitchen, leaned into his wife who stood by the stove, and dropped a kiss on her cheek. He walked over to the table with a slight spring in his step.

Charlotte watched him. He was definitely in a good mood this morning. They were learning to control his diabetes, and it showed. It meant poring through cookbooks and learning how to cook a little differently, but it was, of course, worth it for Bob's health. She had to ease into the changes slowly, so he wouldn't notice it so much.

She scooped the oatmeal into a bowl for him and then placed two eggs, over easy, in front of him with wheat toast. A cup of coffee and a small glass of milk finished his meal.

Charlotte slipped into her seat across from Bob. They folded their hands together, and he said the blessing for their meal.

"You must be feeling pretty good today," she said, sprinkling blueberries into her oatmeal.

"I am." He took a bite of toast. "After I talk to Pete and take a look around the farm, I thought I might go over to AA Tractor Supply and jaw a little with the boys."

Charlotte smiled. Bob was learning to release more and more of the farm responsibilities to Pete. It hadn't been an easy transition for him. After controlling the farm for so many years, it took some rethinking on his part to pass the reins. Walking around the farm and talking with Pete kept him in the loop, but Charlotte knew it was becoming more of a formality.

"Sounds like a good plan," she said.

"Sam start looking for a job yet?" He pinned her with his gaze. The children were a point of contention between them. Bob was old-fashioned and had little tolerance for what he considered laziness. Not that she didn't think Sam needed a job. Still, she was a little more tolerant. Though Sam lacked motivation, she knew he was still trying to find himself after his mother's death.

"He went out yesterday." She hadn't had time to talk to Sam to see if anything had come of it.

"Good. He should find something soon." Bob mopped up the last of his egg yolk with the wheat toast. After swallowing his last bite, he reached for the Bible and read their morning Scripture. They shared a talk with the Lord and then Bob started to leave. He stopped and turned toward Char. "Don't you coddle those kids too long, Char. They need to be up for breakfast with the rest of us. There are chores to do."

"I know. I just wanted to give them a couple of days to celebrate the end of the school year."

He gave a nod, but the expression on his face said he wouldn't tolerate it for long. She understood. But her heart twisted with thoughts of them. Any way she could make life a little easier for them, she had to try, didn't she?

Once Charlotte had cleaned the kitchen, she settled back at the table with her coffee and Bible. Though she and Bob had prayed together, she liked to spend some time alone with the Lord. The kids wouldn't be up for another hour, so she would start their breakfast once she and the Lord had finished their visit.

As she read Paul's words about joy in the book of Philippians, she thought over the recent events in her life, Denise's death, the children moving to Heather Creek. So many changes, and yet Paul said even in the difficulties there is joy. She knew that to be true—some days more than others. She wasn't joyful for the things that had happened. Her joy rested in Jesus. He gave her strength—and joy—for her days.

Charlotte bowed her head and whispered a prayer for her precious family and her friends in need. Tears slipped down her cheeks and onto the table as she named the grandkids one by one and prayed specifically for their needs. She grabbed a napkin and wiped the tears from her face.

Her eyes opened, and she saw Emily standing silently in the kitchen, dressed in her pajamas. For a moment Charlotte could see a younger Emily, an Emily who had yet to be touched by the temptations of youth and the harsh realities of life. When Charlotte saw her, Emily blinked. "Just wondering when we were having breakfast."

Charlotte rose from her chair. "I'm just getting ready to prepare it."

"Um, do you want me to help? Ashley is still in the shower."

"You can set the table if you like; then you have time to get dressed."

Emily grabbed the plates from the cupboard. "You gonna call that lady today?"

"If by 'that lady' you mean Lydia Middleton, then yes. I'm going to call her and see when would be a good time for you and Ashley to talk with her." Charlotte lifted the orange juice from the refrigerator and walked it over to the table while Emily placed glasses at each setting.

"Now, simply because you're meeting with her doesn't guarantee you'll get the job. You understand that, right?"

"Yeah."

"Older people are sometimes fussy about things, and I'm certain Lydia Middleton is no exception."

"It's not like I want to work there." Emily mumbled her words, but Charlotte could just about make them out.

"What?"

"Doesn't that lady have grandkids? Why can't they help her?"

Charlotte shook her head. "She never married." Walking back over to the counter, Charlotte poured circles of pancake batter onto her griddle.

"Doesn't she have any family around?"

Charlotte saw Emily staring at the pancake batter. "Don't worry. There's plenty for you and Ashley."

"Great."

"And to answer your question, Lydia doesn't have any family around. At her age, there aren't many of them left."

"Oh." Emily paused a moment. "You know I found some pretty silk daisies at that garage sale Ashley and I stopped at on Saturday. Do you mind if I put them in a pitcher on the table?"

Charlotte didn't fuss much over her table, but she liked it that Emily thought of that. "I think that would be lovely, Emily."

The teenager brightened. "I'll just run and go get them from my room, and then Ashley and I will be ready to eat."

Before the pancakes could bubble, she had bolted up the stairs. Charlotte shook her head. It seemed her granddaughter was full of surprises.

THAT EVENING, Charlotte knocked on Emily's bedroom door. Music sounded from inside, but Emily kept it to a dull roar to satisfy her grandpa.

The door squeaked open. "Yeah?" Emily stood there with her hair scrunched up on her head and poking out in all directions like sticks of straw. Charlotte just didn't get today's fashions.

"I wanted to let you know I talked with Lydia Middleton. She wants you and Ashley to come over tomorrow afternoon at two o'clock. So I'll swing by Ashley's house tomorrow and take you girls over."

Emily blew out a frustrated sigh. "Do I *have* to do this, Grandma?"

"Emily, I told you. Lydia Middleton is a very nice woman

who needs help. You have the time this summer to help her—and earn a little spending money while you're at it."

"Not that much money," Emily grumbled.

"It's not about the money. It's about helping someone in need. The money is an extra bonus." Charlotte's tone left no room for argument. "It's the decent thing to do. You'd better let Ashley know and see if she's still interested in helping."

Charlotte closed the door on Emily's frown, thankful she could not read her granddaughter's thoughts. She only hoped Emily would be polite during her interview with Lydia.

Stopping at Christopher's room, Charlotte knocked on his door.

"Come in."

Charlotte opened the door. "You ready for me to read to you?"

"Sure."

No matter that he'd be going into sixth grade next year —for now he still allowed her to read a story from time to time. Sam and Emily knew better than to tease him about it. It was a ritual that Denise had started with him from the time he was old enough to sit still, and he couldn't let it go—yet. Charlotte decided the fact that she still had a bookcase of Denise's old books most likely comforted him all the more. Whatever his reasons for allowing her to read to him, she didn't care. She merely savored the moments.

"Which one do you want tonight?"

Christopher walked over to the bookshelf and pulled out *Lad, a Dog*.

Charlotte smiled. "That was one of your mom's favorites."

He grinned in return and settled onto his bed. She read a couple of chapters of the book describing a special bond between a collie and his family. Then she finally called it a night.

"I'll read more tomorrow night," she said, closing the book.

"I like it that you have a dog. Mom didn't let us have one."

Charlotte considered this. "It's hard to have a family and a dog too, especially when you live in the city."

"I guess." He paused. "I'll bet Toby is as smart as Lad in the story."

"Probably," she said, though she wasn't at all sure Toby was as courageous as the dog in the book.

"Sometimes people don't know they have smart dogs unless the dog gets lost and has to find them or save them from something."

"That's true sometimes." She placed the book on Christopher's night table and then looked over at him. The earlier scene of Christopher playing with Toby brought an idea to mind. "You know, Christopher, there's one way we can find out just how smart Toby is."

His eyes lit with excitement. "There is?"

Charlotte nodded. "Our county fair has a dog show. Maybe you should think of entering Toby."

His mouth dropped open. "Really? That would be awesome!"

"Sure. It might be fun for you and Toby. It would take a lot of work though."

He sat up on his bed. "I can do it, Grandma. I know I can. Toby's a smart dog too."

"You bet she is." His enthusiasm tickled her. "Now, you get some sleep, and we'll talk about it more tomorrow. I'll call around to see what we have to do to get you started—if you decide that's what you want to do. We can go to the library too, to check out some books on training dogs."

"That would be great." He smiled and snuggled deeper into his covers.

Charlotte suspected her grandson might have a bit of difficulty getting to sleep tonight. She turned to go.

"Gnily, Grandma," he said.

Charlotte's heart slammed against her chest. "What did you say?"

He grinned. "It's a word Mom said to us every night. I think she made it up. It's an acronym for, "Good night, I love you." Christopher laughed. "It's a funny word, isn't it?"

"It sure is." Charlotte swallowed hard past the knot in her throat.

He grew quiet. "I forgot about it for a long time."

Her heart clenched, and she wasn't sure what to say. "Gnily, Christopher." She closed the door behind her. Tears filled her eyes as she leaned against the wall in the hallway.

She remembered the word well. She had used it every night when she tucked Denise into bed.

THE NEXT DAY EMILY AND ASHLEY stood in front of Miss Middleton's house—the last place Emily wanted to be. She had tried to talk herself into the idea of helping this old woman, but it just wasn't working.

"Well, come on in, girls." Lydia Middleton shifted out of the way so Emily and Ashley could step inside her home. Her voice was a little shaky but also gentle. She was an aged stick of a woman with the whitest hair Emily had ever seen, but her faded blue eyes still had life in them.

"Let's go into the kitchen to have ourselves a chat."

She walked so slowly, Emily figured they'd get there by dinner. Great. Just the way she wanted to spend her summer.

The house was small. The air smelled old and musty. Judging by the smudges on the windows, Emily decided they hadn't been cleaned in ages. A flowered sofa hugged a wall in the living room. A large brown afghan was draped across the top of the sofa. Doilies adorned every table and stand, just like at Grandma's and Grandpa's house.

Once they reached the kitchen, the woman pointed to the chairs around a scrubbed oak table, nicked and scarred but still in good shape. "Go ahead and sit down. I'll get us some lemonade."

"Can we help you?" Ashley offered.

Why did Ashley have to be so helpful? Couldn't she see how boring this was going to be?

"What's that?"

"I said, can we help you?" Ashley repeated, this time in a louder voice.

"No, no, you girls just sit there, and I'll get it. I may be old, but I can still get around."

Emily threw Ashley a what's-up-with-you glance. Ashley shrugged.

Miss Middleton gathered their drinks and placed the chilled glasses before them. The old woman eased herself into a chair across from them, looked up, and smiled.

"These old bones don't work like they used to."

Ashley smiled. Emily marveled that the woman's bones were still working at all.

"Now, tell me about yourselves."

Emily nodded to Ashley. "Go ahead."

Ashley talked about her parents and mentioned that she had a brother—though she left out the part about him being annoying—and that she had lived in Bedford all her life.

Miss Middleton turned to Emily. "And I understand that you are Charlotte and Bob's granddaughter."

Emily breathed an inward sigh of relief. Of course, Grandma had explained everything to her. "Yeah."

"Sorry to hear about your mother, dear."

"Thanks."

"Denise was a lovely young lady."

"You knew her?" Emily hadn't thought of that. Of course this woman had known her mom. Miss Middleton was eighty-eight and Emily's grandma had said Miss Middleton had lived there most of her life. She most likely knew everyone in town.

"Full of life and energy." Miss Middleton chuckled. "And she always made it a point to say hello to me." She looked Emily full in the face. "It's rare when a youngster pays attention to old folks."

That comment surprised her. She knew her mom had been stubborn and rebellious—she had told Emily that herself. So to hear that she took time for old people didn't quite jibe with what Emily knew of her mother. This bit of information made her feel better. But it didn't go so far as to make Emily want to be there. She still had better things to do with her summer.

"But with those grandparents, you can't go wrong."

Emily forced a smile. Sometimes it bothered her when people talked like that. Just because her grandparents were well liked, did that mean she should be glad she had them instead of her mother? She knew Grandma and Grandpa were kind, but they could never take her mother's place.

"Now, as you can see, my house needs a spit shine." Miss Middleton laughed at her own comment, so the girls joined in. "This house hasn't had a good cleaning in quite some time, and I aim to fix that."

Emily's summer was headed south—fast.

"I'll need you to do the normal cleaning, and then I'd like to have you go above the normal stuff and perhaps clean the walls and light fixtures, that sort of thing." She smiled. "At any rate, I think I can keep you busy over the summer if you're up to the task."

"Sounds great to me," Ashley said with so much enthusiasm that Emily wanted to bop her.

"I won't bite you, I promise." Miss Middleton's eyes twinkled.

Despite her mood, Emily couldn't deny that the woman was sweet. Old. But sweet.

"Okay."

"Good. It's settled then." Miss Middleton stood up. "You both come back here on Monday, around ten o'clock—

I need my beauty sleep—and we'll get started on the general cleaning."

"Sounds great." Ashley stood.

"Thanks," Emily said, forcing herself to show good manners. Just as they started to exit through the door, Emily spotted a miniature train on a hallway stand. She wondered why Miss Middleton had a train if she had no children or grandchildren.

They said their good-byes, and Emily stepped into the sunshine. A perfectly good summer afternoon wasted.

Chapter Three

The librarian took Christopher over to a section of books on training animals while Charlotte grabbed a couple of magazines and sat down at a nearby table. They couldn't take too long at the library since she had to get dinner preparations started soon. Still, she knew this whole idea of training Toby would keep Christopher out of mischief for the summer and give him something worthwhile to do. As far as she was concerned, it would do Toby some good, too.

Christopher quickly got engrossed in the books. Charlotte finally decided it was time to leave. She put the magazines back in the rack and then glanced at the bulletin board. A flier about a Diabetes Walk-a-thon caught her attention. The form mentioned getting sponsors for the walk and that the proceeds would go to the Diabetes Foundation in an effort to fight the disease. She wrote down some of the specifics: who to contact, where to get the forms, the date of the event, June 28, and how to get enrolled. By the time they left the library, Charlotte was on a mission.

When they got home, Christopher ran up to his room to pore through his books. While stirring a pot of vegetable soup on the stove, Charlotte considered whom she might contact for donations toward her walk. She'd have to get right to work on that. It was a good thing she was used to walking. Since it was only a couple of weeks away, she wouldn't be able to participate if she weren't in shape—well, at least somewhat in shape.

She looked into the simmering pot of soup. Wouldn't be long till her garden would feed them on warm summer nights. The green beans were already sprouting through the soil. She hoped they'd have enough for her to can abundantly for the winter, now that they had three more mouths to feed. They'd need plenty of tomatoes too. The kids loved chips and salsa. Someone at church had given her a new recipe for salsa, and she could hardly wait to try it out. Nothing like fresh vegetables in the summer.

Charlotte walked over and glanced out the window. Her gaze skimmed over the distant wheat fields. They had just finished planting the cornfields, and they'd soon be harvesting the winter wheat. She sighed. It seemed a farmer's work was never done.

Lightning weaved around Charlotte's ankles, getting her attention. Bending over, Charlotte rubbed the brown tabby which purred like a smooth-running sewing machine. "What's the matter? Are you hungry?" Charlotte smiled and walked over to the cat's food bowl. Her lunch was long gone, so Charlotte poured her a little milk, which Lightning happily lapped up.

The kitchen clock told her everyone would be back for

dinner soon. She hoped Sam had found some leads for work today. Helping Pete with the machinery would keep him somewhat busy, but not nearly as busy as Bob wanted him to be.

After her interview with Miss Middleton, Emily had gone over to Ashley's house for a while. Charlotte was anxious to hear how the interview had gone. Emily had so much potential. These days she wavered between sweetness and teenage crankiness. Picking up on her moods could be tricky, but Charlotte was learning.

She walked into the family room and sorted through the paperwork on her worktable, reading through the flier for the diabetes walk once more. The more she thought about it, the more she liked the idea of participating in the walk. It was one way she could help Bob and others like him.

She shuffled the endless paperwork on the table in the family room that served as her desk. The ink was barely dry on the last check she'd written when she heard the sound of tires crunching gravel and glanced out the window to see Mel's car. Dropping the flier on the table, she went outside to greet her friend.

"Hi, Charlotte." Melody Givens's red lips lifted in a happy smile that could light up a room. Her dark brown hair was scooped back in a scrunchie—at least that's what Charlotte thought Emily called it. Gold hoop earrings dangled from her ears while a necklace with gold beads adorned her throat. Talking with Melody was like a shot of adrenaline. She had an infectious passion for life that made her quite successful in running her diner and also made her a welcome friend.

"Thanks for bringing Emily home, Mel." Charlotte smiled.

On the other side of the car, Emily climbed out and talked with Ashley through the window.

"It was my pleasure. I think the girls enjoyed meeting Miss Middleton today."

Charlotte glanced at the girls, who were engrossed in energetic chatter.

"Did she hire them?"

Melody nodded.

"That's great. It will be good for everyone concerned, I believe," Charlotte whispered. "That's a pretty top you have on," she said, admiring the colorful blouse with the empire waist. It seemed fashion repeated itself. She could remember Denise wearing something like that years ago.

"Thanks. It covers a multitude of sins." Melody laughed.

"I'll have to remember that," Charlotte chuckled, thinking all the while how ridiculous she would look in such a top. The last thing she needed at her age was to look pregnant. Besides, what did a farmer's wife need with fashion?

Once they gathered around the dinner table, Bob prayed over the meal; then Charlotte scooped the vegetable soup into bowls.

"Emily, your grandma tells me congratulations are in order for you and Ashley."

She stared into her bowl. "Yeah."

"You got a job?" Sam asked, wide-eyed.

"Yeah," Emily said, with little enthusiasm.

"Where?" Sam wanted to know.

Emily didn't act as though she wanted to talk about it.

"She'll be helping Miss Middleton around her house," Charlotte said.

"Who's that?" Christopher wanted to know.

"She's an elderly lady from our church."

"What does Emily have to do for her?" Christopher asked.

Emily huffed.

"What? I just asked."

"Do you have to ask so many questions?" Emily said.

"You just asked one. Why can't I?"

Emily glared at him.

Christopher stuck out his tongue. "You're always in a bad mood."

"I am not."

"That's enough," Charlotte said.

"Where did you apply for jobs today, Sam?" Bob asked.

Charlotte cringed at his gruff voice. Though the children were surely used to it by now and most likely knew he wasn't as harsh as he sounded, she still wished he would soften his voice when talking with them.

"See, Grandpa asked a question," Christopher said.

"Make him stop, Grandma."

Charlotte was getting a headache.

Sam's face grew an interesting shade of pink. "Yeah, um, I applied at a couple of places."

Bob studied his grandson while taking a spoonful of vegetable soup. "And where might those places be?" He tore a hunk from his dinner roll.

"Another question," Christopher muttered under his breath.

"Christopher, that's enough," Charlotte said.

Sam rattled off the name of a video store and a library position, neither of which would require much manual labor. Everyone knew Bob heartily believed in manual labor.

Bob nodded, his face set and tight. "Work doesn't come easy. Keep checking." That was all he said, but by the look on Sam's face, Charlotte knew it was enough.

"What about that place Arielle mentioned—Heather Creek Day Care, wasn't it? She said they had a couple of openings. Maybe you could get a job there," Emily said.

Charlotte caught the quick glare Sam tossed at his sister. She suspected Emily didn't want Sam to have any fun this summer if she couldn't.

"That would be a good place for you to check," Bob said, leaving no room for argument.

Children were a big responsibility, and with Sam's past work history, Charlotte wondered if he was up for it. She locked eyes with Bob. He obviously had seen her concerns and gave her a look that told her they'd talk later.

Sam mimicked his brother and sagged farther into his seat, saying nothing the rest of the meal.

"THIS IS LIKE OLD TIMES," Charlotte said to Bob as they walked down their country lane, wrapped in the warmth of the evening sun.

"I know. We should do this more often."

She looked at her husband with surprise. "Are you feeling all right?"

"Yeah, I'm fine. I just wanted to go for a walk."

Charlotte couldn't remember the last time they had gone for a walk together. Bright colors had muted across the horizon to a softness that reminded her of better days before tragedy had struck their home.

"Remember when I proposed to you by the creek?"

"I remember. The leaves had turned beautiful shades of gold and russet. The weather was perfect." A smooth ribbon of contentment meandered through her with the memory.

Charlotte spotted some wildflowers along the side of the road and knelt down to pluck a few stems from the soil. "Oh, can you help me reach those?" she asked, pointing to a cluster of bright yellow flowers.

After they'd lifted a suitable bouquet from the earth, Charlotte dusted her hands on her jeans.

"These will make a gorgeous centerpiece on the table. Alternating with the flowers Emily provided, of course."

Bob nodded. A light breeze whispered across their faces and stirred the grasses. Their shoes scuffed against the ground. "We've had a good life, haven't we, Charlotte?"

His comment startled her. "Yes, we have." Every now and then Bob thought about his diabetes, and it set him to pondering life. Maybe that was what this was about.

"It's not over yet though, just so you know," she said with a grin.

"I know." His hand reached for hers. "But the years sure have flown by."

"I know." *Soon to be forty-six years together. He must be thinking the same thing.*

She leaned into him. Not at all sure what had gotten into him, she decided she'd enjoy it while it lasted.

"Have you talked with Miss Middleton?" he asked.

"No. I hope the girls didn't wear her out on the interview." Charlotte chuckled.

They walked a little farther.

"You think I was too hard on Sam, don't you?"

Charlotte didn't want to spoil the lovely walk they were having, but she had to be honest. "Not hard, really. I just hope Sam is responsible enough to take care of kids."

"He's got to fly sometime, Charlotte. He needs to learn responsibility. A job will help him do that. Sitting around all summer will surely only lead him into trouble."

Charlotte sighed. "I know you're right."

Bob tenderly squeezed her fingers, quieting her fears.

"Did you hear Christopher at the table?" Charlotte chuckled.

"He's like a dog with a bone, that one," Bob said with a laugh.

As they continued down the isolated road, they talked of the neighbors' livestock, broken fences, and the beauty of an early summer's night.

"What do you think about Bill and Anna's news?"

"Another grandbaby? I think I'm old," he said with a smile.

"Hey, you stop that," she said, smiling. "You are not old—and neither am I.

As they walked on, Charlotte felt the eerie quiet of the night settling around them. It might be creepy if she weren't with Bob and feeling, for the moment, that all was right with her world. "I sure wish Pete and Bill got along better. They are such opposites."

"They're men. We don't get all sappy with each other."

"I'm not asking for sap, but a little understanding might be nice."

"Oh, you worry too much. Those boys are fine."

Emotion definitely wasn't Bob's strong suit, which made his behavior tonight a little confusing.

Wrapped in moonlight, they continued on. "Christopher has decided to train Toby."

Bob laughed out loud—something he didn't do often. "Good luck with that."

"Hey!" Charlotte playfully nudged him in the side with her elbow. "Toby's a good dog."

"Not the smartest pooch in the pound."

"Bob." She chuckled.

"Still, it's a worthy endeavor for Christopher. It sounds as though he'll be busy for the summer too. That leaves one."

"He'll get there, Bob. One day at a time, remember?"

He turned and looked at her. "I remember."

SAM PUNCHED HIS PILLOW and stuffed it into place. Clasping his hands behind his head, he stared at the ceiling. The moonlight cast shadows and light across his room as though it couldn't make up its mind whether to make the room light or throw it into darkness.

He could have bonked Emily on the head at dinner. Why did she have to go and mention that stupid day-care job? If that was where Arielle wanted to work, fine. But it was a girl's job. The last thing he wanted to do was to spend his summer watching over a bunch of noisy kids.

Another punch of the pillow. Jake and Paul were lucky. They had gotten jobs at the video store. They thought they might talk the boss into hiring him too, but no such luck. If he worked there, he could borrow videos for free.

They had gotten cool jobs and he had gotten—well, he hadn't gotten anything yet. That idea made him feel better. Who said the day care would hire him? No one else seemed to want him after his last working fiasco. Maybe he could have handled things better, but it was too late to worry about it now.

Why couldn't Grandpa just leave him alone? He helped Uncle Pete now and then, didn't he? Wasn't that enough?

Okay, the truth was he knew he needed something to do. He'd quickly get bored without Jake and Paul to hang with. Another pillow punch. He had so much he wanted to do, and being stuck on a stupid farm wasn't on the agenda. A twinge of guilt pricked him. Yes, he was glad he and his brother and sister had gotten to stay together. His grandparents didn't have to take them in. Still, he couldn't wait to get back to California—where he belonged.

He closed his eyes. He hoped sleep would come. And he wished he'd find a decent job that would not be lame and would still satisfy Grandpa.

He could take a lot of things, but a lame job wasn't one of them.

CHARLOTTE EDGED UP to Emily's bedroom door and knocked softly. "Emily, okay if I come in?"

"Yeah, come on in, Grandma."

Emily sat on the edge of her bed, bristle brush in hand, earbuds draped around her neck. She flipped them off, placed them on the stand next to her bed, and shut off her iPod. "What's up?"

"I just wanted to see what you thought about your visit with Miss Middleton."

She shrugged. "It was okay."

Obviously, Emily was going to make her dig for information. Charlotte settled beside her on the edge of the bed.

"What did you think of her?"

Without a moment's hesitation, Emily said, "She's okay." A quick swipe through the side of her hair.

"Look, Emily, I know this isn't how you wanted to spend your summer, but it will turn out all right. You'll see. Besides, it's only a few hours a week." Charlotte took in the young features of her granddaughter. So much like her mother. Pretty, yet so naïve. And just as stubborn.

Sometimes Charlotte just wanted to scoop her grandchildren into her empty arms and hold them tight, shield them from all the pain and uncertainties of the world. If only she could have done that for Denise.

Emily looked uncomfortable, as though she didn't know what to say next.

"Well, I won't keep you, dear. You get some rest." Charlotte gave Emily a slight tap on the knee. Then she reached over and dropped a kiss on her cheek. "Gnily, Em."

Emily gasped. "Where did you hear that?"

"Christopher mentioned it and—"

"Well, he shouldn't have."

Charlotte's spirit sank. She had meant it in fun, but obviously Emily didn't appreciate it. "Good night, Emily." Charlotte walked out and closed the door behind her. Would she ever be able to reach her granddaughter? Sometimes she felt she had failed Denise. She couldn't bear to fail Denise's children too.

Chapter Four

Humiliation crawled over Sam as he made his way past the kids on the playground of Heather Creek Community Day Care on Thursday morning. His friends back home would have a good laugh at his expense, no doubt about it.

Energetic little people scampered all around the playground. The sun bounced off colors of red, yellow, blue, and bright green, giving him a headache. His boots ground the gravel farther into the pavement as his frustration built with every step. He blew out a hefty sigh before pulling open the door, praying for all he was worth that the position or positions would be filled.

His sister would so pay for this.

When he stepped into the foyer, a woman behind the counter looked up. "Good morning," she said with a pleasant smile. "May I help you?"

"Um, yeah. I wondered if you were accepting applications."

Her eyes widened. "Yes, we certainly are."

His stomach flipped. Right then he remembered a nursery rhyme his mom used to read to them: "The Old Woman

Who Lived in a Shoe." He would be like the old man with a ton of screaming kids around, making him miserable.

"If you'll fill this out and take a seat, I'm sure Mrs. Wilkens will want to speak with you." Her words were pointed and no-nonsense just like her appearance. Tall and thin, she had a bony, pointed nose.

Something told him to run. This woman was far too eager to help him. Maybe there was a reason these positions were open. Maybe no one wanted the jobs. A kid wailed in the distance, causing Sam to jump. He decided if he got the job, he'd ask for a hazmat uniform. The place was obviously dangerous.

He started answering the questions on the application form.

If he tried to blow this, it would get around town and he'd never be hired anywhere. And the truth was he did need a job to keep his car going and hang out with friends.

Not only that, but after his last job failure, he could use a little boost where that was concerned. Presently, he didn't have a great job history.

But a day care?

"Mr. Slater?"

Sam looked up from his finished application. "Yes?"

A plump woman with rosy cheeks stopped short in front of him and flashed a cheerful smile. She reminded him of Cinderella's fairy godmother—without the wand.

Oh, sure, a decoy. They put her out in front so everyone would think the place was harmless. But he'd seen the kids.

"I'm Mrs. Wilkens." She shoved her hand into his and shook heartily. "If you'll come this way, please."

He followed her to her office, shaking life back into his fingers along the way. She was a fairy godmother with a death grip. He couldn't blame her. She probably needed it for survival around here.

"Please, Mr. Slater, take a seat." She motioned to him and took her place behind a small wooden desk.

While she studied his application, Sam looked around and saw a friendly room with murals of happy farm animals and a barn.

A bookshelf held trays of assorted toys, coloring books and crayons, and children's books.

"So you're Charlotte and Bob's grandson?" she asked, pulling his attention from the room.

"Yeah—yes." He had enough good sense to know he should represent them well.

"Good people. I was awful sorry to hear about your mother. I'm sure that was very hard on all of you."

"Yes ma'am."

"My son went to school with your mom. She was a pretty thing." She shook her head. "Such a tragedy."

No doubt she was trying to make small talk, but he didn't want to discuss it—especially with a stranger. So he merely nodded.

"Do you like children, Sam?" Her eyes twinkled when she said that.

He wasn't sure how to answer. No, he didn't want to work around a bunch of squalling kids, but he had nothing against them. The few he'd been around he didn't mind, really. After he thought about it, he decided he could honestly say they were okay, as far as little people go.

"Yeah."

She chuckled. "I know, seeing them swarming all over the place can be a bit daunting at first, but you'll get used to it." More sparkling in her eyes.

Did that mean he was hired?

She glanced over his paperwork and asked a few more questions. Finally, she looked up at him with a smile. "Well, we'll have to run a background check and have you fingerprinted, but once that goes through, if you want the position, it's yours."

Her words jarred him. He hadn't expected the offer. Didn't want the offer. Though he couldn't deny the pleasure that sparked through him for not being rejected yet again.

"Great. I'll take it," he heard his mutinous tongue say.

They discussed salary and how he would be working mostly afternoons. He would need to come in the following Tuesday morning, however, to go over everything with one of their staff members.

That schedule would work well for him. On the days he worked in the afternoons, he could still help Uncle Pete in the morning. It would also make Grandpa happy. Oh, well. With Jake and Paul working, he figured he might as well keep busy too. What else was there to do stuck out on a farm in Nebraska?

He thanked her and headed out of the building. A kid came running down the hall, not watching where he was going, and slammed right into Sam.

"Are you all right?"

Looking up, the kid's eyes grew wide—at the sight of a

stranger, no doubt. Great tears erupted and streamed down his face, followed by a wail that could have passed for an ambulance siren.

This summer was not turning out at all the way Sam had planned.

EMILY BROWSED THROUGH the CD selection in her bedroom. She turned to Ashley. "Want to listen to Hilary Duff?"

"Sure."

"It was really cool of your mom to give me this portable CD player. I love it."

Ashley plunked down on the bed. "Since Brett and I already have one," she said, referring to her brother, "she said someone ought to enjoy it."

"Why did you have an extra one around?"

Ashley shrugged. "Someone gave it to her or something. She prefers her iPod, so she never uses it."

"I like my iPod too, but this way I can play CDs for my friends." Emily smiled at her friend. Then she glanced in the mirror and made a face. "I need to buy some new jeans. Grandma makes me wear them a size too big."

Ashley laughed. "They are not that big. They look good. Wish I looked that good."

"Yeah, right. Look at you with that gorgeous auburn hair." Emily fingered her own. "Mine is so straight," she said with a pout.

"Please. I'd love to have straight hair."

"Whatever."

"I can see why you're so pretty, Em," Ashley said, picking up the framed picture from the nightstand. "You look like your mom."

"Thanks." The mere mention of her mom still caused a stab of pain in her heart. She avoided it at all costs.

"Must be hard being without her."

"Yeah." She wished Ashley would move on to something else.

"Still, your grandparents are cool."

Emily didn't want to sound ungrateful, but they could never replace her mom. "Yeah."

"Do you miss her lots?"

"Of course I still miss her. Wouldn't you miss your mom?" Emily wondered how Ashley could ask such a dumb question.

"I'm sorry, Em. I didn't mean—I didn't—"

"It's all right. I just get a little touchy about it sometimes." Emily was sorry she had snapped at her friend.

Ashley brushed her hair, and Emily looked through Ashley's school yearbook, which she'd brought over. While energetic music filled the room, the girls giggled over pictures and boys and talked of possibilities for the next school year. After lunch, Ashley left for home.

Once Ashley had gone, Emily's mood turned somber. Anytime someone mentioned her mom, it left her feeling that way. She always struggled to shake it off.

"I'm going to feed the chickens, Grandma. Then after I finish my chores, is it all right if I take Princess for a ride?" Emily asked, referring to her favorite riding horse.

"Sure, honey. Go ahead."

Emily stepped outside, took care of feeding her feathered charges, and then made her way to the barn. The door creaked and groaned with its opening. The sharp smell of horses and leather greeted her when she stepped inside. Barn cats mewed and ambled near her in search of food. She glanced at the corner where the plastic food pail was kept. With a sigh she walked over and refilled it with cat food. "All you guys do is eat." The cats ignored her and immediately shoved their whiskers into the pail.

When Emily reached Stormy's stall, she ran her palm over the sleek body of the horse and then patted the white patch on her nose. A fly buzzed annoyingly close, and Stormy's thick dark tail swished it away. Her strong hooves stamped into bits of hay on the barn floor, and she gave a friendly snort. Emily nuzzled into her, talking gently as Stormy whinnied and nuzzled back.

Something about this horse calmed her. Ashley's questions about Emily's mom had put her in a pensive mood—which always made her want to spend time with the horses.

"I'm glad your mom was my mom's horse," Emily said, gently stroking the filly. Stormy glanced at her, and then nibbled on a bunch of hay.

Emily moved on to Princess's stall. Once she was saddled and ready to go, Emily hoisted herself up. Easing her out of the barn, Emily gave her a slight nudge and headed for the open pasture.

Emily wasn't sure why Ashley's comments bothered her.

Her friend usually tiptoed around discussions of Emily's mom, but as time went on, it had become easier to talk about her—or so she thought.

Truth seeped into her thoughts. Tears pricked her eyes. Shaking it off, she pushed Princess harder. The cool breeze chilled the tears on her face. She was cold and hot all at the same time.

Princess's muscles were taut and strong against Emily's legs. The animal pushed forward, almost in a protective way, a way that said she would help Emily through this. Emily hunkered down, leaning into the strong neck of her horse, sensing a closeness she hadn't shared with anyone or anything since her mom . . .

Guiding Princess onto the trail that went down along Heather Creek, Emily was overcome by a frightening thought—could she be forgetting her mom?

Princess's hooves clip-clopped against the ground in hard, steady beats. The evening sun dipped toward the horizon, sending blazing colors of orange and crimson across the treetops—colors Emily normally considered beautiful but tonight seemed angry and harsh. Even the heavens were mad at her.

She couldn't blame them. How could Emily forget? She loved her mother, and yet her image had begun to fade ever so slightly. How could Emily let that happen?

Unbearable aching settled over her, and she gave another nudge to Princess's side. She rode faster and faster. More tears flowed. With impatience, she swiped them away. She would not act like a baby.

Anger released in a torrent. She'd been mad at her mom for leaving them, for forcing them to move to another state and leave their friends and the familiar behind, for not being there to talk with her about boys and growing-up things. But most of all Emily faced the anger with herself, for forgetting.

Slowing Princess, she edged the horse to the side of the path. Cupping her face in her hands, Emily wept. And wept. "I'm sorry, Mom. I'm so sorry." Fresh tears spilled down her cheeks and dripped from her chin onto the saddle.

If what Grandma said was true, that God really did care about people and what they were going through, then maybe, just maybe he would hear her prayers. She decided to try it.

"Please help me, God." As her words mingled with the air, tight and unyielding, she swallowed hard and lifted her eyes heavenward. Her mind flitted to her grandma using her mom's special good-night word. After Grandma had left the room, Emily had tried to remember her mom tucking her into bed and saying that word, but she couldn't envision it because, for a moment, she couldn't remember what her mom had looked like.

"Please, God. Please don't let me forget my mom."

"HOW WAS YOUR RIDE?" Charlotte asked Emily while placing a bag of groceries on the countertop. When she turned to her granddaughter, she caught a glimpse of her red and swollen face before Emily could turn away.

"It was great. I have to go to the bathroom. I'll come down and help you in a second."

An ache clutched Charlotte's heart as she watched Emily leave the room. If only she could fix whatever was bothering her.

Unpacking the groceries from the brown paper bags, Charlotte let out a sigh. Most days she felt so inadequate for the new life they now lived. She knew God saw their circumstances and was guiding them, but there were days when she felt so alone. She lifted her chin. But they *weren't* alone. She knew that.

"Get anything good?" Bob asked, walking into the kitchen.

Charlotte smiled. "Depends on what your idea of good is."

Bob dropped the *Bedford Leader* on the table and walked over to the refrigerator.

"Anything exciting happening in town or the world that I should know about?" Charlotte asked, glancing at the newspaper.

"Same old, same old, I guess." Bob dropped some ice cubes into a glass. "Real estate values are down in the county. Guess banks are pulling back on financing."

Hand clutched to her chest, Charlotte turned to him. "Oh dear. Wonder how that will affect Bill and his real estate deal . . ." She bit her lower lip. "Obviously, it's not the best time to be involved in real estate."

Bob shrugged. "Bill's got a good head on his shoulders. He'll be all right."

Charlotte tried to read Bob, but she couldn't. Sometimes he tried to shield her from worrying about the kids. This time, though, it wasn't working.

A BREEZE, FRESH AND SWEET as the first watermelon plucked from a summer garden, wafted through the porch. Charlotte rocked gently on the familiar wooden swing that gave a mild creak back and forth with the effort. A tractor rattled in a nearby field while the golden blaze of sunlight scrubbed the farm clean. She poked red thread through her embroidery project, a pillowcase, and glanced from time to time at Christopher, who was working with Toby in the yard.

Her Australian shepherd-blue heeler mix appeared more interested in chasing chickens than learning the heel position. She wondered if Christopher had bitten off more than he could chew, so to speak. Fortunately, they had signed Toby up only for the obedience portion at the fair competition. She wouldn't be ready for the agility competition until next year—if Christopher decided to continue another year. Judging from the looks of things, Charlotte had her doubts.

"Grandma, watch this." Christopher turned to Toby and in his most professional voice said, "Ready." Toby momentarily stayed put but watched with great interest as Christopher walked over to his training gear and doggie treats, which lay beside the trunk of a nearby apple tree.

At this point, the temptation was evidently just too great, and Toby decided to join her trainer for a picnic.

Charlotte tried to hide her amusement. Toby certainly had a mind of her own. She was never one to turn down a treat. This endeavor might very well prove to be a battle of the wills.

"Toby, no." With the sharp reprimand, good-natured

Toby trotted back to her original post, tail wagging, tongue lapping with anticipation.

Christopher waited patiently for Toby to assume her appropriate position on her haunches. She decided to oblige.

This time.

Christopher then picked up his training gear and some dog treats, and walked back over to Toby. He placed the food over to the side. Toby's eyes followed the treats, but still she stayed in place.

Charlotte was impressed—with both of them.

Christopher then examined Toby's ears for a few seconds. Then he said, "Good," followed by a treat.

Just as her grandson lifted one of Toby's footpads for examination, Dana Simons's car pulled into the driveway. At that point, Christopher glanced up. Seizing the opportunity, Toby shoved her white snout into his hand and snatched the next treat before Christopher knew what hit him. She then dashed toward the car with the speed of a greyhound, chomping down the treat as she ran, then barking wildly at the happy arrival of a visitor. Charlotte took note that nary a speck of remorse showed on Toby's face.

Christopher, on the other hand, showed obvious frustration, but the whole scene tickled Charlotte to no end. To hide her amusement from Christopher, she steeled her jaws together. Leaving her embroidery on the swing, she left the porch and walked over to her grandson as they headed toward their visitor.

"Don't worry, honey. It takes time to train a dog."

Christopher kicked the gravel with his sneaker. "We're not gonna make it in time."

"Don't be so quick to give up on poor Toby. She's a smart dog. I think she'll make it—especially with a good teacher like you." Charlotte gave him a sideways hug and then glared at Toby as she walked toward Dana's car. "I'll talk to *you* later."

One glance at her dog, and she had no doubt whatsoever that Christopher would have plenty to keep him busy over the summer.

Chapter Five

Hey, Sam. Your uncle Pete's finished with you already today?" Arielle grabbed a sweater on the chair by the door and tied it around her waist. Then she reached down and grabbed the handles of the picnic basket. "See you later, Mom," she called over her shoulder.

"Yeah. He didn't have a lot for me to do. I think he wanted to hurry and get done so he could hang out with Miss Simons."

Arielle laughed. With her usual perkiness, she bounded down the porch steps, causing her black hair to dance upon her shoulders.

"Sometimes I wonder if I'm more in the way than a help anyway."

"Why do you say that?"

They climbed into Sam's Datsun 240-Z.

He shrugged. "You know how it is. When you have someone following you around all the time, they tend to get in the way. And you figure you could get the job done on your own ten times faster. I know this because I have a younger brother."

Arielle laughed. It was a nice laugh. Her smile made his stomach flip.

"Nice touch," she said, pointing to the air freshener hanging from his mirror.

He was proud that he'd bought an air freshener for the car and he'd wondered if she'd notice. She'd told him she loved the smell of car fresheners. He knew it was her polite way of telling him his car stunk.

"Thanks." He shoved the car into gear and backed it out of her driveway. "Where we going for our picnic?"

A curious twinkle lit her eyes. "It's a surprise. I'll tell you how to get there. Head south here." She indicated with her finger. "Hey, guess what! I got the job at the day care."

"Congratulations. I did too."

"What?" She laughed. "You did? You didn't tell me you were going to apply."

He hadn't bothered to tell her because he hadn't wanted her to know in case they refused to hire him. He shrugged. "Didn't want to get my hopes up." Did he really just say that? "I guess I shouldn't say I got the job. They have to check out my criminal record first."

She laughed and said, "I'm guessing it's clear?"

"Don't worry. It's squeaky clean," Sam assured her.

She settled back into her seat. "I'm looking forward to working with the kids."

He didn't really want to go there.

She eyed him. "You don't look very thrilled about it."

"To tell you the truth, I'm a little nervous about working with little kids. I've never done it before."

"Oh, is that all? It's a cinch. They're a lot of fun, really. You'll get the hang of it before you know it."

"I guess. At least it will help me keep my car running." He patted the dashboard of his Datsun.

"You'll see. We'll have fun. They told me I'll be working here and there wherever they need extra help. Most likely, that's what you'll be doing too. Turn right here."

He shrugged, admitting to himself that it might not be so bad after all.

They talked a little about the job and how maybe they could work together to come up with ideas for the long days of summer.

"Okay, turn left here," she said with a smile.

He looked at her in surprise. "The airport?"

She nodded. "My uncle owns it."

"Really?"

"You mentioned to me once that you liked airplanes, and I thought it would be fun to have a picnic here."

Admiration for this girl flooded through him. "This is so cool."

A faint hint of color lit her cheeks. "Thanks."

He pulled the car into the small parking lot, and as they got out, Arielle said, "Let's go to the office first. Uncle Ed knows we're coming, and I want to say hello."

Sam straightened himself and hoped he looked presentable. It wasn't every day that he met the owner of an airport. Just then a white Cessna with orange stripes across the center taxied down the runway. Shielding his eyes from the sun, he watched as the plane slowly edged forward, gained momentum, and then eased into a cloudless sky without a hitch.

A friend of his mom's had a pilot's license and had taken him and Emily on a short ride. Christopher didn't want to go. Emily hadn't been crazy about it, but he'd never forgotten how it felt to glide over land, to feel as though nothing could touch him up there.

"You ready to meet my uncle?" Arielle tugged on his arm, her bright smile in place.

"Sure." He followed her into the office, where a couple of upholstered chairs, complete with tears and snags, sat in front of the counter area. The room smelled of cigarette smoke and day-old coffee. Fine dirt, cigarette butts, and fragmented wrappers littered the cement floor. Crumpled papers bulged from an overflowing trash can.

Sam's grandma would have a fit.

After Arielle had made the appropriate introductions, her uncle Ed offered to take them around the airport.

There was an office building and four big hangars that housed four airplanes each. A ribbon of tarmac ran through the property. Fuel pumps were located in another area. A few people milled around.

"I hear you like airplanes," Uncle Ed said to Sam.

"I sure do."

"Ever been in a small one?"

"Once. It was awesome."

Ed smiled. "How about I take you two up for a ride?"

Arielle clapped her hands together.

Sam felt as happy as Arielle but, of course, guys didn't

show it. He merely shoved a hand in his pocket and said, "That would be great."

His hands were sweaty. His heart thumped in his ears. When was the last time he'd been this excited about anything—well, next to taking Arielle to the prom?

Inside the plane, Ed Haffner explained some things on the control panel while Arielle checked her makeup in a small mirror.

"I don't know how you guys remember all that stuff," Sam said with true admiration.

"It becomes second nature after a while." He adjusted a few knobs and turned to Sam. "Why don't you sit up here in the copilot seat?" He looked at Arielle. "That okay, kiddo?"

"Sure." She scooted into the rear seat and lifted a smile of sheer pleasure to Sam as he moved to the front.

The upholstery squawked when he strapped himself into the seat. The engines roared to life. The cab of the plane made him glad he didn't suffer from claustrophobia. Looking at the size of the control panel spread out before him, Sam suddenly knew the true meaning of *cool*.

Arielle's uncle talked over the handset of the radio, saying things Sam couldn't understand, and the next thing he knew, his stomach gave a slight twinge and they were airborne.

He stared out the window and tried to drink it all in. Not a cloud in the sky. The sun bleached everything clean below them.

Once they reached altitude, the plane settled into a

pleasant cruising speed. Ed went on to explain some of the controls and let Sam push a button here and there.

"See that farm over there?"

Sam nodded.

"That's Heather Creek Farm."

Sam looked at him in surprise. "You know where I live?"

Ed smiled. "I make it my business to know the boys my niece is dating."

Sam blinked.

"Uncle Ed!" Arielle said from the backseat.

Ed gave a hearty laugh. "Okay, the truth is, she told me where you live."

Sam nodded with relief, and then turned his attention back to the ground below. He could make out the silvery feed bin, the red barn, and the white farmhouse. A car the size of a matchbox ambled slowly down the lane.

They eventually landed, but even after they had reached the ground, Sam's head stayed in the clouds. Right then and there, he felt certain of his destiny. He wanted to pilot an airplane. Right now he didn't have the money or the equipment to make it happen, but somehow he knew it was meant to be. Surely his grandparents would agree. Though he suspected his grandma might worry. 'Course he wouldn't tell them just yet.

THURSDAY EVENING WAS WARM and still, and after dinner, Dana, Pete, Bob, and Charlotte decided to sit on the front porch. The wooden floor groaned beneath them.

Flowery, plump pillows graced the wooden swing. Bob had replaced the chains that held the swing in place, and their silver links glistened in the light of the evening sun.

"Sam still out with that girl?" Bob asked.

Charlotte gave him an impatient look. "Yes, he's still out with Arielle." In reality, it wasn't so much that she was upset with Bob calling Arielle "that girl" as she was with the fact that Sam was spending more and more time with her.

One of the barn cats perched on a fence post. Mama cat sat nearby, grooming her paws. Cattle stirred in the distant pasture.

"Sit, Toby," Charlotte heard her grandson say. Toby immediately fell back on her haunches, eyes eager with anticipation. They had obviously played this game before. Christopher tossed Toby a treat. She sprang to her feet and with one easy jump, lapped the doggie treat in midair.

The porch audience cheered and clapped.

Evidently assuming the show was over, Toby trotted most pleasantly in the opposite direction. The proud plume of her tail and triumphant arch of her head made her appear every inch a show dog.

"Will you look at that," Bob said, pure wonder in his voice.

"I told you Christopher was working hard." Charlotte felt a tad smug about her grandson's determination.

Bob scratched the evening whiskers on his chin. "I have to say, I wouldn't have imagined him taking this so seriously."

"Kids can surprise us."

Dana and Pete settled beside one another on the porch swing while Charlotte sat in the corner wicker rocker and Bob brought a folding chair from the house to sit on.

Charlotte took in the damp scent of the air. Swallows fluttered and chattered from treetops. The orange blaze of the evening sun exploded across the horizon, granting another perfect setting on a summer's night in the country.

Charlotte sat on the cushion and eased into a gentle rocking motion. "I guess Pete's told you our good news," she said to Dana.

Dana's eyebrows shifted upward. "What news?"

"Bill and Anna are expecting."

Large brown eyes fringed with thick lashes opened wide with the happy announcement. Dana turned to Pete. "You didn't tell me." Her voice held disappointment rather than accusation.

He shoved the bill of his baseball cap up his forehead and looked at her. "Didn't think about it."

She waved him off and looked back to Charlotte, who rolled her eyes. "Men."

A wide smile split Dana's face, causing faint wrinkles to crowd the corners of her eyes.

"Besides, if you ask me, I think he's too old to have more kids," Pete mumbled.

"Oh, I don't know," Dana said wistfully. "As long as you're able, a family is a good idea anytime."

Charlotte felt her jaw go slack. Pete looked as though someone had just taken his one and only copy of *The Princess Bride*. Bob kept his nose stuck in the *Farmer's Almanac*.

"Well, it's not for us to say one way or the other, Pete. It's their business." Charlotte wanted to put an end to Pete's grousing.

"Anna must be so happy," Dana said.

There was more in the air than the scent of Charlotte's leftover spaghetti and garlic bread.

Pete cleared his throat and shuffled his feet. "Mom, that iced tea sure was good. Mind if I get some more?"

Charlotte started to get up.

"No, you stay seated. I'll get it." Pete turned to Dana. "You want some?"

She gave him a glazed stare.

"Dana?"

"Huh? Oh, no, no, thank you, Pete." Her eyes went back to dreaming.

Pete's gaze locked with Charlotte's. His eyes held unadulterated fear.

With no time to lose, Pete skedaddled into the house, practically leaving skid marks as the screen door slammed behind him.

Charlotte swallowed her giggle. Glancing at Dana, she could see the woman had no idea about the worries she had set in motion for Charlotte's son. Charlotte glanced at Bob, focusing intently on the almanac. How a man could study the moon's effect on crops when his family had so much drama going on right in front of him was beyond her.

Chapter Six

"Do you suppose she's up?" Ashley asked as she and Emily stood at Miss Middleton's front door on Monday morning.

Emily looked at her reflection in the glass storm door and adjusted her bangs. "Of course she's up. Old people don't sleep late. Besides, she told us to come at ten."

Ashley bit her lower lip. "I hope she's not sick."

Emily sighed and looked at her friend. "You worry too much. She's not sick. She's just slow."

Just then footsteps shuffled on the other side of the door as Miss Middleton slowly made her way to them.

Emily tossed an I-told-you-so glance toward Ashley as the door crept open.

"Good morning," Miss Middleton said with a sweet smile, her dull, blue eyes sparking to life at the sight of the girls, causing a twinge of guilt in Emily.

They stepped inside. Midmorning sunlight lit the room, revealing dust that had collected on tabletops and the faint line of cobwebs hanging in ceiling corners. By the looks of things, Emily figured she'd be getting a new pair of jeans and money toward her digital camera this summer.

"Well, girls, I thought today we would concentrate on the kitchen. I haven't been able to entertain for some time in this room. How can I show I love Jesus if I can't show people I love them?" She turned around and looked at them. "And we all know the best way to reach people is through their stomachs."

Emily and Ashley exchanged a glance. Was she kidding? This lady was eighty-eight years old, and she was worried about reaching out to others? Emily couldn't quite wrap her mind around that one. Though she wouldn't be surprised if her grandma would be the same way when she became really old.

Emily and Ashley spent the next two hours emptying cabinets, washing them down, and then putting the dishes back inside. The room smelled fresh and lemony.

Once that was done, they cleaned the oven and the refrigerator. Emily noticed the refrigerator didn't have much inside, but she doubted that Miss Middleton needed very much for herself.

"Now, you have to join me for lunch," Miss Middleton said.

Emily couldn't imagine what they would eat.

Miss Middleton reached into the refrigerator and pulled out a large covered bowl. "I made this vegetable soup just last night. It was my mother's recipe." Admiration shone in her face.

The girls helped her set the table, and they soon sat down

in chairs covered with plump green cushions. Experience had taught Emily to wait a moment before digging in. Her grandparents always said grace before the meal, and she wondered if Miss Middleton might do the same.

She did.

"That's a neat train you have in the hallway," Ashley commented.

Miss Middleton took a sip from her iced tea and then leaned against the cushion on the back of her chair. "Ah, the Orphan Train," she said.

The two girls looked at her.

"You've heard of that, of course . . ."

Ashley shook her head, and Emily knew they were done for. Showing interest like that to an old person was like saying, "Sic 'em!" to a dog. Now they were in for a history lesson, for sure.

"Oh, my, my. Well, I was two years old when my sister was born in New York. We never knew our papa. Times were hard, and Mama had to take care of us all by herself." She rubbed her knobby fingers while thinking. "When I was seven and Rose was five, Mama got sick with smallpox. She died later. We didn't have any family that I knew about, and I heard some grown-ups talking about us having to go to a home for children. I'd heard kids talk about it before, and I wasn't going to let anyone hurt Rose and me, so the night our neighbor stayed with us, I packed up a suitcase, grabbed some bread, and sneaked my sister out of the house."

Ashley gasped.

"Weren't you scared?" Emily asked, scarcely aware she was caught up by the story too.

Miss Middleton chuckled. "Didn't have the sense to be, I guess."

"Where'd you go?" Ashley asked before taking a spoonful of soup.

"I found a spot by the bridge near our house. Other homeless people were there too. One old woman watched over us. She didn't look like much, but she had a kind heart."

Emily took a bite of french bread but wished she hadn't. She was afraid crunching the crust would make her miss something Miss Middleton might say.

"One night some man came along. All whiskers and meanness, that's what he was." She gave a visible shiver. "That old woman shooed him away from us. Rose cried, and I wanted to, but I couldn't." She looked at the girls. "I had to be brave for her."

Always thinking of others. Just like Grandma. Emily wondered how some people could do that when others, like her, were too busy thinking of themselves.

"What did you do after that? Where did you live? Who took care of you?" Ashley peppered her with questions.

"Let's save that for another day, shall we? I'm tired, and you girls must have other things to do." She stood and they followed suit, cleaning up after themselves, putting the dishes away, and saying good-bye. They would come back at ten on Friday.

Surprisingly, Emily could hardly wait.

"ARE THE GIRLS BACK from Miss Middleton's house yet?" Hannah wanted to know.

"No. But Melody is picking them up when they're done, and I left a note for Emily that I was walking with you, so we're good." Charlotte saw evidence in the trees and shrubs that summer was in full bloom.

"Where's Christopher?"

"He's upstairs. I told him I was leaving too. He's reading some books we picked up at the library. They're books on how to train dogs." Charlotte chuckled. "He is determined to make Toby a winner if it kills him."

"How's Toby taking it?"

"Oh, Toby's good-natured for the most part, especially when she gets treats."

"Did Sam find a job yet?"

"Yeah, he got a job at the day care in town. So that's good."

"But?"

Charlotte turned to Hannah.

"I heard a *but* in there somewhere," Hannah said.

"No buts. It's just that—"

"Uh-huh, just as I thought."

"Okay, so there is a *but*."

Hannah laughed. "I thought so."

"Arielle works there too."

"I thought you liked Arielle."

"I do, but that doesn't mean I want them together all the time."

"I see." Hannah suddenly got quiet, and Charlotte wished she hadn't said anything.

"I'm trying not to worry though. The Lord will help us."

Hannah gently grabbed her friend's arm. "He will, Charlotte. He surely will."

Charlotte cleared her throat before tears could pool in her eyes. "So did I tell you why I want to walk more?" Charlotte picked up the pace a little, her sneakers spitting gravel behind her.

"Whoa, don't go too fast or I'll never make it," Hannah said between gulps of air.

Charlotte slowed down. "Sorry."

"Is it the apple pie?" Hannah asked. "Is that the reason for the sudden interest in exercise?"

"No, that's not it. I want to train for a walking event. While I was at the library, I noticed a brochure on the bulletin board about a walk for diabetes. I was hoping to get a few sponsors and walk. You know, do my part to help out."

"Does Bob know?"

"No. I'm afraid it might embarrass him. But I feel so . . . so . . ."

"Helpless?"

"That's it."

"I understand. My uncle felt that way when my aunt was diagnosed. I remember he always contributed to the cause after that."

"When it strikes home, it has a way of making one more aware and more charitable."

"That it does."

Sparrows collected on a telephone line as though they

were having a community gathering. That's what the diabetes walk was about too—a community gathering together to help others in need.

"Well, this is a good way to get in shape. Count me in."

Charlotte turned to Hannah. "You mean you want to train with me?"

She shrugged. "Why not? Could be fun—in a grueling sort of way."

Charlotte looked at her again. "You're the best, Hannah; do you know that?"

"I'm not all that noble. If I walk, it also means I can eat more dessert."

Their laughter carried into the afternoon air, and Charlotte knew she would be hard-pressed to find a better friend than Hannah Carter anywhere.

WHEN CHARLOTTE GOT HOME, she heard Emily milling around in her bedroom. Charlotte knocked on the door.

"Em, I'm getting ready to fix dinner, and I could use your help in the kitchen."

Charlotte heard a heavy sigh but ignored it. Instead, she walked down the stairs and hoped she wouldn't have to climb back upstairs to remind Emily. Just as Charlotte reached the bottom stair, she heard Emily's door crack open. With a purposeful stride, she continued toward the kitchen.

"What's for dinner?" Emily asked when she walked into the kitchen.

Charlotte pulled a large pie plate from the cupboard. "I thought we'd have pot pie." Charlotte placed the flour canister on the counter along with a few other necessary ingredients for a pie crust and set to work. "How was your time with Miss Middleton?"

Emily shrugged. "Okay. Did you know she was on the Orphan Train?"

"Oh yes, I'd forgotten about that. Did she tell you girls about it?"

"A little bit."

Charlotte could hear the interest in Emily's voice and was pleased. This would be a good job for her.

"So what did she say? I haven't heard her story in a while." Charlotte sprinkled a dusting of flour on the counter, and then plopped the ball of crust on it. With her rolling pin, she began to roll out the dough.

"Can we talk about it another time, Grandma? I really don't want to go into it now."

"All right. Why don't you wash up so you can help me set the table."

"Why can't the boys help? I've been working all afternoon. I'm tired."

Her voice teetered on disrespect, and Charlotte felt obliged to deal with it. "Emily, we all have to do things we don't feel like doing from time to time. The boys will help with cleanup."

Emily blew out a long, dramatic sigh, and then stomped off to the bathroom.

Charlotte blew a strand of hair from her forehead as

her strong arms finished rolling the dough. It was pro-ba-bly good that she had dough to work out her frustrations on.

SOMETIMES GRANDMA drove her crazy. Emily plunked down on her bed. She was tired and didn't want to help with dinner. Why couldn't someone else do it? She'd done her share around the farm and at Miss Middleton's. She did more work than her two brothers put together.

She loved her grandma, but sometimes she felt that Grandma wanted to control her life.

Well, she would get through the next few years and move on. One day she would have her own place and get to do what she wanted, when she wanted. No one would be there to boss her around.

After dinner, Emily asked her grandma if she could take Princess out for a ride.

"That will be all right if you don't stay out too late. You would be hard to spot on a dark horse at night."

"Okay. Thanks." Emily turned and quickly went outside before anyone could stop her. She needed some time to herself.

Emily saddled up Princess and took off down the path toward the Norris house. The wind was soft and warm on her skin. The smell of freshly tilled soil swirled in the evening air. She took in roads and meadows as far as the eye could see. Typical.

The isolation used to make her crazy. When they had

moved to Nebraska after her mom's death, Emily considered the town of Bedford a dead place too. She wondered why her grandparents couldn't see that they needed their friends, people around them, to keep their minds off . . . things.

Now, though, she had to admit there were times when she welcomed the solitude. Just the sound of Princess's hoofbeats pattering a steady clip-clop was so soothing to Emily. When life overwhelmed or frustrated her, the horses offered a safe retreat. She patted her filly.

Emily didn't mean to get so upset with Grandma. She knew her grandparents were trying their best. It was just that life was so out of sorts. Memories of her mother had sustained her up to now. But the memories were coming less frequently, and it frightened her that her mom's image sometimes eluded her.

Emily leaned into Princess and stroked her thick, strong neck. "Help me, girl."

The chestnut horse rewarded her with a comforting whinny.

Satisfied, Emily sat back up on the saddle, feeling better already. She gave herself over to Princess, holding the reins loosely between her fingers, allowing her thoughts to turn fuzzy while the filly led the way.

Princess seemed to know what she needed. The horse pushed when Emily needed to work through an issue and meandered at a pleasurable clip-clop when Emily needed calm.

The sound of approaching hoofbeats shook her to attention.

"Fancy meeting you here."

Emily turned to see Hunter Norris, a boy from her English class at school. Hunter lived down the road, and they rode together from time to time. Hunter had dark, rugged good looks and sometimes hinted that he might have a crush on Emily, but she was more interested in his friendship than a boyfriend-girlfriend relationship.

"Hi, Hunter. Haven't seen you since school let out."

"I've been busy helping out at the grocery store twenty hours a week."

"Oh." It seemed everyone had to work around here.

"What are you doing this summer?"

"I'm helping a lady clean house." She felt kind of stupid saying that. It would have sounded much cooler to announce that she had a job at the mall. But of course they had no mall in Bedford. Still, she was glad she had a job or she might sound lazy.

"That's good."

She didn't know what was so good about it.

"It feels great to ride again," he said, taking in a sweeping view of the landscape. "I've been too busy to take Rambo out, and I've missed it. I need to be ready to compete in the barrel races at the county fair later this summer." He patted his sorrel quarter horse.

"Cool," Emily said. She felt comfortable riding with Hunter. He was a good friend who understood her love for Princess.

While their horses' strong hoofbeats drummed a steady rhythm through the evening air and the moon slowly rose in the sky, Emily and Hunter talked of school and future goals.

"Well, it's getting late. Guess I'd better get home," she said.

"Yeah, we don't exactly have reflectors on these things."

Hunter followed her to the farm. "See you next time, Em." He waved and headed on home.

Chapter Seven

Tuesday morning Sam took a deep breath and stepped into the day-care center.

"Good morning, Sam." A middle-aged woman with a sharp chin and sensible eyes took crisp, precise steps over to him and gave his hand two curt shakes. "I'm Deborah Trent, and I'll be training you with the kids over the next week."

The way she said *training* made him feel he had wandered into a zoo. He scanned the crowd of kids. There was not a single one over five feet tall. How hard could it be?

Another woman came into the room and promptly began working with the children while Deborah motioned Sam to follow her into another room.

"First of all, we're hoping that you will be able to keep the more, shall we say, rambunctious kids entertained." She flipped through a voluminous notebook filled with day-care stuff, and he silently prayed he wouldn't have to read all that.

"We have two adults in the room at a time—one teacher, one assistant. You won't make the lesson plans, but you'll help keep the kids under control and keep them busy and active during playtime. Here it is." She swiveled the notebook toward him so he could read it. "This is the games section. You may read through these pages and get some ideas. What we want—" She pointed to a chair. "Let's go ahead and sit down."

He complied, still staring at the notebook, swallowing hard so his tongue wouldn't stick to the roof of his mouth.

"You'll plan the games, help keep an eye on the children at recess, read stories during storytime, that sort of thing. You won't stay with any one class. We'll shift you around as needed. You will help with field trips as well. We might even need you to help in the kitchen."

Despair shot straight to his heart. If there was one thing he hated, it was kitchen duty. It was bad enough he had to do it at home.

And to think he had imagined this as an easy job. Couple of games of kickball a day and he could go home, that kind of thing. This was not turning out at all the way he imagined. If he didn't have to face his grandpa every night, he'd tell her thanks but no thanks.

Mrs. Trent finished explaining the inner workings of the day care, and before he knew what hit him, it was time to leave.

Backpacks and papers cluttered the doorway while kids tugged and shoved one another as they waited in line for their rides. Boys teased, and girls huddled and giggled. Sam had never understood why girls giggled all the time.

The teachers welcomed him with open arms. Now he could

see why. This was a scary place. Little people everywhere. He'd seen *Dennis the Menace,* so he knew very well what kids were capable of.

The longer he stood there watching them squirm and wiggle about, the more convinced he was of one thing: He did not want to be there.

"IT FEELS GOOD to get those tarts finished," Hannah said later that afternoon while she and Charlotte took a walk together.

"Who did you say you were making them for again?" Charlotte asked, feeling a tad out of breath.

"Oh, we're trying out different desserts for the mother-daughter tea. Our committee is meeting tonight and bringing desserts to taste and test. Since it's our first official tea, we wanted it to be really nice."

Charlotte looked at her in surprise. "What mother-daughter tea?"

Hannah frowned. "You didn't know? I thought Emily would have told you by now."

"She hasn't."

"I hope I haven't spoiled her surprise. They announced it at church last Sunday during the teen and children services to give the kids a chance to ask their moms before they hear about it this Sunday."

Charlotte felt her stomach plunge.

Hannah picked up on her friend's feelings. "I'm sure she'll ask you, Charlotte. Don't worry."

"I'm sure she will." Charlotte hoped she sounded more confident than she felt. "But if she doesn't say anything, it's all right. I'm not her mother, after all. I don't want Emily to ever feel as though I'm trying to take her mother's place."

"I know. I'm sure she doesn't feel that way. I truly admire the way you and Bob have taken the kids in and adjusted as a family. You've made it work. No matter how rough the road, you've made it work."

"Thanks, Hannah. We love the kids, and we're blessed to get to know them and be a part of their lives—even though the circumstances surrounding that were hard."

"Yeah."

They walked a little farther in silence. "By the way, would you like to try any of the desserts, give me your two cents' worth on them?"

"Sounds heavenly, but I'd better not." Charlotte didn't mention that the whole tea thing had taken away her appetite.

After their walk, Charlotte worked on the farm books and the evening meal. She made hints over dinner that she hoped would prompt Emily to discuss the tea, but her granddaughter never mentioned it.

Following dinner, Charlotte scrubbed the kitchen so clean she wondered if someone would slip on the shiny floor when they walked into the room. Sometimes it just helped calm her when she used a little elbow grease.

She'd discuss the matter with Bob. He was so levelheaded. He'd help her see it in the proper perspective.

Still, she couldn't help thinking how nice it would be to attend the tea with her granddaughter.

THE NEXT AFTERNOON Christopher dragged the big tin washtub across the grass into the middle of the backyard. Chickens squawked and fluttered out of the way. Toby probably wasn't going to like getting her bath out here in front of God and everybody, but Grandma wouldn't let him wash Toby in the house, so he had no choice. He wondered if Toby would like bath time any better than he did.

Christopher looked at the low-slung clouds overhead and thought they looked dirtier than Toby. He could smell the threat of rain. That's what his mom used to say, but he had never really known what it meant. Sparrows chattered in nearby trees.

He gathered the soap and finally the hose. Filling the tub, he left room to add some hot water from the house. Running back and forth a couple of times to the house, he filled a large bucket with hot water and poured it into the tub. Toby had sneaked into the house when Christopher was carrying out the last bucket of water, so he had to go get her.

He heard Grandma working in the kitchen. He went in to talk to her. She wrung out a dishcloth and then draped it over the faucet.

"Have you seen Toby? She got inside when I carried out the water."

"Oh, dear." Grandma picked up a kitchen towel and dried a plate. "You'll no doubt find her under one of the beds."

Christopher rolled his eyes. How could he make a show dog out of a chicken?

"Toby, come here, girl," Christopher called out as he went from room to room, checking under beds. He was glad he found Toby under Grandma and Grandpa's bed before he had to check under Sam's. Sam had a messy room, and he was afraid of what he might find under his bed.

"Come on, girl," Christopher said, yanking at Toby's collar. "I don't like to take a bath either, but it feels pretty good once you're all done." The fear in Toby's eyes said she didn't believe him.

"Now, Toby, you get yourself outside," Grandma said, hands on her hips. "It's high time you had a bath, young lady."

Christopher appreciated Grandma's help, though he could see it wasn't doing a whole lot to motivate Toby. She panted hard and loud, almost like she was gearing up to take off or something.

"Here, let me help you," Grandma said, scrunching down onto the floor. Christopher heard her bones crack. He tried not to worry.

Once she folded into a kneeling position, she pulled Toby out from under the bed. Christopher had his doubts as to whether Grandma could get up without breaking anything. He offered to help her, but she assured him she could manage by herself.

Once Toby was in clear view, Christopher snapped the leash onto her collar and stood to lead her outside. He tugged on the leash, but the stubborn canine dug her paws into the carpet.

Grandma proceeded to give her a good tongue-lashing, as she called it, and Toby whipped right into shape. With her tail tucked between her legs, Toby lagged behind Christopher as though he were leading her to the pound where she would breathe her last.

As Christopher and Toby headed for the door, he saw Grandma watching them. She covered her mouth with one hand and rubbed her backside with the other. He hoped she hadn't broken anything.

Arriving outside, they stopped in front of the washtub. "Okay, Toby, time to jump in," Christopher said in the most authoritative voice he could muster.

Toby sat back on her haunches and with large, melting eyes gazed up at Christopher. She mustered a sympathetic face and pathetic whine.

Christopher tried to stay tough, but his heart dipped a little. "Toby, you have to do this."

More whining, pleading eyes.

Christopher recognized an actor when he saw one. "Don't make me pick you up, Toby."

Toby inched backward, tugging on her leash.

Christopher sighed. "Okay, that's it." He wrapped his arms around Toby's underbelly and with a grunt and a heave, pulled her up. Toby would not go willingly. She struggled and squirmed; Christopher tugged and pulled. They were, for the moment, a tangle of arms and paws.

Finally, Christopher shoved her over the tub's rim, causing an enormous splash of water and puffs of fluffy bubbles to land on the surrounding ground. Toby shook herself, sending a spray of sputtering bubbles everywhere. Christopher's entire front side sagged with water. Toby began to pant again. Christopher did too.

With sheer determination, Christopher got the dog brush and set to work. When he turned away to get more soap, Toby shook herself with great vigor once again, causing water and suds to spray everything within a two-mile radius. Christopher let out a yelp and was almost sure he saw a doggy smile play on Toby's mouth.

Rolling up his sleeves, Christopher determinedly grabbed the dog soap and the brush and scrubbed the dog so thoroughly, they were both soon lost in a sea of bubbles. Toby finally settled in to her plight, though sympathetic whimpers filtered through the air.

As the suds flew, the clouds grew darker.

"Christopher, it's not that cold out here. You go ahead and rinse Toby off with the hose when you're done washing her," Grandma said, casting a worried glance at the clouds.

"Okay."

Grandma turned toward the door. Just as Christopher watched her step inside, one of the farm cats decided to trot his completely soiled and unkempt self past Toby. The tomcat seemed to delight in Toby's total and utter humiliation.

That was his mistake.

Before Christopher could blink, Toby clambered out of the tub, shook hard enough to strip bark from the trees, and went after that cat like there was no tomorrow. Yapping and barking, suds flying everywhere, Toby chased the cat. Christopher chased Toby, and Grandma chased all of them while chickens flapped out of the way and squawked at the indignity of it all.

Just then Grandpa showed up on the scene, got out of the truck, and with mouth gaping, stood still and watched everything.

Gravel scrunched and twigs snapped beneath Christopher's feet as he burned rubber going after Toby. To top it all off, the clouds suddenly burst, and a thunderous downpour drenched the lot of them, so much so that Christopher didn't have to hose Toby down for a final rinse.

Perched atop a high tree branch, being whipped around by the wind and the rain, the tomcat hung on for dear life. In the meantime, Toby gave the frightened feline a piece of her mind—or at least that's what the barking sounded like to Christopher. No doubt, the cat had learned his lesson.

With Grandma's help, they were able to haul Toby away from the cat and tug the rebellious hound onto the porch.

"You keep Toby here, and I'll get a towel so you can dry her off," Grandma said, her hair clinging in wet strands around her face and her clothes sopped with rain. Distant thunder growled, and lightening flickered across the sky.

It was then that the faint sound of a chuckle reached

them, and they both turned to see Grandpa standing in the doorway, struggling to catch his breath between spells of laughter.

Christopher had never seen Grandpa laugh so hard. He barely even smiled usually. He sure was making up for it now.

But when Grandma looked at him, it didn't last long.

JUST THEN PETE AND DANA drove up. Charlotte waved and headed into the house. Pete and Dana soon followed, dropping an umbrella by the door.

"Got room for one more for dinner?" Pete took one look at his mom and stopped in his tracks. "Whoa, you sure got drenched."

"I don't want to talk about it." Charlotte turned to Dana.

"We'd love to have you join us for dinner, Dana. You're always welcome here."

Charlotte and Christopher dried off and changed clothes. Sam and Emily emerged from their rooms to join the rest of the family. After a fine dinner of meatloaf, mashed potatoes, green beans, and salad, everyone soon settled into comfortable conversation in the family room.

Charlotte tried not to stare, but she caught the way Dana threaded her fingers through Pete's and took note that their relationship seemed to be growing closer. She wondered where that would take her son.

There were days when Pete's life was so entangled with the farm, she wondered if he would ever marry. Charlotte hoped that she and Bob didn't make him feel that he couldn't have a life beyond the farm.

Of course that was silly. Pete had loved the farm from the time he was born. One of his first words was *tractor*. She smiled at the memory. *They sure do grow up fast.*

One of these days, Pete would have little ones of his own running through the yard, laughing, squealing, and scaring the chickens. She glanced once more at her son. By the look of things, it could be sooner than they figured.

Chapter Eight

Emily sorted through Miss Middleton's linen closet while Ashley worked in the front hallway closet. Miss Middleton stood within earshot of both, advising what to toss and what to keep. By the end of the afternoon, they had a pile to pitch and another pile to give away.

Emily was glad it was Friday. She could use a couple of days off.

Miss Middleton shook her head. "My, my, will you look at that," she said, staring at the piles. "Years of memories right there." She shook her head and looked at the girls. "Well, it's time to let go." She shrugged. "Now, let's have that tea."

They followed her to the kitchen, where they helped her get the glasses and ice cubes for their tea, and then they all settled at the table.

"Still want to hear about the Orphan Train?" she asked.

Emily and Ashley nodded eagerly. Though Emily did not want to be there, she had to admit she looked forward to hearing more about the Orphan Train.

Miss Middleton smiled and then tapped a knobby finger against her chin. "Let's see; where was I?"

"You left off at the bridge with your sister and some woman protecting you from a whiskery man," Ashley said with enthusiasm.

Miss Middleton chuckled. Then her face clouded with remembrance. "Yes, that woman took care of us. She helped us find food. We'd go to a few of the restaurants and wait till they tossed out food at night. One evening when a man at Luigi's Italian Restaurant took out the trash, he saw Rose and me waiting in the darkness. The next night, and every night thereafter, when we came back, that man—I assume it was Luigi—had a bag of warm food waiting on the back doorstep." She turned to the girls. "And it was mighty good food. Lasagna, spaghetti, fettuccine, garlic bread, salad. I'll bet I gained ten pounds eating that stuff over time." She clucked her tongue. "Yes, ma'am, that man was a godsend. We prayed every day that God would bless him real good for his kindness to us."

Emily and Ashley listened with rapt attention while sipping their tea.

"What else happened?" Ashley asked.

"Life was hard in those days. New York winters can be brutal. Icy winds, biting cold. The bridge offered a little shelter, but hardly the warmth of a home. The old woman shared her tattered blanket with us. Our thin coats offered little protection. Fortunately, it was early winter, so we hadn't suffered from frostbite yet.

"Then one night when we went to pick up our dinner at Luigi's, we found three bags where our one bag normally sat. Peeking inside, we saw our hot meal—which seemed more plentiful every night—in one bag. The other bags held two small coats, hats, scarves, mittens, and blankets! We thought it was Christmas. I wanted to share with the old woman, but she said they were too small for her. She looked awful cold though. And she had a bad cough."

Emily couldn't imagine how awful that would be.

"We shared our meals each night with her, of course. We became a sort of underground community. If anyone wandered into our 'homestead' and threatened anyone in any way, the grown-ups stood together and got rid of him.

"I remembered hearing Mama pray, so I made the old woman pray with us every night. She didn't seem to like it at first, but as time went on, she prayed longer and with more punch." Miss Middleton chuckled. "I think she started believing what she was praying.

"God continued to work through that man at Luigi's Restaurant to help us. I truly believe he saved our lives." She looked at the girls. "The night we found the coats in the bags, we put them on, along with the scarves, hats, and mittens. Rose and I swirled around and around, we were so happy. That's when I caught a glimpse of the man's smiling face through the window. When he saw me looking, he slipped out of view so I couldn't see him. He was an angel; that's what he was."

Miss Middleton yawned and rubbed her eyes.

"You've given us a lot to think about till next time," Emily said. "We'll let you get your rest for now."

Ashley nodded, obviously thinking the same thing. "Thanks for sharing with us, Miss Middleton. We'd better not bother you anymore today. But we'll look forward to hearing more next time."

"I'll look forward to that, girls," she said as though she truly meant it.

Once Emily got back home to the safe confines of her room, she thought over what Miss Middleton had said. She imagined the old woman as a little girl watching over a younger sister. She thought about the woman at the bridge who watched over them. She thought about the prayers and wondered if that's what truly made the difference or if her life would have turned out the same no matter what.

Then she thought of the man at Luigi's. He did seem to have been an answer to their prayers. What would have happened to them if he had not helped them? Maybe God did use people to help each other. But what if they weren't listening to him?

Then Emily thought about her own situation. No, she didn't have to live out in the cold, but her mother had been taken from her, and they had been uprooted from their home and had come to live on a farm in corn country. Even as she defended herself, a thread of shame inched its way into her heart. She knew things could be much worse.

And then there was her grandma and grandpa. Maybe they were answers to prayer too. Where would they be without them? Their dad was nowhere to be found. Would they have become wards of the state? Would they have been split up? Put in foster homes? She shuddered to think about it, yet it *was* interesting to think about—that they might have been there because of someone's prayer.

Maybe there was something to what Grandma and Grandpa tried to teach them about God.

FRIDAY NIGHT AND SAM DIDN'T HAVE anything to do. This was so not San Diego.

His buddies had to work, and Arielle was out with her girlfriends. Sam had started to feel sorry for himself when he thought about the airport. He had nothing else to do. Might as well go hang out there.

Once Sam arrived at the airport, he could hardly believe it was so deserted for a Friday night. He should have known.

"Where is everyone?" he asked, sagging into a chair across from Ed Haffner's desk.

"Two planes just left. Most folks wait till Saturday for their trips, rather than flying at night. Just depends."

"Boy, it must be something else to pilot a plane."

"You think?" Ed's eyes flickered with amusement.

Sam nodded. "One of these days I'm gonna learn how. I told my dad that years ago, and I meant it."

"What's holding you back?"

Sam blinked and then coughed. "Well, money for one thing. A plane for another. They seem to go hand in hand."

"They do at that." Uncle Ed rubbed his jaw. "I've been thinking. Ari told me you're working at the day-care center in the afternoon."

Sam nodded.

"I could use somebody to come out here and help fuel up the planes, clean 'em out, sweep the hangars, all that. What if you came out here in the mornings and helped me around here, and in turn, I would give you a few flying lessons?"

Sam's breath caught in his throat. He could hardly find

his voice. "Free lessons?" Adrenaline shot through him. This was beyond his wildest imaginings.

A broad smile split Ed's face. "Well, not exactly free. You'd have to work for them. And this will just whet your taste, really. Won't be enough to get you a license. To do it right, you'll need more airtime than I can provide for you and about five weeks of ground school before the big final exam. But this experience might show you if you're really interested or if it's a passing fancy."

"I understand." Nothing could deter his excitement.

"Get here at eight o'clock. We'll go up before the customers start trickling in. After we land, you can work till around eleven thirty, take time for lunch, then head to your other job. How does that sound?"

Sam could hardly sit still. "It sounds awesome."

Dressed in overalls with a red kerchief hanging from his back pocket, a tall, lanky man stepped into the room. "Hey, Ed, we need you out in hangar three."

"Okay, Roy, be right there."

Roy disappeared through the door.

"That was Roy Greene. He works here as a mechanic for our planes. Well, listen, kid, I've got to go. I'll see you here on Monday morning, eight o'clock sharp." He extended his hand and gave Sam a good hearty shake. "Oh, one more thing." He poked his head back through the door. "I'll need a written permission slip from your grandparents since you're underage."

"Thank you, sir," Sam said. When he walked out of the airport, he decided he didn't need an airplane.

He was already flying.

It was only after he got home and came face to face with Grandma that he realized he couldn't tell her about his new job. Not yet. She'd worry and might not even let him take the lessons.

Maybe he could talk Grandpa into signing the permission slip for him. He didn't know how he would do it. He only knew he would. No matter what.

"SO, WOULD YOU CARE for any *tea* and cookies, Emily?" Charlotte asked, extra emphasis on the word *tea* in a last-ditch effort to jog Emily's memory about the upcoming event before they announced it at church tomorrow.

"Yeah, that would be great."

Emily grabbed a glass from the cupboard and put ice in it while Charlotte lifted the pitcher from the refrigerator.

"Get me a glass too, will you?" Charlotte asked.

Emily retrieved another one, and they soon slid into their seats at the table.

Charlotte placed a plate of chocolate chip cookies in front of them with a couple of saucers and napkins.

"How are things going with Miss Middleton?" Charlotte wanted to keep communication open with Emily and had to start somewhere.

"Okay. She talked some more about the Orphan Train."

Charlotte noticed how Emily's eyes sparked with interest. "Anything you want to share?" She wasn't sure whether to push her or not. Emily had been fairly tight-lipped about it all up to now.

Emily told her what Miss Middleton had said about the coats and the worker at Luigi's Restaurant.

"Sounds like God was watching over them," Charlotte said.

"That's what I don't understand," Emily said before munching on her cookie.

"What's that?"

"If God was watching over them, why did he take their mom and dad in the first place? Wouldn't their parents being alive have been the better answer?" Emily looked at Charlotte with earnest eyes that caused a dull ache in Charlotte's heart.

"God doesn't always shield us from life's hurts, but he does walk through them with us."

"*Hmm* . . . I have to admit it seems God did take care of them through that man at the restaurant."

"I quite agree," Charlotte said, greatly encouraged by this conversation and by Emily's thoughts on spiritual matters.

"Could I have some more tea, Grandma?"

"Oh, you want more *tea*? Sure, let me get it for you." Charlotte still hoped the word would jostle something loose in Emily's brain.

"Grandma, are you hearing all right?"

Her question caught Charlotte by surprise. "Hearing?" Understanding dawned on her. "Oh, yes. Yes, my hearing is fine, honey." She poured Emily some more tea.

Emily quickly took a few swallows. "Well, I think I'll go to my room for a while," she said.

"Don't forget to feed the chickens this afternoon," Charlotte said.

"Okay. Remember Ashley's on her way over," Emily said as she stood up.

"Oh, Emily, here's your glass. Be sure and empty your *tea*."

Emily studied her a moment. "Are you sure you're all right?"

"Yes, why?" Charlotte was hopeful.

Emily shrugged. "No reason. Just wondered."

Someone knocked at the front door.

"I'll get it." Emily was out of the room before Charlotte could blink. Charlotte carried her empty plate and glass to the sink. She could hear Emily and Ashley giggle in the other room, then the scuffle of their feet clamoring up the stairs. She shook her head. The only tea Charlotte could see in her future was iced.

Just as she started to leave the kitchen, the girls reappeared.

"Hey, Grandma, can Ashley have some cookies?"

"Sure." Charlotte placed the plate of cookies on the table.

Emily fetched them both glasses of iced tea. Charlotte wondered how her granddaughter stayed so skinny.

"I've got some bad news," Ashley said.

Charlotte and Emily turned to her.

"Mom said I can't work for Miss Middleton for a while."

Charlotte noticed that Ashley's fingers held onto her plate of cookies as though she were afraid that with her news they might snatch it from her.

Emily's jaw dropped. "You're kidding." She sagged in the seat across from Ashley. "Why didn't you tell me earlier?"

"She just told me today. She said I needed to let you know in case you wanted someone else to help you."

"I think I can do it until you come back."

Ashley nodded. "One of her busboys quit, so I have to help clean tables."

Charlotte wondered what was going through Emily's mind.

Emily felt sorry for her friend, but not too sorry. At least she didn't have to take care of chickens.

"It shouldn't be for too long," Ashley said.

Emily turned to Charlotte. "Grandma, if I put this paper beneath my hands, can we polish our nails?"

Obviously, Emily wasn't about to let it throw off her day.

"I guess that's all right. Just make sure the table is protected."

"Okay." Emily plucked a bottle of purple polish from the pocket of her jeans.

Charlotte couldn't imagine ever in her lifetime wearing purple polish.

"You'll have to keep me posted on the Orphan Train story," Ashley said, snacking on her cookie.

"I will. Can you believe all Miss Middleton went through as a kid?"

Ashley shook her head.

"I can't imagine what I'd do in that situation," Emily said.

"I know what I'd do."

"What?"

"I'd cry."

"Oh, that would help," Emily said, putting the finishing touch of purple nail polish on her thumb. "There." She stuck the brush into the jar and twisted the cap back on.

Ashley shook her head. "She had to have been so frightened. Can you imagine your little brother taking charge like that?"

"Christopher? No way. But then I can't imagine taking charge myself either."

"Yeah. It's mind boggling."

"I know." Emily held out her nails and admired them.

Charlotte shamelessly kept herself busy in the kitchen so she could get a little more of a glimpse into Emily's world.

"My brother sure wouldn't take care of me that way. He'd let me rot somewhere," Ashley said.

Charlotte gasped, and then covered her mouth. The girls looked at her. Emily rolled her eyes and Ashley grinned.

"Well, he would."

"You might be surprised, Ashley. When faced with dire circumstances, our siblings sometimes come through for us. God gives us the strength we need when we need it," Charlotte said.

Emily shrugged. Ashley went back to her cookie. So much for Charlotte's great words of wisdom.

"Well, I'm just glad we don't have to live like that." Emily blew on her nails. "You got any of that fast-drying polish you put on as a topcoat?"

Obviously, the girls weren't ready to be bogged down with the cares of the world.

"I don't carry it around with me," Ashley said with a laugh.

Emily made a face. "I'm out of it too."

"You're in luck," Charlotte said. "When I bought your

last bottle, they had a two-for-one sale, so I bought two. The other one is in your bathroom cabinet, second shelf on the right."

Emily looked surprised. "Thanks, Grandma."

The girls ran up the stairs, leaving Charlotte feeling quite gratified. Finally, she'd done something right.

WHEN SAM GOT HOME from clocking some skateboarding time with Jake and Paul, he found Grandpa in the living room reading the paper. "Where's Grandma and Christopher?"

Grandpa peered around his paper. "They're out in the barn checking on the cats."

Sam took a deep breath, figuring now was as good a time as any. He wished he'd been more of a praying man. It could have come in handy right about now.

"Grandpa, can I talk to you a second?"

To Sam's surprise, Bob immediately folded the paper and laid it on the floor.

"What do you need?"

"You heard about my job at the day care?"

"Yeah, I did."

Though his grandpa didn't show a lot of emotion in his expression, Sam could see the pleasure in his eyes.

Sam gazed at the floor. "You ever go up in an airplane?"

Bob studied him with unblinking eyes. "I've been up a time or two. Why do you ask?"

"Just wondered." He cleared his throat. "I'd like to fly one someday."

"Planes deserve our respect. They're powerful . . . and dangerous."

"Yes sir." Hesitation. "Um, Arielle's uncle runs the county airport. Ed Haffner's his name."

"Is that right?" Bob said, still staring.

Sam squirmed in his seat and then stopped himself. "He, um, offered me a job too." Before Grandpa could say no, Sam blundered on. "Of course, I would work there in addition to the day care. Mr. Haffner said I could work at the airport in the mornings, maybe even earn some free lessons." He dared to peek up at Grandpa just then to see if he was still breathing. He was.

"I see."

"I'll be real careful and won't do anything stupid. I know Grandma would be nervous about it, but I was wondering if you would be willing to sign a permission form . . ."

Bob continued to study him with intensity; finally he let out a sigh. "I don't see why I can't, but you'll still need to clear this with your grandmother." He reached for the paper.

In a flash, Sam pulled a consent form from his back pocket as quickly as possible before his grandpa could change his mind. He had printed it from the Internet as soon as he had gotten home from the airport.

Bob signed the paper, handed it back to him, and then picked up his newspaper. "Thanks, Grandpa," Sam said. "Um, would you mind talking to Grandma with me? You know, just in case she doesn't think it's a good idea."

"Think what's a good idea?" Charlotte asked as she and Christopher returned from the barn.

"Your grandson here was offered a job at the county airport and can earn some free flying lessons for himself," Bob offered.

"Flying lessons?" Charlotte gasped.

"Yeah, Grandma. It's a great opportunity. It might even be something I'd like to do after high school, you know, earn a pilot's license." Sam hoped this fact might convince his grandma that flying was something he would take seriously.

"And you think this is a good idea?" Charlotte asked Bob with a hint of disbelief.

"Well, we have been hounding him to keep busy and take responsibility. This seems as good a way as any," Bob mumbled.

"Well, I can't say I like it," Charlotte went on, "but I'm willing to let him give it a try if you are. Sam, don't let us regret this."

"You won't Grandma. I promise," Sam said, breathing a sigh of relief.

Chapter Nine

"I can't be gone too long. I've got a roast ready to come out of the Crock-Pot soon," Charlotte said when she met up with Hannah for their walk on Saturday afternoon. "Nothing worse than keeping teenagers waiting when they're hungry."

"The kids are home on a Saturday evening?"

"We try to make it a priority to be home together for meals when possible. Sometimes that's a real challenge."

"I can only imagine. So how are things going with Toby and Christopher?" Hannah asked.

"It's interesting; that's for sure. The nice thing is, he's taking Toby for her daily walks, which allows me to take these longer walks to gear up for the walk-a-thon," Charlotte said.

"Yeah, that is good." A swallow swooped in front of them and landed on a nearby fencepost. "I still get a kick out of that whole tub-washing fiasco you told me about."

"That was something. These kids sure have livened things up at our house. Speaking of which, Sam is going to take flying lessons at the Adams County Airport and I'm worried sick. You know how I hate flying." Charlotte was glad she was wearing her sweater since the late afternoon air carried a slight chill.

"What inspired that?" Hannah asked.

"Arielle's uncle runs the airport and he offered Sam a part-time job there in exchange for some free lessons."

"Well, maybe it will be a good thing for him. Teach him some real responsibility."

Charlotte appreciated her friend's offer of encouragement. "You're right. I just can't help but worry."

"That's part of your job description, isn't it?" Hannah joked, lightening the mood.

"I guess it is," Charlotte agreed.

They continued along the path, breathing in the scents of early summer and enjoying the comfort of friendship.

"I saw Dana at the grocery store yesterday. Are she and Pete getting serious?"

Charlotte's surprise stuck in her throat. "I'm not sure. I know he likes her a lot, but I don't know if Pete's feelings go that deep. 'Course, with Pete and feelings, one never knows."

Hannah laughed. "That's just like a man, isn't it?"

"Yeah."

"So does Bob know you're doing the walk-a-thon yet?"

"No. I don't want him to know. He hates being fussed over, and that's the way he would see it. I'm just going to do my part, and that's that. He can't say anything once I've raised the money and participated in the walk."

"Isn't he curious about why you're walking longer these days?"

Charlotte grunted. "You know Bob. He doesn't notice

those things. He's too busy with his nose stuck in the *Farmer's Almanac* or the newspaper."

"Or watching TV."

"Exactly."

"Well, he's sure to notice the weight dropping off. I can tell you've lost a little already."

"Really?" That comment pleased Charlotte. She wouldn't mind losing a couple of pounds. Though that was certainly not her reason for doing the walk-a-thon.

After Bob's diagnosis she had felt so helpless. She knew plenty of people suffered with diabetes and got along just fine, and most likely, Bob would too. But she had never been one to sit around and do nothing. Her personality pushed her to do something. She would never understand people who gave in to their illnesses without a fight.

"Well, I won't lose any weight if you keep bringing over those delectable desserts for the kids," Charlotte said.

Hannah waved her off. "No need to worry. I told you I use sugar substitute so you, and especially Bob, can eat them."

"That's really very, um, sweet of you, Hannah. But need I remind you that even with sugar substitute, desserts have calories?"

Hannah laughed. "That's true enough. But you know what they say, if the ladies on the *Titanic* had known they were going to sink, they wouldn't have skipped dessert the night before."

"Only you." Charlotte shook her head.

Their laughter swirled about them, and Charlotte realized once again just how thankful she was for Hannah's friendship. She looked up at the sky. "Either it's getting dark early or a storm is brewing."

Hannah glanced upward. "Yeah, I'd say the latter. I heard it was supposed to rain tonight."

"I hope we make it home in time."

"We'll make it," Hannah said with confidence, though Charlotte noticed she had picked up her pace.

"So, how's Anna getting along?"

Charlotte smiled. "She's doing well. I talked to her yesterday, and she's all aflutter with renovations and baby plans."

Hannah glanced at her. "Uh-oh, what's that worry line doing between your eyebrows?"

Charlotte looked at her. "What? Oh, it lives there. Didn't you know?"

Hannah laughed. "Don't change the subject. What's up?"

"I'm not sure, really. I just think the baby might have caught Bill by surprise, that's all."

"How so?"

"Oh, I don't know. It's probably nothing. He just seems a little different this time around."

"Well, they are older."

"That's true enough." Charlotte paused then took a deep breath. "He's also in the middle of a real estate venture. Bob read in the newspaper about how the banks weren't giving out loans as freely due to plummeting real estate values."

"Yes, I read that article. Frank and I talked about it just this morning. It will most likely have a great impact on our community."

Charlotte didn't like the sound of that.

"You know, that explains something," Hannah said.

Charlotte turned to her. "What?"

Hannah shrugged. "I thought I overheard someone at the bank mention Bill's name. The customer was talking with a bank representative, and I heard him mention the name of a housing development—can't remember it now—and he mentioned a couple of other names, one of which was Bill's."

"Probably trying to work out the financing."

"Yeah, probably."

Charlotte wanted to ask her friend if it looked as though the banker was about to bear good news or bad. But then she decided she was better off not knowing.

"OH, MY GOODNESS, we barely made it inside before the storm hit," Charlotte said, looking out the door at the torrent of rain hammering the ground. A low thunder growled from the heavens like a crouching wolf ready to pounce on a chicken. Jagged shafts of light cracked through the menacing sky.

Christopher climbed on the sofa and stared out the window. "Cool."

"Dude, what's cool about it? You can't go outside and play," Sam said, looking none too happy when he plopped down on the sofa beside his brother.

Christopher shrugged. "I know. But it's still cool to watch a thunderstorm."

"You're weird," Emily said, frown in place, as she sat

across from her brothers. "It never rained in the summer in California."

"Oh, it's not so bad, really," Charlotte said. "You just have to make the most of a rainy evening."

They looked at her as though she'd sprouted horns.

Bob shook his head and settled in his easy chair.

"But before we do that, it's almost time to eat. Emily, would you please help me set the table?"

Charlotte didn't miss Emily's expression of displeasure, but she said nothing.

The kitchen window cast gray shadows on the walls. "Why don't we light some candles for the table tonight," Charlotte suggested.

Once the table was set, Emily retrieved the matches from the drawer and lit the three tapered candles that stood in the middle of the table along with her flowers.

After everyone was seated, Bob prayed over the meal while thunder moaned an ethereal chant and the rain played an accompanying patter on the windowpanes.

The beefy scent of pot roast and onions hovered over the table, joined by the aroma of a hefty side of vegetables for Emily. After Bob's prayer, Charlotte lifted a dish filled with beef and passed it around. The sound of silverware scraping plates, the faint tinkle of cubed ice, and the thump of glasses settling upon the wooden table rose gently above the patter of rain.

"I'm hungry." Christopher speared a big piece of roast and dropped it onto his plate, spattering a bit of meat juice.

Charlotte and Bob exchanged a glance and a smile.

"These potatoes look awesome, Grandma," Sam said,

scooping a hefty helping onto his plate and then adding gravy.

"Thank you, Sam. I hope you enjoy them," Charlotte said.

"So how's summer going for you kids?" Bob wanted to know.

Their words were lost on Charlotte as she gazed around the table and offered a prayer of thanks to God for moments like these, which made all the hard work worthwhile. It seemed only yesterday that she and Bob had sat at this very table with a young Bill, Denise, and Pete.

After the kids helped clean the kitchen, they settled down to a movie while Charlotte worked on her embroidery and watched with them. She couldn't think of a nicer way to spend a rainy Saturday evening.

Bob sat reading in his chair, the light of his lamp casting a soft glow among the stormy shadows. Every now and then he would glance up at the kids and crack a smile. One thing everyone knew about Bob was that when he smiled, the recipient deserved it. He didn't hand smiles out freely. It wasn't that he was stuffy and mean. He just took life more seriously than most folks. He often said life wasn't a laughing matter.

Charlotte begged to disagree. They were opposites in that regard, but she always felt the Lord brought them together to complement one another. He toned down her silly side, and she loosened up his serious side every once in a while.

June 29 would mark forty-six years together for them. They must be doing something right.

MONDAY MORNING, bright and early, after breakfast and chores, Sam headed for the front door, "Hey, Grandma, I'll see you later."

His grandma appeared in the doorway of the living room. A blue-and-white-checkered apron covered her T-shirt and jeans. She wiped her hands on a towel that had pictures of chickens all over it. "Where are you going so early this morning?"

"I'm heading out to the airport, remember?"

Charlotte pressed her lips together.

"Okay, well, be careful. Have a nice day."

"You too," he said with a smile and then scurried out the door before she could change her mind about him taking flying lessons.

Sam was surprised to realize that after the year or so they'd been in Nebraska, he actually was settling into the quieter side of life. A California boy at heart, he never would have dreamed he could handle living on a farm. Not that it had been his choice, but these days he was learning to deal with it.

From the research he had done on the computer over the weekend, Sam knew it took about eight months to get in enough flying hours to qualify for a pilot's license, so that wasn't a feasible goal—at least for now. Still, the few lessons he could take would let him know if this was an avenue he wanted to pursue. Who knew where this might take him? The very thought sent a shiver of excitement through him.

The airport was fairly quiet when he arrived. When he walked into the office, Arielle's uncle was talking on the phone. His eyes brightened and he gave a nod when he saw Sam. He held up his finger to indicate he'd only be a minute.

Once he'd hung up, he looked at Sam. "So how you doing today, son?"

"Doing good."

"Great. Why don't I get you a soda, and then I'll walk you out to hangar one." Dressed in dark work pants and a gray shirt, Ed led the way, stopping briefly at a soda machine to buy Sam a Coke, and then they walked to the hangar.

"Looks like a nice summer day," Ed said, shielding his eyes from the sun. "Mornings are always quiet out here. It's the best time to fly too. Just when the birds are getting up."

Sam smiled, feeling like he had butterflies in his stomach.

Opening the hangar, Sam saw the tanned Bonanza and wondered if that was the one they would be taking up.

"We'll be taking this one up," Ed said, confirming Sam's suspicions.

He took Sam around the airplane and explained the pre-flight checks such as determining the status of the engine oil and the fuel tank on the wings, checking for debris and water in the fuel with the fuel tester. Then he unlocked the doors. Sam climbed inside. The cabin smelled of upholstery and stale smoke. Dust and dirt particles covered the floor. Bits of paper were strewn about. The seats had nicks and scars on the upholstery, and Sam was beginning to wonder if this was a good idea.

"I know she looks a bit rough, but this is a good plane. Just needs some tender care. That's where you come in. The planes I use for lessons will need to be swept out and washed down on the inside as well as the outside each day they're used. Don't want to make people nervous when they go up." Ed seemed to think his joke was funny. Sam wasn't convinced.

As they taxied down the runway, Ed explained in detail about the different instruments on the control panel. Upon liftoff, Sam's stomach flipped. The ground grew farther away, and they seemed to float into a shroud of blue.

"Wow, you can practically see the entire state of Nebraska from up here," Sam said above the roar of the engine.

Ed chuckled. "On a clear day, you can see pretty far, no doubt about that."

Sam's ears popped as they climbed higher into the sky. He yawned to ease the pressure.

"Here, take this. It helps." Ed handed him a piece of gum.

"Thanks." Sam popped it in his mouth and started chewing, and the pressure in his ears let up.

Ed turned a few knobs and poked a couple of buttons. "So what got you interested in flying?"

Sam shrugged. "I'm not sure, really. Probably watching Superman or something."

Ed let out a belly laugh. "Well, this won't be quite the same as that, but I think you'll enjoy it."

Sam went on to tell him some of the things he'd discovered in his Internet research.

Ed nodded. "The FAA requires a minimum of forty hours of flight time, twenty with an instructor," he said. "Most folks put in around sixty to eighty hours' flight time before getting a license. Half the flight time is with an instructor, and the rest is going solo. Obviously, our lessons will be hit-and-miss this summer, but like I said, at least you'll get a taste for it. Either the lessons will give you flight fever or you'll be glad when they're over."

Glancing out the window, feeling free as a bird, Sam knew in his gut that he would not be glad when they were over.

Chapter Ten

Headed toward the chicken coop, Charlotte looked up when a silver Toyota sedan entered their driveway. She couldn't imagine what Bill would be doing here on a Monday in the middle of a workday. She walked toward the car and met him halfway.

"Hi, Mom."

"Everything all right?" She searched his face, looking for any signs of distress.

"Everything is fine." He put his arm around her. "I was in town clearing up a few minor details for our proposed addition. Since I was so close, I thought I'd drop by and see how my folks were doing."

Charlotte warmed to her son. Times like these made her wish he was little and living at home again. The years disappeared quicker than she could imagine.

"Where were you headed just now?"

"Oh, just going to check on the chickens, gather some eggs. It can wait a little bit."

"I thought that was Emily's job."

"Yeah, it is. She's doing a good job of it, but you know those hens. Sometimes they lay eggs in peculiar places, and I'm scouting around for those."

He scrunched up his nose. "I was going to follow you, but on second thought, I don't think I want my suit to smell like chickens."

"I'm sure you don't," she said with a laugh. "I just baked a couple of apple pies. Want a piece?"

He wiggled his eyebrows. "Don't have to ask me twice."

They started for the house.

"So where's Dad?"

"He's out in the barn. Should be in shortly. He'll smell the pie." Charlotte chuckled. When they reached the kitchen, she put on a pot of coffee and then retrieved plates and silverware. Bill slid into a kitchen chair and stretched his long legs as though he was glad to get the load off them.

He stared out the window, deep in thought, and she studied him. His sandy blond hair had a tinge of gray starting at the temples. When did that happen? She hadn't noticed that before. Bill was a nice-looking young man, if she did say so herself. With the determined set of his jaw, the warm yet purposeful eyes, he wore confidence well. And why not? He had succeeded in everything he had put his hand to. Bill had been their "golden child." Never caused them a day of worry.

Of course, she was proud of all her children. Her heart squeezed with the flickering thought of Denise. Charlotte placed the coffee and pie servings on the table.

"Is Anna feeling all right?" Charlotte slipped into her place at the table.

"Anna's fine," he said. Something in his voice got her attention.

"You're sure."

His eyes met hers. "Everything is fine. Her health is fine. Her plans for the baby—fine. Everything is . . . fine." He lifted a smile that never reached his eyes.

That let her know without a doubt that everything was not fine. The real estate news was worrisome indeed. Still, Bill was not one to be pressed on personal matters. His training in confidentiality procedures had taught him well, and to get anything out of him, one practically had to hogtie him and squeeze it out. Over the years she had learned that he would talk when and if he was ready.

"I'm glad to hear that."

"Mmmm, this is great pie, Mom. Remember how Denise loved apple pie?"

Charlotte smiled with the memory. "She sure did."

"I always told her I wouldn't want to be stranded on a desert island with her and only one apple pie between us."

They both laughed.

"I miss her," he said.

It surprised Charlotte to hear Bill open up this way. "I miss her too."

"So who's the other pie for?" he asked.

"The one on the counter is for your dad. It's made with sugar substitute. You kids get the good stuff." She winked.

"Poor Dad," Bill said.

Just then the door opened and Bob walked in.

Charlotte winked at her son and got up. She cut Bob a piece of his sugar-free pie and then slid it onto a plate.

"I figured this was where I would find you two," Bob said, giving his son a pat on the shoulder. "What are you doing in our neck of the woods this time of day?" Bob walked over and washed his hands at the sink before joining them at the table.

Charlotte placed the pie in front of him and served him a cup of coffee.

"Had some details to work out for our housing deal."

Bob nodded. "Look like it's gonna work out?"

"Oh, sure. Just the usual glitches. You know how it is."

Charlotte studied the look in Bill's eyes. He turned away.

The screen door bounced against the doorframe when Pete entered. "Do I smell apple pie?" His voice bellowed through the hallway as his footsteps carried him to the kitchen.

"Like father, like son." Charlotte rose from her chair to get another plate.

"Hey, big brother, what are you doing here?"

Bill looked weary from answering the same question, but he obliged.

"Well, looks like this pie isn't going to make it to dinner," Charlotte said, scooping a piece for Pete.

The conversation drifted over to farming concerns, a few sick chickens, the price of feed corn, and how farming had changed over the years.

"Well, if those white-collar types don't leave our farmland

alone, we're not going to have anything left to farm anyway." Pete took an aggressive bite of his pie.

A muscle twitched in Bill's jaw. "I believe we've already had this discussion a few times."

"Yeah, and I haven't changed my mind on the matter," Pete pressed.

"We need both types of people, I guess," Bob said, trying to keep the peace.

"Well, I'm not the only one unhappy about it," Pete said. "There was talk down at the tractor supply that the farmers are getting tired of the honchos in business suits coming in and taking over. You'd better give it some thought, big brother."

Bill studied Pete—more like glared at him—but kept absolutely still.

"Anyone want any more pie?" Charlotte knew Pete felt passionate about this issue, but why couldn't he just agree to disagree with his brother over the matter and be done with it?

"How are those renovations coming?" Bob said.

Pete frowned and went back to his pie. If he had been looking for a good scrap with his brother, he wasn't going to get it today.

Bill finally tore his gaze away from Pete and turned to his dad. "They're coming."

It was then that Charlotte noticed the flush that spread across Bill's neck and worked its way up his face. She was thankful when Bob changed the subject.

"Might be nice to have a boy this time around," Bob said.

"You never know." Bill shoved away from the table. Tension filled the air. Then he said, "Besides, it's Pete's turn to churn out a grandkid."

Pete choked on his pie while Bill watched with slight amusement.

"He'd better not since he's not married yet," Charlotte said.

"It's time he worked on that too." Bill gave his mom a quick kiss and then headed toward the front door, his earlier frustrations seemingly under control.

"I've got my hands full just watching over the cows and the chickens." Pete loaded that comment with full importance, leaving no room for doubt that he was far too consumed with farmwork to worry over a personal life.

"Say what you will, but the look in Dana's eyes says otherwise, little brother. I'd say it's just a matter of time," Bill called out. "Thanks for the pie and coffee, Mom." The door closed behind him.

Bob and Charlotte walked to the front door and waved as their son pulled out of the driveway. Pete finished off his pie in the kitchen and then walked past them.

"You might want to give that matter some thought," Bob said.

"What matter?"

"Marriage, kids, all that."

"I'm going back to the field." Pete pushed through the door in a huff, leaving Charlotte and Bob chuckling behind him.

MISS MIDDLETON ASKED EMILY to concentrate her efforts on the master bathroom today. Emily listened as she laid out her instructions, and then spread an afghan across her lap and leaned back in her rocker.

"I feel a little guilty taking a nap while you do all the work," she said with a chuckle. "I hope you don't mind."

Her last words were barely audible as her eyes drifted to a close.

Emily set to work scouring the bathtub and sink. She pulled an old toothbrush from the supplies and used it to scrub the grout between the ceramic tiles. Once that shined, she polished the mirror, and while she was at it, checked her teeth and straightened her hair. She polished the ceramic goose that served as a soap dish. She swept and mopped the floor, and then shook the rug. For reasons she couldn't explain, she wanted the house to sparkle for Miss Middleton. Once she felt confident she had done a good job, she put the supplies away.

"My, my, I must say, I've never seen the bathroom shine like that before," Miss Middleton said when Emily met her in the hallway a little later. "How about we sit down to tea, and if you want, I'll tell you more of my story about the Orphan Train."

"Sure."

They quickly sat down to tea, and Emily blurted out a question before Miss Middleton could get settled.

"What was it like when you were out on the streets, Miss Middleton? You were so little. Weren't you scared?"

"I sure was. I can still remember our first night out on our own. Rose held on to my hand as I took her through the streets of New York. We passed kids who begged for bread with smudge-streaked faces and tangled hair, tattered clothing, and worn-down shoes." Miss Middleton's eyes took on a faraway look. "One little girl stole a big loaf of bread from the bakery. The baker ran after her with a broom, but she held on tight to that bread."

Emily couldn't imagine being that hungry, that desperate for food.

"It snowed that day. A little boy sat in a corner by a building, shivering and cold. I wanted to give him my coat, but I was afraid if I got sick, no one would be around to protect Rose. Instead, I gave him my crust of bread from Luigi's and told him about the kind man there who had given us coats. Then we moved on.

"The old woman who watched over us, her name was—" She thought a moment. "Zana. I never knew her last name."

Emily made a face. "That's a funny name."

Miss Middleton chuckled. "It's one they don't use today, that's for sure."

"She was nice to you though," Emily said.

"Yes, she was. She watched over us for a long time—at least it seemed that way. It's hard to tell when you're a kid." She took a drink of tea. "Then one day a man came through the streets talking about a train that would take us to families and homes where we could eat and be warm. Zana told me I needed to take Rose and go on the train."

"Were you afraid?"

Miss Middleton shook her head. "I was mad at first. Thought she didn't want to take care of us anymore. But Rose had gotten sick and was never quite the same after that. So I figured Zana was right. I needed to get Rose a home. Any home would be better than New York winters under a bridge."

Emily thought about the coldest time she could remember. When they lived in California, it never got very cold, but one winter's night had brought rain and with it a cold chill. She got caught in a downpour with little protection. And then there was winter in Nebraska. She was still thawing out from last winter. Still, sleeping under a bridge in the winter? Unimaginable.

"Zana built a fire to keep us warm, but the icy chill still turned our noses and toes to stone. Some kids suffered frostbite. Zana took us to a church that offered us a warm bowl of soup three times a week for lunch, and more warm blankets.

"After we got the extra blankets, I went back to find that little boy to give him one, but he was gone. I thought of him a lot over the years, wondering if he'd survived the winter. Prayer sure helped us through it all," she said.

How could she say that? Emily wondered. They were homeless, and her sister had finally died. To her, it made no sense. Same as it made no sense that her own mom had died. She didn't understand a God who allowed things like that to happen.

As if seeing the questions in her face, Miss Middleton looked at her point-blank and said, "God didn't say life would be easy. But he did say we wouldn't walk alone. He never left us. Not one single moment."

Emily didn't want to talk about it anymore. It was great that Miss Middleton felt that way. But she was old, and after all this time her memory had no doubt blurred. Sometimes talk like that made old people feel better.

Even when it wasn't true.

THE NEXT AFTERNOON while working at her chores, Charlotte ran a dust cloth over the television. They'd had it forever.

She couldn't believe they had been married so long. She still felt like a spry nineteen-year-old bride. Well, most of the time.

The lemon spray scented the air as she wiped the television screen. Their TV might be getting old, but Bob had a way of squeezing the last bit of life out of things. No doubt, he would do the same with the television.

At least, she hoped so. If the TV went out, what would Bob play the DVDs on that she had bought him for their upcoming anniversary? Three seasons of *The Real McCoys* were sure to keep him busy for a time. She chuckled at the thought. She couldn't count how many times he'd told her how much he loved that show as a boy. She couldn't believe her good fortune to find it available on DVD.

"Any chance I can sneak in here and watch a little TV?" Bob's voice startled her, and she whipped around.

"Sure. I was just finishing up."

He settled into his chair with a groan.

"You all right?"

"Yeah. Just ready for a little snooze."

Bob liked his afternoon naps.

"Wait. I thought you said you wanted to watch television." She couldn't hide her amusement.

"I do. What's a good snooze if the television isn't on?"

Charlotte shook her head. "I'll finish up the dusting and leave you to your nap. I thought I heard a car outside."

"Yeah, it was Dana."

Charlotte's eyebrows shot up. "Oh?"

Bob shrugged. "Don't ask me. I just live here."

Her husband seemed oblivious to everything around him. If it didn't have to do with farming or television, he didn't have anything to say about the matter. Though Pete could get him stirred up on politics every now and then.

Charlotte put the dust cloth and furniture polish away and walked to the kitchen. She needed to think about dinner preparations, after all. Carefully, she peered out the kitchen window. Not that she was nosy or anything. Just curious.

Pete stood out in the driveway talking with Dana. She was looking up at him with obvious affection. Pete took a step backward. Charlotte's hand flew to her mouth to stifle a giggle. That boy was scared, pure and simple.

Bill's words to Pete played back to her. Could he be right, or were they all reading too much into Dana's behavior these days? Judging by the look of fear on Pete's face, Charlotte didn't see a wedding in their family happening anytime soon.

But then again, she'd been wrong before.

Chapter Eleven

Watering can in hand, Charlotte bathed the flowers in the large pottery tubs on her porch. After sprinkling the last petal, she stood and stretched her back. At the edge of the porch, Charlotte stared out at the land. Their land. Where the earth touched the heavens. The place where they had made a life for themselves. She loved life on the farm. Oh, it was hard work, to be sure, but there was something very satisfying about it all.

In her mind's eye she could still see Denise, Bill, and Pete running across the yard, breathless with laughter. A flash of Pete chasing Denise with a chicken surfaced, causing her to smile. She blinked, and her babies had turned into adults. She blinked again, and Denise was . . . gone.

She couldn't go there. Not now. Not when the day held such promise.

Another sweeping glance. The sun left a blazing trail across the horizon as it inched upward. Birds twittered in distant trees, and a warm breeze stirred through the porch. A perfect summer's day.

Emily had been working hard lately, so Charlotte had let her sleep in again this morning. Bob said she was coddling Emily. Maybe she was. Charlotte sighed. Some days it was hard to know what to do.

Sam was probably at the airport, as usual, till he had to go to the day care.

He hadn't said much about his job at the day care. She'd tried to squeeze information out of him, but he was tight-lipped, just like the other men in her life. She sighed. At least he was working. That made Bob happy, which, in turn, made her happy.

She started to go inside when she spotted Christopher. He was exploring already this morning. Her heart melted as she watched him, poking and prodding with a stick at something on the ground. Too young to go through all he had already endured.

She walked out to him. "How's it going with Toby?"

He shrugged, looking a tad glum.

"It takes a while to teach dogs, you know. Maybe if she doesn't make it this year, she'll be ready next year."

Christopher kept digging and poking with the stick.

Maybe he'd been working too hard. Every time Charlotte looked at him, he had Toby working at something. Charlotte placed her hand on Christopher's shoulder. "You know, we haven't seen Dylan in a while," she said, referring to Christopher's friend. "Why don't you call him and see if he can come and spend the day on the farm with you?"

Christopher's eyes rounded and sparkled like full moons. "Really?"

Charlotte chuckled. "Yes, really." Before she could say another word, he dashed to the house to call his friend. He obviously needed a little time off from dog duty. She looked up just in time to see that as Christopher entered the house, Toby exited.

Guess they both needed a little time off.

EMILY TRUDGED OUT to the chicken coop. No matter how many times she did this, she couldn't get used to it. Dirty, smelly chickens flopping around everywhere. How did people live like this? At least Grandma had let her sleep in this morning. She supposed she should be happy about that.

She tried to think kindly of the chickens. She really did. Even named a few. Tried to muster up the cartoon images, complete with the cast of *Chicken Little*. Nothing worked. She just didn't find them endearing. Why, if she weren't vegetarian, she'd have no problem eating them.

She allowed clean, fresh air to fill her lungs; then she bravely opened the door and stepped into the still, dank air of the chicken coop. The poultry clucked and flopped about, scratching the floor, plumping on their nests, fluttering out of her way as she fumbled through the straw in search of eggs.

Her nose scrunched when she grabbed an overly soiled egg. Oh, for the city life where eggs were plucked from a clean carton rather than a dirty nest. She was a city girl, through and through. No wonder her mom had left this place.

No, wait. She was beginning to like the farm, the town, wasn't she? She felt a stab of pain—not only for the reminder of her loss, but also for thinking her mom was right to leave here. Despite how old-fashioned her grandparents could be, she did love them. And she knew without a doubt they loved her. She was old enough to realize they'd sacrificed plenty to let them live there. She wondered how they must have felt when her mom left them. Probably the same way Emily had felt when her mom left her.

Still, that didn't mean she had to like the chickens.

One by one, she checked the nests and inched the complaining chickens out of her way. They obviously didn't appreciate her visits any more than she did. But it was what it was, and they needed to get on with it.

Besides, once this was done, she would go to Miss Middleton's for a while.

She thought of how she complained about her life and felt sorry for herself because her mom had died. Some days she criticized everything her grandma did, but she wasn't sure why. She usually blamed her attitude on what had happened to her and the fact she'd had to move to a Nebraska farm, far from her home, friends, and life in San Diego.

But as she heard Miss Middleton's story, she couldn't help wondering how the woman could be so pleasant. She'd been through so much more. Emily thought about the aching hole in her heart after her mom's death. It was still there, but not as painful as it used to be. She wondered if that was normal. Fading memories, easing pain . . . was she a bad daughter? She didn't want to forget. Not ever. And yet . . .

She looked forward to Miss Middleton's story. It stirred a place deep inside her, though she couldn't say why. She knew only that she wanted to know more about the Orphan Train and the young passengers who rode it.

Once her chores were finished, Emily got a ride to Miss Middleton's house, where she was put to work polishing silverware.

"Okay, dear, here is the silverware I want polished," Miss Middleton said. "Here's the rag and polish. I'll be in the living room working on cards if you have any questions."

"Isn't it a little early for Christmas?" Emily teased.

"Christmas?" Miss Middleton looked puzzled, but when she saw Emily's expression, she grinned. "They're not Christmas cards. Some sympathy, one for a sick friend, a couple of birthdays, that sort of thing."

Her explanation surprised Emily. She'd remembered seeing Miss Middleton hovering over cards before but thought little of it. "Do you send out cards every day?"

"Most days."

"Why?"

The old woman's bony shoulders lifted up and down. "Why not? People need encouragement. I'm old, and it's one thing I can still do for my Lord."

Emily watched after her as she shuffled into the next room. She'd never met anyone quite like Miss Middleton. So old and yet still acting as though her life had purpose.

Her grandparents were like that too, but they still had

energy. It amazed her that someone as old as Miss Middleton wouldn't just do what she wanted with the rest of her life. She'd earned it. She'd been through a lot. Didn't life owe her something for her final days? Emily wouldn't spend her life that way. She had plenty of things she wanted to accomplish and she aimed to while she was still young.

After all, she knew life had no guarantees.

One by one, she picked up the heavy silver pieces and polished them to a sparkling shine. Afterward, Miss Middleton insisted they sit out on her front porch.

"Now, let me see, where did I leave off last time?" she asked while her arthritic fingers worked on a crocheted hat.

"You said a man came through the streets announcing an Orphan Train."

"Ah, yes. Let me see." Still holding the yarn, her fingers paused a moment; then she made a face. "Zana told us we had to go."

"And you didn't want to go."

She shook her head fiercely. "I most certainly did not." She continued working her stitches. "Zana had kept us safe. If we left her behind, who would take care of us?" She paused. "At least that's what I thought."

"What happened next?"

"Well, I think I told you Rose's health wasn't good. Living outside had taken its toll on my sister. Zana insisted we go on the train. She said Rose wouldn't last another year out in the elements. Zana refused to help us anymore. Until I got older, I didn't realize she actually did us a great favor."

"Do you know whatever happened to Zana?"

Her face downcast, Miss Middleton shook her head. "Never saw or heard from her again. How could I? She didn't know where we were, and I had no address for her. What would I put, 'To the woman under the bridge'?"

Emily could see her point.

"Remember Luigi's Restaurant?"

Emily nodded.

"She took us there, and Luigi let us go in the bathroom so she could clean us up the day the train was leaving. Luigi even gave us a few clothes he'd gotten somewhere. Rose and I looked halfway decent by the time they'd gotten through with us."

"So you went to the train station?"

Miss Middleton worked a stubborn stitch and then went back to the routine of her crocheting. "Yes, we did. There were lots of kids waiting there, each hopeful they'd find a place off the streets. Big billows of steam were pouring out of the engines." She smiled. "And the whistles were loud. I remember it hurt my ears. Rose's too. She clung to me like the last leaves of summer cling to the branches. The thick smoke made her cough, so we moved away."

Emily thought it sounded exciting, but she knew in that scenario it might not be so much fun.

"Then a man with a long gray beard came around and looked us over. He had a kind face. He had a gold chain looped across his vest. He pulled out a pocket watch to check the time. 'You, you, you,' he said, pointing over the crowd. I held Rose tight against me. We were going together, or we weren't going at all."

"Did he choose you?"

"No." A shadow crossed her face. "He chose Rose."

Emily gasped. "She went without you?"

Miss Middleton shook her head. "She refused, and I didn't want her to go. I should have forced her, but I didn't."

Emily heard the sadness in her voice, and it made her feel bad for Miss Middleton.

"Well, I think that's about all I can tell you for today." Miss Middleton stood up to signal the session was over. She looked weary and stooped over.

Though Emily wanted to know more, she would let it drop unless Miss Middleton brought it up the next time. She didn't want to bring back painful memories, and something told her today's part of the story did that very thing.

CHARLOTTE PICKED EMILY UP from Miss Middleton's and then the two of them went to Jenny's Creamery for an afternoon treat.

Bedford seemed a little quiet today, but then Wednesdays were like that. Slow-paced living, tree-lined streets—that was the life for Charlotte. She couldn't imagine anything else. She supposed the kids couldn't have imagined anything else but life in San Diego.

"Here we are," Charlotte said, maneuvering the car into a parking spot.

In no time at all they had bowls of hot fudge sundaes in hand and had settled down in a high-backed booth. They faced the town green across the street. Park benches dotted the lawn where local talent gathered in the evenings to share their gifts with the community.

"Where's Christopher this afternoon?" Emily asked.

"He and Dylan are playing basketball in the schoolyard."

"Oh, that sounds fun."

"Yeah, he's been a little frustrated lately. I thought it might do him some good to be with his friend."

"I don't blame him for feeling frustrated. Toby's not exactly Wonder Dog." Emily laughed.

Charlotte tried not to feel defensive for her pet. "No, not Wonder Dog, but she'll get the hang of things soon." Doubt fringed her words. She decided to change the subject. "So how do you feel your summer is going so far?"

"Pretty good. I like working for Miss Middleton, and it gives me extra money to put toward that digital camera I've been wanting to buy. Might even get a new pair of jeans—if I can find some around here. You know, Grandma, you could use a new pair of jeans too. Though, like I said, I don't know where you'd find any around here."

"Brenda's Boutique carries jeans."

Emily scrunched her nose. "I don't know. They're probably not the cool kind."

"Sure they are. Let's go over there, and I'll show you."

Emily's eyes sparked with excitement. "Really?" She looked genuinely pleased.

"Really." The laundry could wait.

Charlotte enjoyed the look on her granddaughter's face. Why hadn't she thought of it before—treating Emily like a young woman, instead of always looking at her critically?

Asking her opinion. That's what a mother would have done. That's what Denise would have done.

After ice cream, they went over to Brenda's Boutique. Brenda was running errands, and Tiffany Reddick, her assistant who helped out from time to time, was filling in.

"How are you, Tiffany?" Charlotte said while she and Emily rummaged through a stack of jeans on a shelf.

"I guess I'm fine."

Charlotte stopped her search and looked at the young woman. "You don't sound convincing."

She smiled. "It's just that Rod and I are trying to buy a house, but the banks are making it hard for us to get a loan."

A twinge went through Charlotte's heart. "Oh?"

"Yeah, I hear things are getting bad." Her eyes were wide, fearful.

This sounded foreboding. If young married folks were affected, Charlotte felt sure the real estate crunch would impact Bill and his family. "Oh, don't worry, honey. These things come and go. It will work itself out." Charlotte tried to convince herself.

Tiffany brightened. "Thanks, Mrs. Stevenson. I sure hope you're right."

Charlotte smiled and then disappeared into the dressing room with her arms full of jeans that Emily had chosen for her.

She tried not to think about Bill and his real estate venture while trying on her jeans. She was determined to enjoy her time with Emily and worry later. Charlotte stared at the jeans hugging her hips, the flat front and flared legs. Boot cut, she thought Emily had called them. She wondered if they should have tried on jeans *before* the ice cream.

"I don't know, Emily. Don't you think they look a bit young for me?" They didn't appeal to Charlotte all that much, but the look on Emily's face kept her considering them.

"Grandma, they look awesome! You need to wear those. You aren't too old. In fact, they make you look younger."

Charlotte wondered at the wisdom of a fifteen-year-old. But the more she looked at her reflection in the mirror, the more she thought she could at least tolerate the jeans. And by the look on her granddaughter's face, she knew it would make her very happy.

"All right, if you say so."

Emily clapped. Truly clapped with glee. Charlotte didn't think she'd ever seen her do that without her friends around.

"Now we need to find you a cute top," Emily was saying as she headed off in search of something.

Charlotte wanted to stop her, but she was in the dressing room, and she couldn't exactly traipse after Emily in her underwear.

Before long, Emily had returned with a couple of tops for Charlotte.

"This one looks really artsy, Grandma. I like it," she said, shoving a glittery, long top into Charlotte's hand.

This was not at all the type of top one would expect a farmer's wife to wear. What on earth would Bob have to say about this?

"Try these on, Grandma." Emily flopped another "artsy"

top over the door of the dressing room and flung a hat over the door too.

Charlotte gasped. "You can't be serious." She was glad Brenda had gone on some errands and had a young girl tending the store. Charlotte wasn't sure she wanted Brenda to see the clothes Emily was picking out for her.

"They're really cool, Grandma. Just try them on. Please?"

Charlotte decided to humor her, but no way would she wear the hat in public.

Once she stepped into the hallway outside the dressing room and faced the three-way mirror, she burst into uproarious laughter. Emily came around the corner and joined her.

"I look—I look—" Charlotte could hardly get anything out, she was laughing so hard. "I look like a Cher reject."

Emily laughed all the more. "Okay, maybe the hat and top are not for you, but the jeans are definitely a go, don't you think?"

When her funny bone finally settled down, Charlotte looked at Emily and smiled. "I think." In that moment, she wanted desperately to hug Emily, but they were having such a good time, she didn't want things to turn awkward. "Well, I guess we'd better get going. Emily, this has been fun."

Emily looked her square in the face. "I've had fun too, Grandma. Thanks."

They walked over to the register to pay for her purchases. One look at Tiffany, and Charlotte remembered that some people had a lot bigger worries than how their jeans fit.

Chapter Twelve

Boy, that was a good walk," Hannah said, dabbing at her face with a tissue. "I think we set a new record for endurance each time we walk."

"I don't know about that, but my poor legs are sure feeling it," Charlotte said.

"I'm surprised you're not wearing your new jeans," Hannah said with a chuckle.

Charlotte grinned. "Those are special jeans, you know, meant for special occasions—like when Emily is around."

"I think it's great you girls had a nice afternoon together. Worth the cost of a pair of jeans, for sure."

"Sure was. You know, I felt like we were having some real grandma-granddaughter bonding time. The pretenses were gone. No hormones getting in the way. Just pure fun."

"I'm glad," Hannah said. "I know you both needed that."

They walked a moment in silence then Hannah spoke up again. "Has Bob said anything about you walking so much?"

"No. When he watches TV, he doesn't know if I'm gone or in the house."

Hannah let out a grunt. "Frank is the same way. When he watches the Cornhuskers play, he doesn't even know I exist." She took a sip from her iced tea.

"How are things coming along with the house?" Charlotte asked her friend.

"We're getting back to normal, slowly but surely. The flood really did a number on the place."

"Well, I sure appreciate how you still manage to look out for us with all you've been through," Charlotte marveled.

"You know cooking is my creative outlet. I have to cook. Frank can't eat it all, so it has to go somewhere. You're the closest neighbor."

This time Charlotte laughed. "Well, I'm glad we are. The kids always love what you bring over, and it keeps them filled up, for the most part. I'm telling you, they have bottomless pits for stomachs."

"I remember you saying that about your kids too."

"I guess I did. It must run in the family."

"Kids might have helped my figure and Frank's. Guess we should have had some." She grinned.

Charlotte's heart twisted for Hannah. She knew her friend had wanted children, but it had never happened. Frank tried to make up for it by spoiling his wife. He showered her with cards, romantic notes, flowers, and surprise gifts. They had each other, he had said, and they'd get through it together.

Hannah filled the hole by being an "aunt" to everyone else's kids. It suited her. One thing Charlotte knew: Her friend had touched a lot of lives over the years.

Hannah glanced at her watch. "Oh my, will you look at

that. I'd best get home and start dinner or Frank will trade me in for a younger model."

"Oh, you." Charlotte waved her friend off. They both knew that Frank was as devoted to Hannah as any man could be to a wife. Sometimes Charlotte wished some of that would rub off on Bob. She loved her man, but if he told her he loved her once a month, he figured he'd covered things. She told him once that she liked to hear it and asked why he didn't tell her more often. He responded with, "If I say it once and nothing has changed, why do I need to say it again?"

How could she argue with that? But Frank? He never missed a birthday, anniversary, or holiday, especially Valentine's Day.

And thinking of anniversaries, Bob had yet to mention anything to indicate he remembered theirs was fast approaching. But there was still time.

She smiled at the memory of the Valentine's Day dinner the kids had come up with for them. Maybe they would put a bug in Bob's ear about the anniversary too. Not that she and Bob celebrated much, but they usually acknowledged the event with something. A card and dinner out would be nice.

Her mind was made up. If he didn't say anything soon, she'd just have to resort to dropping hints.

Bob poked his head out the front door and spotted Charlotte.

"Hey, what's for dinner?" he asked.

She headed toward the door. "I'm making barbecue chicken." She slipped inside, stopped in front of him, and looked up into his eyes. "I remember when we first got married you told me that was one of your favorites." She smiled and batted her eyelashes a couple of times.

He stared at her. "Something wrong with your eyes?" He looked concerned and leaned toward her.

Charlotte frowned. "Nothing is wrong with my eyes." She turned and stomped into the house, leaving him absolutely speechless.

STEEL CLENCHED AGAINST STEEL with a screech as Sam slammed his car door closed the next morning. Rain pelted him, but he had no protection. If only he'd worn a jacket today. Sloshing through puddles, he dashed for the airport office. Once inside, he shook his wet hair like a dog shaking fur. Thankful that the room was empty, he grabbed a soda and took a minute to calm himself. In inclement weather, the place seemed dead. No roaring of engines, twirling of propellers, tires rolling on pavement. Planes stayed captive in their hangars.

"Nice out there, huh?"

Sam turned at the sound of Ed's voice.

"Yeah."

Ed walked past and thumped Sam's shoulder. "Don't look so glum. You'll get more time to fly."

Sam lifted a half smile. "Yeah, I guess."

"In the meantime, I have a flight manual book you might want to browse through. Not the most interesting reading you'll ever see, but it might give you some insight into things."

Sam looked at the thick manual and felt an adrenaline surge. Totally different reaction than the one he'd had over the day-care manual. It sure made a difference when you got to study something you actually wanted to learn about. He thought it was pretty cool that Ed would think of him like that. With a glance up, he caught Ed smiling at him.

"I thought you might like it," Ed said.

"I can hardly wait to look through it."

Ed looked beyond Sam toward the window. "Well, you can't do much here today. You've already cleaned the office, and there's nothing going on out there. Might as well kick back and read a spell."

Sam couldn't believe his ears. "Really?"

"Sure, why not?"

Sam really liked this guy.

LATER THAT AFTERNOON, Christopher and Dylan threw paper airplanes around Christopher's bedroom. One landed in the trash can.

"Yes!" Dylan punched the air with his fist.

"Oh, let me try." Christopher would not be outdone.

He missed.

They laughed together—though Christopher noticed Dylan laughed harder than he did—and spent a few more minutes aiming toward the target, sometimes hitting, sometimes missing.

"How come Toby isn't around?" Dylan asked, settling on the edge of the bed, his face twitching with Tourette's-like symptoms, eyes blinking in rapid succession.

They had been friends long enough now that Christopher hardly noticed his friend's tics.

"She's avoiding me." Christopher took a piece of paper from his notebook and made sharp folds in it, forming another paper airplane.

"Why?"

The paper plane missed its mark. Christopher groaned and fell back on his bed. Staring at the ceiling, he said, "I've been trying to train her for the fair."

"Train her to do what?"

Christopher sat back up. "Sit when she's supposed to, stay when she's supposed to, that kind of thing."

"Doesn't she have to be a purebred for that?"

"Well, she's a hybrid. Part Australian shepherd and blue heeler. They have a category for mixed breeds."

"Hey, she's like me," Dylan said.

Christopher punched him. "You're not Australian shepherd and blue heeler." He laughed.

Dylan playfully punched him back. "No, but I'm a mix of Dakota Sioux and Winnebago."

"Maybe we should enter you in the dog show."

Dylan shoved him on the floor, and the boys tumbled about like a thick ball of yarn.

"We'd better stop or Grandma will come up here," Christopher said finally, quite out of breath.

Dylan flipped the hair from his eyes and wiped his face with the crook of his arm. "Okay." He picked up a small ball and began to toss it up and down. "Wish I had a dog to work with."

"Hey, maybe you can help me with Toby." Christopher

was getting bored with doing it by himself and figured it would be more fun working with his friend.

Dylan brightened to the idea. "That would be cool."

"It's hard work," Christopher said with authority. "I have to groom her too." Made him tired just thinking about it. "Let's go find her."

Dylan nodded and followed Christopher. They stopped in the kitchen, where Grandma stood at the counter, rolling out pie dough.

"Grandma, is Toby outside?"

She turned to the boys. "Um, I'm not sure. You might check her doghouse."

"What're you doing Mrs. Stevenson?"

"Oh, I'm making pie crust for a strawberry pie for dinner."

Dylan licked his lips.

She smiled. "Do you like strawberry pie?"

He nodded enthusiastically.

"Well, then you'll have to ask your parents if you can join us for dinner."

He and Christopher locked eyes.

"Awesome!" Christopher said. "Let's go call your mom."

They'd deal with Toby later. Right now, they had a call to make.

A BASKET PILED WITH EMILY'S JEANS and assorted tops sat at the foot of the stairs. She had just finished her chores, and already she was barricaded in her room and on the phone.

Charlotte sighed, bent over, and grabbed the basket.

She'd get it for her this time, but she didn't want Emily to get in the habit of having Charlotte do everything for her.

Just as she was about to knock on her granddaughter's bedroom door, she stopped in midair when she heard Emily say, "What tea?"

Charlotte had taken the call, so she knew Emily was talking with Ashley. She shamefully listened at the door.

"No, I didn't ask her. She's not my mom."

Charlotte's heart dipped. Not that she wanted to replace her daughter in her granddaughter's life. She just wanted a closer relationship with Emily.

"Stop. I don't mean that bad. Grandma's cool, as far as grandmas go. She's just not my mom. It wouldn't feel right to go to something like that without my mom."

Charlotte thought she heard a catch in Emily's voice. The familiar pain gripped her own heart and held it captive. Would it ever go away? Sometimes it seemed to ease; other days, the loss of her daughter seemed unbearable.

"No, she hasn't mentioned it. She wouldn't expect me to ask her. She's not like that."

Shame washed over Charlotte. She had been selfish to want Emily to ask her. Emily had her reasons, and Charlotte needed to respect that. They'd build their relationship on what they had.

Charlotte knocked on the door before she could hear any more.

Emily came to the door. "Oh, sorry," she said when she saw her grandma holding the basket of clothes. "Hang on, Ashley." She put the phone down and grabbed the basket of clothes.

Just as Charlotte turned to leave, Emily said, "Grandma?"

She turned around. "Yes?"

"Were you—" She looked toward the door. "Oh, never mind."

Charlotte smiled and quickly walked out the door before Emily could change her mind. With the door closed behind her, Charlotte breathed a sigh of relief. That was a close one. She couldn't lie to her granddaughter so she would have had to tell the truth if Emily had asked if she'd heard anything.

There was more than one reason for the kids to carry up their own laundry.

THAT EVENING AFTER DINNER they all congregated in the family room, mulling over how to entertain themselves on yet another rainy night.

"I've sure been thirsty today," Bob said, finishing off his iced tea. He kicked the foot of his recliner in and headed to the kitchen to fill up his glass.

A rerun of *Family Feud* squawked from the television, and Charlotte attempted to talk over the noise. "You been taking your medicine?" The soft glow of the lamp encased the colored embroidery thread in her hands.

"Yes, I've been taking my meds." He disappeared through the doorway.

Hearing the soft patter of rain against the window, Charlotte looked at the beads of water on the windowpane. She knew they needed rain, but it seemed they'd sure been getting their share lately.

"Is his diabetes very bad?" Emily whispered.

Charlotte noticed the worry lines that etched her granddaughter's young face.

"It's under control. He'd do a whole lot better if he would get some exercise."

"He walked to the kitchen," Sam pointed out.

Charlotte shot him a look.

"Hey, we men have to stick together." Sam's lopsided grin softened her.

Charlotte was about to mention the diabetes walk to the kids, but Bob came back into the room. She'd talk to them later.

"That's right," he said, fresh glass of iced tea in hand. "Besides, I get enough exercise walking around the farm."

"And just how much walking do you think you do?"

"I do a lot," he defended.

"Yeah? You walk out to check on Pete, and you take a car if you have to walk very far, so just how much walking?" Charlotte hated sounding like a nagging wife, but there was his health to consider. Her nagging had absolutely nothing to do with the fact he had not mentioned their upcoming anniversary so much as one time.

He grunted. "Why, I'll bet I walk three miles a day, easy."

"I know how you can find out, Grandpa," Christopher piped up.

All eyes turned to him. Charlotte couldn't help but notice Bob's eyes didn't look all that friendly.

"How?" He said the word as though he didn't really want to know but felt pressured to ask.

"Wear a pedometer," Christopher said with all the innocence of a child.

"Oh, that's right," Emily joined in. "You can get those

almost anywhere. Our gym teacher said it was a good way to keep track of how much exercise you get each day."

"Why, that's a wonderful idea," Charlotte said, feeling a tad lighter knowing they could monitor his walking. It was the perfect solution.

"I don't need a pedometer," Bob argued.

"Don't be afraid, Grandpa. You probably walk even more than you think you do, and that will help Grandma not to worry." Sam winked.

"Put on a movie, Sam," Bob said. He turned to Charlotte. "Go ahead and get me one of those. I'm not afraid to wear it. I'll show you; I get plenty of exercise. Then you can stop being such a worrywart."

Emily looked at Charlotte and smiled. The boys did the same. If she didn't know better, she'd say they had the whole thing planned, to help her out. Maybe they were concerned about their grandpa too. After all, they'd lost their mother already. They didn't need to lose their grandpa too.

Satisfied, Charlotte went back to her embroidery, every stitch making her more determined than ever to get that pedometer first thing in the morning.

Chapter Thirteen

Friday afternoon had finally arrived. Soon Sam would have the weekend to himself.

Kids screamed and chased one another on the playground when he passed by. He groaned. Sam couldn't believe he was stuck with this stupid job, babysitting a bunch of kids.

He kicked at a clump of dirt. At least he got to work at the airport. That was cool. Jake and Paul were pretty impressed by that. Maybe one of these days he could ask Ed to take them up for a ride.

The airport had been plenty busy this morning. Ed wasn't able to take Sam up. They had some big CEOs fly in, and the airport crew all pretty much catered to their whims. Some days were like that and Sam had to be patient—though he didn't like it. Still, he knew he was lucky to get any flying lessons at all.

"Hey, big guy, how's it going?" Arielle walked up beside him with a broad grin, shining eyes, and looking as pretty as ever, dressed in jeans and a light blue shirt. His heart jumped.

"Okay. How about you?"

"Good. I tried to call you last night, but your cell phone wasn't on." They stepped inside the building.

"Sorry. We were having—" he gestured quotes "—family night."

Her eyebrows raised. "Oh?"

He told her about it.

"That's pretty cool."

He made a face. "I think it's pretty lame. I'm seventeen years old. I don't need a family night."

She laughed. "Sure you do. Everyone needs family. No matter how old you are."

Something about her saying that made him feel better. Not that he needed her permission, but it kind of validated the idea in his mind. Truth be known, he liked spending time with his family but figured it wouldn't sound all that cool to say so.

"Well, I'm about to get my exercise for the day," he said before entering the classroom.

"Yeah, me too. By the way, I've been meaning to tell you something."

He turned to her.

"Doesn't your grandpa have diabetes?"

"Yeah. Why?"

"There's a Walk for Diabetes in a couple of weeks. I thought it might be fun to participate. Figured you'd want to join me to help out your grandpa."

"Don't we have to get money from people?"

She shrugged. "So ask a few people. It's a worthy cause.

Maybe you could get Emily and Christopher to do it too," she said.

He stared at her. "What's in this for you?"

"My mom is heading it up. Diabetes runs in her side of the family. Mom says we won't go down without a fight." She smiled and shrugged. "See ya."

"See you later," he called after her.

Maybe he would check with Emily and Christopher about the walk. It might be a way they could help their grandpa—and Sam could impress Arielle all at the same time.

Taking a deep breath, he prepared himself to enter the room filled with people five feet and under. And old people said his generation's music was too loud. Maybe they should visit a day care.

CHARLOTTE HAD NO IDEA there could be so many different pedometers from which to choose. They ranged from fancy ones that could tell people more than they ever wanted to know about themselves, to simple ones that merely told the number of steps one took in a fixed period of time.

She picked up the simple one. They didn't need all the bells and whistles.

"You gonna get yourself one?" Hannah asked, a full-fledged twinkle in her eyes.

"Me?"

"Sure, why not? I think I'll buy myself one while we're

at it." Hannah lifted one off the rack. "We all need to stay healthy, and this will keep me accountable."

Charlotte's tummy twisted a teensy bit. She hadn't thought of keeping herself accountable. But what was the big deal? She was "training" for the diabetes walk, after all, so she would have plenty of steps in each day, to say nothing of all the roaming around the farm that she did. She had nothing to worry about.

"In fact," Hannah continued, making Charlotte wish she hadn't invited her neighbor along, "you and Bob could sort of challenge each other. You both like a little competition. So make it one. Tell each other at the end of the day how many steps you got in."

This was beginning to sound like work, and Charlotte was on the verge of regretting the whole thing.

"Yeah, I guess," she offered in a weak voice.

"Though it might not be fair. We both know you'll win, hands down."

Charlotte studied her friend with suspicion. She wasn't sure if Hannah was baiting her or what but decided in that moment that perhaps she was right. In fact, the more she thought about it, the more she was positively sure her friend was right. Besides, the competition would encourage both of them to get back into shape.

And that's all it was. Friendly competition for a worthwhile goal.

MISS MIDDLETON hadn't mentioned the Orphan Train today, and Emily was disappointed but still didn't push the older woman. The last conversation had obviously been painful for her, so Emily had decided to wait until Miss Middleton mentioned it herself.

They sat down in the living room with their tea. The room smelled fresh with Emily's cleaning. Curtains fluttered with the summer breeze. Emily wasn't sure when she had started looking forward to the visits instead of resenting them. It certainly wasn't because of the money. She actually liked hanging out with Miss Middleton.

"What's that?" Emily asked, pointing to the rows of soft pink yarn Miss Middleton held in her hands.

"It's a baby blanket I'm working on for a young lady at our church. See these gnarled hands?" She lifted her right hand. "I've never been able to keep them quiet. I suppose that's why they look this way." With a crochet hook, she pulled a loop of yarn through an opening in the work she'd finished earlier; then she flicked the yarn around the hook to pull another loop through, and another. "I can't seem to give it up. I've done it too many years to remember."

Emily watched her with interest. It looked like fun. She really liked the skull caps kids were wearing these days. Maybe she could learn to make one sometime.

Miss Middleton looked up and caught her watching. "Want to learn how to do it?"

Emily brightened. "Could I?"

"Sure you could. It's easy. Come over here." Miss Middleton patted the flowered sofa seat beside her.

For the next hour, Miss Middleton mentored Emily in the craft of crocheting, and by the time they were finished, Emily had learned to make chain stitches, double crochets, single crochets, and a few other basic stitches that would enable her to make a worthwhile project.

A project she would keep to herself.

"LET ME GET THIS STRAIGHT," Bob said, holding the pedometer in his hand. "You want me hook this onto my pants and wear it all day long?" Checking the tap water, he then filled his glass and took a drink.

Charlotte nodded. "You said you weren't afraid."

He put the glass on the counter and straightened. "I'm not."

"I guess two thousand steps is around a mile. To lose weight, you need to walk approximately ten thousand steps."

"Ten thousand?" He looked as though someone had just told him the price of feed corn had shot through the roof.

Charlotte smiled. "You don't have to walk that many. It's just a goal you might want to reach down the road—if you want to lose weight or anything."

"Are you telling me I need to lose weight?" He looked offended.

"No, honey. I'm only concerned for your health."

He didn't appear all that pleased with her concern. If she didn't know better, she would say he wasn't enjoying this conversation in the least.

"Don't be concerned. I'm fine. I'm on medication. I don't have to do all this other stuff."

She tried to keep her frustration at bay and her words

light and encouraging. "The doctor mentioned these other things to do in addition to the meds, Bob."

"I have to go to the barn." He turned and stomped off, muttering something indiscernible under his breath.

Charlotte sighed. She turned and picked up Bob's glass from the counter—and spotted his pedometer.

Good thing she hadn't mentioned the competition part.

EMILY KEPT THINKING of Ashley's words about the mother-daughter tea. Did Grandma expect an invitation from her? She wasn't her mother, and Emily didn't want to invite her. It seemed a betrayal to her mom.

The more she wrestled with the idea, the worse she felt. Why did Ashley have to bring it up at all? She still had her mom; it was no big deal for her.

In the confines of her room, Emily grabbed her stuffed teddy bear and squeezed it close to her heart. Her mother had bought it for her when she was little, and she'd slept with it most nights since her mom died—except for when Ashley spent the night. She didn't want her friend to think she was a baby.

She blinked her eyes closed and squeezed a tear from them. "Mom, I miss you. I wish you were here so I could talk to you. I have so many questions about girl things, and I just can't talk to Grandma like I could talk to you." She curled into a fetal position, holding Teddy close. "I love Grandma, but you're the one I want to take to the tea. I wish you were here." Her eyelids grew heavy.

A knock on her door startled Emily awake.

"Emily, are you all right?" her grandmother's voice called out.

"Yeah, Grandma, I'm fine."

"May I come in?"

"Yeah, sure." Emily pushed Teddy over to the side of her bed.

The door opened.

Emily sat up and ran her fingers through her hair. "Guess I fell asleep."

Charlotte smiled. "You work hard at Miss Middleton's. Everything go okay over there today?"

Emily nodded and glanced around the room for her crochet project; then she remembered she'd put it in her closet.

"Any more talk of the Orphan Train?"

"Not today."

"Well, just wanted to check on you and let you know that dinner is ready."

"Oh, I'm sorry I didn't help you set the table, Grandma."

"It's all right. You can do it next time." Charlotte turned to walk out of the room.

"Grandma?"

She swiveled back to Emily. "Yes?"

"Do you want to go to the mother-daughter tea at church?"

Charlotte studied her. "I would love to do that . . ." She paused but kept her eyes on Emily. "But I promised to go with your grandpa into Harding to an auction that day. They're selling a tractor he has his eye on. If you want me to cancel . . ."

"No, no, that's fine. I just thought I should—I would ask."

Charlotte gave an understanding smile. "Thank you for asking, Emily."

Something in the way her grandma said that made her realize her grandma had sensed her hesitation and in that moment made a sacrifice.

"Grandma?"

Charlotte looked at her.

"Thanks."

Charlotte smiled and walked out the door.

Chapter Fourteen

First thing Saturday morning, Pete and Christopher stepped into Filly's Flower Shop. The perfume from the flowers made Christopher nauseous. Reminded him of funerals.

"How come we're here, Uncle Pete?" Christopher asked.

"I wanted to look around for a minute, and you insisted on coming with me."

"How come you're whispering? Don't we want some-body to help us?" Christopher decided he wanted to get out of there as soon as possible.

"Yes, we do. And I'm not whispering," Pete whispered. He took a few steps and made a face. "I don't know why women like flowers so much. I think they stink."

"Me too." Christopher was glad Uncle Pete understood.

Pete looked all around while glancing out the window from time to time.

"You meeting somebody here?"

"No. Why?" Pete fingered a petal, and it dropped to the ground.

"Uh-oh, look what you did." Christopher pointed to the fallen petal.

Uncle Pete glared. Christopher couldn't figure out why he was all tense and grumpy.

"The truth is, I don't want anybody to see me here."

"Why not?"

"For someone so quiet, you sure are a chatterbox today," Pete hissed.

Christopher shrugged.

"I don't want people to think I'm henpecked, that's why."

"What's henpecked?"

"Forget it." Pete took off his ball cap and swiped his forehead with the crook of his arm. His boots scraped the floor, sort of like he was dragging them.

"Are these for Grandma?"

"If you must know, Mr. Nosy, they're for Dana."

Christopher's eyebrows arched.

"Cut that out," Pete snapped again.

"What?"

"Doing that thing with your eyebrows. Like it's a big deal that I'm getting Dana flowers. Don't go filling your head with notions. I'm just getting her flowers."

"Okay." Christopher wished he'd stayed home.

Pete sighed. He ruffled Christopher's hair. "Sorry, kid. Guess I'm just a little on edge."

Right then the front door shoved open.

"Hey, Pete, how's it going?"

Silas Maynard stepped into the flower shop. Bib overalls covered his paunchy midsection. Christopher wondered why it seemed farmers always wore overalls. The right cap could make Mr. Maynard look like a railroad conductor. His gray hair was buzzed to his scalp. He walked with an easy gait toward Pete and lifted a friendly smile.

"What are you doing here?" Pete asked.

"Oh, you know how it is. Our milk cow, Old Betsy, has been giving us fits. Things have been a little tense at home. I figured it was a good time to give my Betsy some flowers."

"You're giving your cow flowers?" Christopher asked.

Silas laughed. "No. My wife Betsy."

"How come you named your milk cow after your wife?" Christopher asked, standing by his uncle.

Pete nudged him from behind, causing Christopher to scoot forward two inches.

Silas laughed. "Guess it does seem funny to outsiders, doesn't it?"

Christopher wondered how his wife liked having a milk cow named after her.

"Gonna spoil her, huh?" Pete asked.

Silas nodded. "And just what are you doing here?"

"Well, I don't believe in spoiling women, but sometimes you gotta keep 'em happy."

Silas roared with a laugh loud enough to shake the windows. Christopher didn't know what was so funny.

"So you got a little trouble with your woman too?" Silas asked, leaning in to Pete.

"No trouble." Their gazes collided. "Well, okay, maybe a little." Pete cleared his throat. Christopher wondered what kind of trouble.

Silas laughed again and gave Pete a good swat on the back. "You're in the right place, my man."

They talked a while about their farming operations, and Christopher got bored. He'd rather be home with Toby.

"Guess you know my uncle died recently?" Silas said.

"Yeah, I'd heard that. Sorry, Silas."

Christopher wished people didn't have to die.

"Don't be. He lived to the ripe old age of ninety-five."

Pete nodded.

"Anyway, he didn't have any kids, and since we were close, he left me some money." He leaned in to Pete again. "A good amount."

"Well, good for you."

"Yeah. Except now I got to figure out what to do with it."

Pete laughed. "That's a good problem, right?"

"I guess. I'd like to invest it in something. Not stocks. Those things scare me. I'd like something a little more tangible."

Christopher wondered why grown-ups used big words like *tangible*.

"Sounds like a plan," Pete said. "The old Martin homestead is up for auction. You could buy it, fix it up, and rent it out."

Silas scrunched his nose. "Sounds like too much work to me. I have my hands full just taking care of the farm."

Christopher wished Uncle Pete would stop talking so they could go home. He shifted from one leg to the other.

"Yeah, I know what you mean."

"Well, I'll figure out something. In the meantime, I'd better get back home or the flowers aren't gonna help. Good to see you, Pete, Christopher." Silas walked up to the counter and talked to the woman standing behind it. Together they picked out a colorful bouquet for Betsy—or was it Old Betsy? Christopher couldn't remember which was the cow and which was his wife.

After smacking some bills on the counter, Silas walked out with his purchase and waved at Pete.

"Wow, that's a big bunch of flowers," Christopher said about Silas's purchase.

"Yeah. Wonder if he'll have enough money left for his investment."

Pete walked over to the lady and said he wanted the same thing Silas had—only half the size.

"I think next time I'll just shut up and listen to Dana," Pete said, holding onto the flowers with one hand and shoving open the door with the other.

Christopher had no idea what his uncle was talking about, but he was glad to go home.

Grown-ups were so weird.

"GRANDMA, OKAY IF I MEET ASHLEY over at her mom's restaurant?" Emily asked.

Charlotte stopped sweeping the kitchen floor and looked at Emily. "They're pretty busy on Saturdays. Did Mel say it was okay?"

"Yeah."

"And your chores are done, right?"

"Yeah."

"All right, you can go for a little while. Do I need to take you?"

"No thanks. Sam said he would take me over."

Her grandma took two steps closer. "That's a big bag you've got there."

Emily glanced down at the bag holding the project she was working on for her grandparents. "Yeah. Used to belong to Mom."

"What did she use it for?" Grandma wanted to know.

Emily shrugged. "Just stuff. Well, I'll see you later, Grandma. I'll be back before dinner."

"Oh . . . okay. Have a nice time with Ashley."

Emily couldn't wait to get out the door. If she weren't careful, Grandma would look in that bag. She hoped Grandma wouldn't snoop.

"Come on, Em. I've got to get going," Sam said.

Grandma held open the screen door and called out, "Make sure you get back by dinner, Sam."

"I will."

Emily breathed a sigh of relief when she clicked on her seat belt.

"What's up with you?" Sam asked.

"I was afraid Grandma was going to look in my bag." She patted it beside her as though to double-check that it was safe.

"What's the matter with that? Did you rob a bank or something?" Sam backed the car out of the drive.

"Ha, ha. No, I didn't rob a bank. I'm making a lapghan for their anniversary, and I didn't want her to see it."

"A what?"

"It's a small version of a crocheted blanket, something she or Grandpa can lay across their lap while they're watching TV." She pulled the unfinished product from her bag to show him.

When they pulled up to a stoplight, he looked over. "That's pretty cool. When did you learn how to do that?"

"Miss Middleton showed me."

"You really like her, don't you?"

"Yeah, she's nice."

"Well, don't start acting like an old lady. Next thing I know, you'll have lots of cats and watch mysteries."

"You never know," she teased.

Sam shook his head. "I'll get you a rocking chair for Christmas."

She ignored him. "It's fun. I like making something for them. It's more fun than just buying a gift. It's like giving a part of myself."

He turned to her. "Whoa, you're starting to talk like an old lady too. Cut it out."

She laughed. "What are you doing for Grandma and Grandpa for their anniversary?"

"When is it?"

Just like a guy. They never seemed to remember the important things. "It's on the twenty-ninth. Next Sunday."

He scratched his jaw. "I don't know yet. I'll have to think about it."

"Well, you'd better hurry up; there's not much time."

Sometimes the groan and wheeze of Sam's car reminded Emily of an old man. It stalled, and they had to wait while he tried to start it again. The engine finally kicked in.

"What are you doing today?" she asked.

"Arielle and I are going out in hopes of getting sponsors for the diabetes walk."

"The what?"

"Oh yeah, I've been meaning to tell you. There's a walk for diabetes coming up, let's see, the twenty-eighth, I think. Hey, that's the day before Grandma and Grandpa's anniversary."

"Next Saturday?"

"Yeah. Anyway, Arielle's mom is heading it up. I guess we have to get people to pledge so much money per mile that we walk or something like that. It helps the Diabetes Foundation. Anyway, I thought it might be a good idea to, you know, help Grandpa."

"That's a great idea, Sam."

He turned to her. "Yeah?"

She nodded.

"So you think you want to do it too?"

"Sure! I'll ask Ashley; maybe she'll want to join me."

"That would be great. I'll see if I can get the information you need from Arielle."

"Okay." She thought a minute. "I haven't seen Jake and Paul in a while. What are they up to these days?"

"Working, just like the rest of us. It's been hard to get together."

She sighed. "I guess we've all joined the working class."

"I guess."

"We're meeting up with them later today."

"That's cool. Hey, maybe Arielle can give you some ideas for Grandma and Grandpa's anniversary." Emily smoothed her hair.

He brightened. "Yeah, that's a good idea. She's good at that stuff."

Sam turned on the radio. They rode the rest of the way to Mel's restaurant in silence. Emily was excited to help her Grandpa in this way. It was one way they could "give back" for what their grandparents were doing for them. That thought scared her. Maybe Sam was right. Maybe she really was starting to act old.

After Sam dropped her off at the restaurant, Emily promptly told her friend about the diabetes walk. They mentioned it to Ashley's mom, and she immediately set things into motion. It seemed she too was involved in organizing the walk. One thing Emily had noticed about small towns: When a worthy cause came along, it appeared almost everyone got involved.

Before they had time to do anything else, Mrs. Givens pulled out a couple of pledge forms and handed them to the girls. "Now is as good a time as any to get started." She winked.

"Thanks," they said in chorus.

They turned to walk out the door. Emily considered buying a chocolate chip cookie before they left the restaurant but decided she needed to save her money.

She breathed in the scent of coffee and glanced at the

colorful silk flowers on the wooden tables. The restaurant made her feel better. It had a cozy feel about it.

"Hey, I like those," Emily said, pointing to the grouping of pictures of outdoor cafés and coffee cups.

"Thanks," Mrs. Givens said. "Those café paintings seem to be all the rage these days."

"Thanks again for the pledge forms, Mrs. Givens," Emily said. She was glad Sam had encouraged her to do this.

"Oh, no problem. I have a lot of them to hand out." She smiled. "And if you'll look on your papers, you'll see that Mel's Place is your first contributor." A twinkle lit her eyes.

Emily glanced at her paper and saw that Mrs. Givens was donating a dollar for every mile they walked. "Wow. Thanks a lot."

She lifted a sweet smile. "You're welcome." Mrs. Givens wiped her hands on her apron. "Well, I'd best get back to my customers. Hope you get lots of support." She leaned over and gave Ashley a peck on the cheek. "Bye, honey."

"Bye, Mom."

The girls turned to leave.

"By the way—"

They swiveled back around.

"I think it's a wonderful thing you're doing. I'm sure it will mean a lot to your grandpa, Emily."

"Thanks. It was my brother's idea." She couldn't take credit for it.

"Well, it's a good one," Mrs. Givens said. "Bye."

The girls stepped into the warm summer air. Emily had to admit she liked this place. It was way different than

San Diego, but it was still cool. The tree-lined streets, the little shops, and the small-town feel . . . she liked it. Funny, when they first got there, she thought it was a hick town. Now, it made her feel safe in a way her other home hadn't. She wasn't sure why.

"We've picked a perfect day to do this," Ashley said. "It's so warm and sunny."

"Yeah. Thanks for going with me on this, Ashley. You didn't have to do it."

"I wanted to. It will be fun," she said, her auburn curls stirring in the gentle wind. "Let's stop here." Ashley pointed to Kepler's Pharmacy.

"Yeah, this is good. Grandma gets Grandpa's medicine here."

The jangle of the bell sounded when they opened the door. Medicine smells assaulted her nose the moment they stepped inside. It made Emily think back to a time when she had the croup. Her mom had put a vaporizer in her room and slathered her with vapor rub. It took years for her to get that smell out of her head.

Big black letters, evenly spaced across the back wall, read APOTHECARY. Small towns must like to call it that instead of *pharmacy*. Pictures of old pharmacies hung about, reminding Emily of *The Andy Griffith Show* reruns her grandpa watched.

The dark wooden floor groaned and creaked beneath them. Shelves, from floor to ceiling, were stocked with medicine bottles. A wooden ladder with wheels leaned against the shelves. Emily had seen a store like this once in an old movie.

"Hi, Mr. Kepler," Emily said when she saw the elderly man stocking a shelf. His thick gray hair and bushy mustache reminded her of pictures she'd seen of Albert Einstein. Since Mr. Kepler was a pharmacist, she figured he was probably as smart as Mr. Einstein too. She could almost imagine him standing over steaming test tubes, concocting some sort of brew for what ailed people.

"Well hello, ladies. What can I do for you?" His back stooped a bit when he shuffled over to the register.

"We're participating in the diabetes walk that's coming up next weekend, and we wondered if you would consider pledging money for our walk," Emily said.

The old man studied them for a moment, and Emily figured his decision could go either way. The overhead lights flickered and buzzed while they waited.

"You're Bob Stevenson's granddaughter, aren't you?"

She didn't know if he was implying that was a good thing or a bad thing by the way he said it.

"Yes sir."

"Good man."

She breathed a sigh of relief.

"It's a shame about the diabetes. They get his medicine here. 'Course I'll do it." He reached for their papers and signed his name and pledge.

"Thank you, Mr. Kepler," the girls said in unison.

Encouraged by their pledges, they made their way outside. They continued on around a few city blocks, visiting the shops and collecting pledges before they decided to call it a day and ended up at Jenny's Creamery.

They stepped inside onto the black-and-white-checkered

floor and slid into their seats at a high-backed booth.

"I'm so hungry I could eat a horse," Ashley said. "Stormy excluded, of course."

Emily laughed. "I'm starving too. But at least we got a lot of pledges." She couldn't be more pleased with their work today. Though her grandpa wouldn't directly benefit, he would be helped in the long run. And it meant a lot to her to be a part of it.

"Your grandpa will be surprised," Ashley said right after ordering a large hot fudge sundae with crushed nuts and a cherry on top.

Emily hoped they didn't get diabetes. "Yeah. I sure hope no one tells him though. We want it to be a surprise."

"Tells who what?" Emily's grandma stepped up to their table.

"Grandma, what are you doing here?"

"Well, I was trying to gather up some pledges for the diabetes walk, but from what I hear, you've already contacted every potential sponsor in the county."

Emily and Ashley both grinned.

Charlotte pulled a chair up to their table. "I think it's really sweet that you two are participating in the walk. It will mean a lot to your grandpa, Em."

Emily was embarrassed that her grandma was acting all sappy in front of Ashley. "We wanted to do it. No big deal."

"Well I, for one, happen to think it *is* a very big deal. I think your grandpa will too."

"You won't tell him, will you? I mean, it will be a surprise, right?" Emily asked.

"That's fine by me," Grandma said. "I haven't told him about my participation either."

"Great. Sam's going to walk too, in case you didn't know. In fact, he's the one who told me about it."

Her grandma smiled. "Is that right? Well, it seems this family is full of secrets."

The grin Grandma turned her way made Emily feel very proud.

"Well, I'll let you girls enjoy your sundaes. I've got some pledges to get." She grinned and returned her chair to its table. "See you later."

The girls waved good-bye. Once they had finished their hot fudge sundaes and talked Jenny into making a pledge, they called it a day.

By evening, Emily considered it a day well spent.

Chapter Fifteen

"You can't do that, Dylan. It doesn't work that way." Frustration filled Christopher. "Toby has to sit over there and stay there until the judge tells me to call her. When I call her, then she has to run to me and sit in front of me. Then I will command her to finish, and she has to go to heel position."

Dylan looked totally disinterested in what Christopher said. He looked past him and shouted at Toby to come to them. Christopher sighed. It had been hard enough taking care of Toby before, but with Dylan interfering, it was really messing up things.

Christopher had to take charge. "Toby, you come over here." Toby happily trotted to Christopher's side. She sat down where Christopher pointed.

Dylan opened his mouth to speak. Christopher walked past him and whispered, "Don't say anything. You'll break her concentration."

Dylan promptly clamped his lips together in a huff.

Christopher walked across the yard and turned to face Toby, who obediently sat opposite him but now had her eyes fixed on a sparrow that had caught her interest.

There was a kid at school like that who couldn't keep his attention on anything. The teacher said he had ADD. Christopher wondered if Grandma should have Toby checked for that. Then he wondered if it was catching.

Just as he raised his arm to give the signal, hoping all the while that Toby would see and obey, his grandma opened the screen door and hollered out, "I've got peanut butter cookies."

Toby shot across the yard, ears blown back by the wind, freedom in her face, and bounded up the porch steps two by two.

Christopher moaned, "Thrown over for a cookie." Dejected, the boys climbed the steps.

"We never should have started letting Toby in the house." Grandma held the screen door open for the boys. "I'm sorry, Christopher. Did I mess up your training session?"

"It's all right. She wasn't in the mood anyway."

Christopher dragged his feet as they headed to the kitchen. Cookies usually made him feel better, but he was just tired of working with Toby. He didn't think that dumb dog had learned one thing since they started. Seemed she'd get something figured out, and the next day they'd have to start all over again. It sure didn't help with Dylan contradicting his every move. He liked his friend, but he wished he wouldn't try to tell him how to take care of Toby. Christopher had been reading plenty on dog training, and he figured he knew more than Dylan did about it.

After washing their hands, the boys sat at the table as Grandma placed plates of cookies and cold glasses of milk in front of them. The milk made Christopher think of

Old Betsy; then he wondered how Mr. Maynard's wife had liked her flowers.

Dylan bit into one. "These are great, Mrs. Stevenson."

"Yeah, they are," Christopher quickly agreed.

Grandma kept looking at him, and Christopher wondered if he had cookie crumbs on his face, so he swiped his cheeks with his fingers, just in case.

"You boys have been working awful hard today."

Well, Christopher knew *he* had. He wasn't so sure about Dylan.

"I've got an idea. How about you have a campout in the backyard tonight?"

Adrenaline shot through Christopher. "Really?"

"You haven't done that in a while." She smiled and nodded. "Uncle Pete was just in here for cookies, and he's the one who mentioned it. Said he'd help you put up the tent if you wanted to camp out tonight."

Dylan and Christopher exchanged grins and a high-five.

"Let's ask your mom when we get done," Christopher said.

"Yeah."

Grandma smiled and tousled his hair. Christopher didn't like it when she did that, but right now, he didn't care.

They were going to camp out!

BILL PULLED THE CAR into the drive at Heather Creek Farm and cut the engine. His girls jumped out and ran up to the porch.

"Hi, Grandma. Hi, Grandpa," Jennifer said, hugging each one.

Madison followed suit. Though Madison was older, most of the time Jennifer led the way.

Charlotte hunkered down and pulled her granddaughters into an enormous hug. "How are our girls?" she asked, dropping a kiss on their cheeks.

"Good," they said simultaneously.

"That remains to be seen," Bill said when he climbed the steps.

Still stooping, Charlotte looked up and searched his face. "What does that mean?"

Before he could say anything, Anna waved him off. "Oh, it's nothing. We went to the dentist yesterday, and Bill is still pouting because the dentist said the girls would likely need braces in the future."

"They can tell that already?" Grandpa wanted to know.

Charlotte tried to get up, but her muscles were working against her—from all that walking she'd been doing, no doubt.

"I told her she shouldn't let them suck their thumbs," he said, clearly agitated. "Now we're gonna pay for it. Big time."

"Don't you have insurance for that?" Bob asked.

"Sure, we have insurance. But I don't know how much it will cover. I'll have to check into all that." His jaw tensed.

Something was troubling her son, and it was more than braces. Charlotte hated to interrupt, but she would really rather have this discussion without talking to their knees. "Could someone help me up here?"

"Well hello, kids." Hannah and Frank stepped up to the porch, along with Pete and Dana. Hannah passed a covered dessert plate to Frank; then she walked over and gave Bill a side squeeze.

"How's my favorite aunt?" Bill teased.

"Oh, you!" Hannah walked over and helped Charlotte up from her awkward position. Charlotte heard a crack and prayed everything would still be intact once she stood upright.

Frank and Hannah visited with everyone for a few minutes.

"Won't you join us for dinner?" Charlotte asked.

"No, no," Hannah said. "We've already eaten. Just wanted to drop off this dessert and see how our kids were doing." She grinned and winked at Bill and Anna.

They took a few minutes to catch up on things and then Frank announced he had to get back to work. After waving good-bye to Frank and Hannah, everyone went inside to eat.

Conversations about their busy week swirled around the dinner table, but Charlotte said very little. Instead she studied her son. She wondered if his glum mood had anything to do with his real estate deal.

Once dinner was over, they settled on the front porch. The gentle stir of the air smelled fresh and welcoming, like a cold glass of tea on a hot summer's day.

"So glad you could come over tonight," Charlotte said to Bill and Anna. Then she looked at Pete and Dana. "You too."

"Well, it seems I never get to see you," Pete said with a wink.

"So how are you feeling, Anna?" Dana's eyes were wide and full of smiles.

"I'm feeling great." Anna lifted her feet onto the porch ledge. "Though I'm not that far along yet, sometimes my legs ache at the end of a long day."

Charlotte could so relate, but she thought it best to keep silent.

"Must be wonderful to feel the flutter of a baby inside your belly," Dana said, all starry-eyed and full of dreams.

Pete choked on his tea.

Everyone turned to him. Bill used the opportunity to swat his brother on the back. Charlotte couldn't help but wonder if the swat truly had anything to do with Pete choking.

With a frown, Pete looked at Bill. "I'm fine. Thanks." The look on his face said, *Whop me again, and I'll whop you back*.

Charlotte sighed inwardly. Would those boys ever get along? She didn't know why there always seemed to be tension between them, especially on Pete's part. Hadn't she and Bob treated them the same over the years? There shouldn't be any jealousy. Bill was doing the work he'd always wanted to do, and Pete was running the farm the way he'd always wanted. So what was the problem?

Maybe she just couldn't understand the male psyche. She glanced over at Emily. Charlotte had enough problems trying to figure out her own gender.

"Sounds like a lot of responsibility to me," Emily said. Charlotte wondered if Emily was thinking about Miss Middleton and all she'd been through with the Orphan Train.

"It sure does." Pete agreed with her before the words had

barely escaped her lips. The quick response seemed to catch everyone's notice except Dana, who still had that dazed, cloudy look in her eyes.

"I'd like to learn how to crochet or knit," Dana said. "Wouldn't it be fun to make a cute little pair of booties?"

Emily was about to say something, but then she seemed to think better of it.

Anna waved her hand. "Oh my, no, I could never do that. I'd just as soon go to the baby boutique in town and find cute things. It's a lot less hassle, and they are simply adorable."

The chair groaned as Bill shifted in his seat.

"Shhh. Did you hear that?" Pete said, eyes large.

Everyone got quiet.

"What?" Bob asked.

"Just an owl or some weird bird," Emily said.

"Are you sure?" Pete pressed.

Charlotte couldn't figure out what he was getting at. He caught her attention and winked. He was teasing the boys. No doubt getting them into the mood for sleeping out in the tent tonight. She shook her head.

One glance at Christopher and Dylan told her Pete's teasing was working. Their eyes were the size of chocolate chip cookies—the extra large kind. She looked back at Pete and shook her head.

"Probably nothing," Pete said, stretching his legs. "Can't be too careful nowadays though, what with all that talk about werewolves and vampires . . ."

Charlotte gasped. "Pete!"

Christopher jumped. Dylan's eyes twitched.

"Aw, I'm just teasing." Pete scratched his jaw and grinned at Dana. "Still, with that full moon blazing, a fella can't help but wonder."

Charlotte frowned at Pete. "You boys go get your stuff, and don't you listen to him." She left no room for argument this time. In fact, the boys didn't argue.

"You shouldn't tease those boys like that, Pete," she said.

Pete thumped back in his chair and let out a hearty laugh. "Just having a little fun, Mom."

"Well, you should be ashamed, trying to scare them that way."

"Hey, I remember Dad scaring us boys plenty when we were kids."

Bill nodded. "He sure did."

Bob feigned innocence. "Me?"

Charlotte gave up.

"You having any problems with the banks over that housing development deal?" Bob asked Bill.

Charlotte glanced at Bill, who shook his head. This was never a safe topic, but she was just as curious as Bob about the development.

Bill and Anna locked eyes. "Everything will be fine," Bill said.

Charlotte wondered if he said that more to convince Anna than anyone. Charlotte loved Anna, but sometimes it seemed she wasn't easily satisfied.

"How are the renovations coming along?" Charlotte did not want Bill and Pete to get into another match, so she moved the conversation to what she hoped were safer waters.

"Slow," Anna fumed.

"At least you have plenty of time before the baby gets here," Charlotte said.

"Yes, but it seems with every change we make, I see a need to do something else."

Bill noticeably sighed, and everyone glanced at him.

Anna playfully tapped his arm. "Oh, don't mind him. He stews about everything." She flashed him a smile. "Don't you, sweetie?"

He shrugged.

Charlotte thought of the renovations and expenses facing them, and frankly, she couldn't blame him for sighing. She tried to shake off her attitude. Like Bob said, Bill had a good head on his shoulders. He'd make out all right. They'd never worried a day about him. She wasn't about to start now.

Well, not if she could help it.

Chapter Sixteen

"This is so cool," Christopher said, shining his flashlight against the tent walls. The air was quiet and dark. Spooky. Prime for ghosts and goblins. Now that he thought about it, prime for werewolves and vampires too. Goosebumps shivered up his arms. Not a sound. Anywhere.

Dylan swatted at an insect and smacked his arm. "Got it." He flicked off the squashed bug. "I hate mosquitoes."

"Here. Grandma said to use this." Christopher passed the bug-repellent spray.

"Want to play outside?"

"We can't. I promised Grandma we'd stay in the tent after ten o'clock." After what Uncle Pete said, he was sort of glad they couldn't play outside.

Dylan shrugged. "Too bad we have church tomorrow. We could have played out later."

"Yeah. We'll have to do this on a Friday night sometime."

Christopher propped the flashlight between them in the middle of the tent to use as a lamp. The slant of the light made Dylan look ghoulish, his eyes shadowed. The twitches didn't help.

"You look scary," Dylan said, pointing at Christopher's face and laughing.

"So do you."

Dylan put his hands out like a monster, and the boys tussled about a moment, whopping each other with pillows. When they finally stopped, Christopher readjusted the flashlight so they could see and used his arms and hands to make shadow figures on the tent wall. Anything to get his mind off of werewolves and vampires.

"Oh, cool. Let me try," Dylan said. He created a perfectly formed giraffe.

"Look at this one," Christopher said, spreading his fingers and giving a wild hair impression.

"What is it?"

"It's Sally Bender on a bad hair day."

They both rolled with laughter, and the stress began to melt away until . . .

A rustle sounded outside the tent. And then a slow growl.

"What's that?" Christopher said, every nerve in his body on end.

Dylan sat up and straightened his hair. "What?"

"Didn't you hear that?"

They sat perfectly still. Christopher's heartbeat plugged his ears from hearing anything else.

They looked at each other; then Dylan said, "You're just trying to scare me." He whopped Christopher again with his pillow.

"No, I'm not. Knock it off."

"Where's Toby?" Dylan asked.

"Grandma was gonna leave her outside with us, but she would have been here by now. I'll bet Grandma forgot."

"Maybe you should go let her out to be with us."

Fear shot through his veins. "Me? Why me?"

"Well, you live here, doofus," Dylan said. "Besides, what are you worried about? Nobody lives that close to you. And who comes out this far in the country? Nobody. It's just us and the ghouls," he said, all freaky-like.

Suddenly the air in the tent grew very thin. Christopher's throat tightened. His mouth was dry as peanut butter. Dylan was right. They did live a ways out in the country. He tried to swallow but didn't have a lick of spit left in his throat. They were away from everything. Everything. Who would even hear them if they got into trouble? He'd heard Grandpa snore before, so he knew nobody inside the house would hear anything going on outside. The horses, chickens, cows, they wouldn't help.

"What if it's a coyote?" Dylan asked, suddenly concerned.

Christopher wasn't so much afraid of coyotes as he was the unknown. He'd seen too many scary movies.

A dog's cry filled the air in the distance. Just as Christopher got the courage to peek out the zippered slit in the tent, they heard a rustling. A close rustling.

Their gazes collided and locked into place. They froze like figures in a wax museum.

IN THE QUIET OF HIS ROOM, Sam browsed through the book Ed had given him so he could get a better handle on flying. He mentally went through the checklist of the instruments in the cockpit. The altimeter, airspeed indicator, tachometer, oil pressure gauge, turn coordinator. He sighed. Would he ever get it all?

Arielle's uncle Ed was very cautious to Sam's way of thinking. It hadn't been raining all that hard when he wanted to go up yesterday, but Ed said no. He said one of the rules of flying is using your head to make smart decisions. By the time he had finished explaining, Sam felt stupid. He figured Ed thought he was an immature teenager who thought the plane was a toy. He hoped he had convinced him otherwise.

Still, he thought Ed was overly cautious. But he would bide his time and play by the rules until he could fly his own plane someday. Then he would be in charge and could fly when he wanted.

He loved the way flying made him feel as though he hadn't a care in the world. It was almost as if nothing bad could touch him up there. He didn't know all that much about God, but if there was one, Sam figured when he was flying in the clouds, God couldn't be too far away.

He read a little longer, and finally put the book down. He wasn't one for reading. He was a doer. He'd much rather be in the airplane cockpit right now, studying the instruments, learning hands-on. He sighed. He'd have to get used to the idea of studying if he wanted to become a pilot.

A light beam flashed through the window and across his ceiling. He got up to check it out. When he peered out his window, he saw the flashlight shining through an opening in the tent. Toby was scratching to get inside. Christopher opened the tent and let the dog in before zipping it back up.

Sam had forgotten the boys were out there tonight. A smile tugged at his mouth.

This night showed more promise than he thought.

Sam knocked on Emily's door and whispered, "Hey, Em, can I come in?"

"Yeah."

The door squeaked when he opened it and stuck his head inside. "Wanna go out and scare Christopher and Dylan?"

Emily was sitting on her bed, brushing her hair. Her eyes brightened. "Sure."

He put his finger to his lips to quiet her. They slipped down the stairs and outside without their grandparents noticing.

Sam pointed. They sprinted quietly across the yard, meeting up in the barn.

Once Sam closed the door behind them, Emily took a gulp of air and asked, "What are we going to do?"

He glanced around. "I don't know yet. Help me look around for something."

"Like what?"

"Something that can cast a shadow on their tent," he said, rattling through metal cans and rusted tools.

"All that clanking will alert them for sure," Emily said.

"Hey, how about this?" Sam pulled out a large broom, put a plastic bucket on the end of it, and then covered it all with a tattered sheet.

The light seemed to dawn in Emily's eyes, and her mouth curved upward. "That's a great idea. And I can take this," she said enthusiastically, grabbing trimming shears. As she snapped them open and closed, the shears made a creaking, cutting, snapping sound.

"Better not. Someone could get hurt with that." He looked around. "How about that rusty bucket over there and the hand spade?"

"Yeah, that's a good idea," she said, picking them up.

"Great," Sam said. "Let's go."

CHRISTOPHER HEARD DYLAN SWALLOW. Not a normal swallow either. It was more the sound of someone trying to swallow an elephant whole. The chill bumps on Christopher's arms brought reinforcements. The pale color of Dylan's skin brought his Native American heritage into question.

"You gonna open it?" Dylan squeaked.

Christopher took a deep breath and nodded.

Just as his hand reached for the zipper, they heard another scuffle outside and then the looming shadow of a dog strode up to the tent. A dog whose tail was wagging. A happy dog. Dylan and Christopher released a collective breath, and Christopher peeked through the zipper at Toby.

"Why on earth did you scare us like that, Toby?" He unzipped the tent the rest of the way and let the happy dog inside.

She was a welcome sight.

They wrestled and cuddled her, both clearly relieved to have a guard dog beside them through the night. Everything was sure to be all right now.

Christopher pulled out the container of popcorn and soda that Grandma had sent outside for them. They both began to relax and enjoy things again. Christopher decided this wasn't such a bad idea after all. He really liked staying out in a tent. Maybe Grandma and Grandpa would let him do it more often.

That was his last thought . . . until Toby started barking wildly and they turned around in time to see the giant dark shadow hovering over their tent.

"What is it?" Dylan's voice quivered. Christopher had never heard his friend's voice quiver. His twitches were worse too. In fact, the bottom of Christopher's eyelid started twitching. He gulped. Loud. Toby wouldn't stop barking. She kept jumping at the side of the tent to get to the shadow that did not move. Something—or someone—was standing outside their tent. Since the person wasn't saying anything, Christopher could only assume he or she wasn't friendly. Did werewolves or vampires speak English? Christopher broke out in a sweat.

"Uncle Pete, is that you?" Christopher asked in as courageous a voice as he could muster. He wanted to prove his bravery, but it sure was hard right now.

No answer.

"Are you going to go out there?" Dylan asked.

Christopher's legs turned to concrete. A good indication he had no plans of going anywhere soon. Besides, he was getting tired of Dylan bossing him around. "No."

"Are you scared?"

"No. But I'm not stupid either. Why don't *you* go out there?"

Dylan's right shoulder twitched. That was a new one. Christopher felt bad that camping out was causing his friend extra stress. Although, presently, he thought he could match him twitch for twitch. They should have stayed inside.

"We have Toby. She'll protect us," Christopher said, though he had his doubts. If the intruder offered Toby a bone, they were so in trouble.

Just then an eerie sound came from outside. A ghostly sound. Light, yet creepy.

The boys turned wide eyes toward one another. Toby's bark took a dark turn. Her lip curled into a snarl, baring her teeth.

"Can you run fast?" Christopher asked.

Dylan nodded with gusto.

"I'm gonna unzip the tent quietly; then we'll make a run for it." Christopher's heart leapt to his throat. He prayed Toby would be able to ward off the attacker.

SAM MOTIONED FOR EMILY to stop giggling while they listened to the boys freaking out inside the tent. Toby's barking was driving Sam to distraction, but he hadn't had this much fun teasing his little brother in years.

He lifted a ghostly call into the night air that sent Dylan and Christopher tumbling around in the tent. Sam could smell their fear.

Inside and outside the tent, they waited. Finally, Christopher carefully, methodically, unzipped the tent and peeked out with one eye.

It was then that Sam gave the signal and Emily started beating on the rusty bucket with the hand spade like a wild drummer at a rock concert, causing a ruckus loud enough to wake the dead. The boys tumbled out of the tent and blurred into the dark night as sheer adrenaline carried them to the house with Toby barking and wildly zipping across the lawn behind them.

Just when things were getting good, Grandma came out the front door.

Sam motioned for Emily to stop whopping the bucket, but she just kept laughing and belting it out for all she was worth. In spite of everything, they had a good belly laugh, but when the two of them got a better view of Grandma, they stopped laughing.

"GRANDMA, ARE YOU ALL RIGHT?" Christopher said when Sam and Emily ran up beside him.

Dylan looked as though he wished he could go home. Sam wished he could go with him.

Grandma tried to move, and then she groaned. "My back. I think I've hurt my back again."

"I'll get Grandpa," Emily said, dashing into the house.

"I'm sure I'll be fine," Charlotte said, but Sam had a feeling he would be grounded till he was thirty-five. He'd only wanted to have a little fun with Christopher. Now this. The last thing he wanted to do was hurt his grandma.

Bob came out looking dazed—until he spotted his wife.

"Charlotte, what happened?" He bent down to reach for her.

"I'm not really sure," she said. "I think I missed the last step. It's possible I've strained my back again."

"Here, let me pick you up—"

His hands reached around her, and Sam stepped up to help him. Once they got her inside the house, they situated her comfortably on the sofa. Emily ran for the heating pad.

"You kids are spoiling me." Grandma shivered. She turned to Christopher. "I'm so sorry, honey. I've ruined your night in the tent."

"Which reminds me," Bob said. "What were you doing out there anyway, Charlotte?"

She paused. "Oh, I remember now."

They were so busted.

She turned to Sam and Emily, but before she could say anything, Christopher piped up.

"It was you?"

Sam didn't so much as flicker with the hint of a smile. He knew better.

"Sam?" Bob asked. "What were you and Emily up to?"

One look at his grandpa's face and something told Sam this was going to be a very long night.

Chapter Seventeen

"No, we don't need any meals. I'll be fine, Pastor Evans. I just wasn't able to make it to church this morning." Charlotte explained the strained-back problem to her pastor.

They talked awhile longer and Pastor Evans assured her the church family would lift her health needs in prayer.

She thanked him and they said their good-byes. Charlotte appreciated how their church was like a close-knit family, each member looking out for the others.

A quilt her grandmother had made for her lay in soft folds around her body. The air was pleasant this morning, but the night chill had sent Emily searching for a blanket for Charlotte.

She smiled. It pleased her that her granddaughter was fussing over her this way. No doubt guilt motivated her, but Charlotte would take what she could get.

"The chickens are fed, and I've collected the eggs, Grandma," Emily announced when she stepped into the family room.

"Thank you, dear."

"Can I get you anything? Grandpa had a meeting after church. Said he'd be back soon. He'll stop and pick you up a sandwich on the way home." Emily tucked the folds of the quilt around her grandma, checked the cord on the heating pad, and then slumped into the big armchair opposite the sofa. Despite her visit to the chicken coop, a sweet flowery scent trailed behind her.

Charlotte appreciated this nurturing side of her granddaughter. Though Emily tended to keep it hidden like many teenagers, it was nice to know it was there.

Charlotte sighed. She hated to be such a bother. She could have made lunch, but Bob insisted she stay down till her back was better.

"How's your back?"

Charlotte focused her attention on how it felt. "It seems better. When are you going to Miss Middleton's? Sam said he would take you."

"Yeah, he told me."

"Where is he?"

"He and Christopher took Arielle home from church. Hannah and Frank brought me home so I could check on you." She kicked off her sandals and curled her legs beneath her. "Sam's taking me and Christopher to lunch and then he'll drop me off at Miss Middleton's after lunch. Are you sure you're all right with me going? I'm just checking on her, not working or anything."

Charlotte studied the young lady unfolding before her. A woman-child in so many ways. Still, every day a new petal bloomed. Now and then the shy bit of childhood poked through, but most days she radiated confidence. Sometimes that confidence made her a smidgen unteachable, causing them all a snatch of grief.

"I'll be fine, honey."

A car rattled into the driveway, tires biting gravel.

"Sounds like Sam," Emily said with a smile, bounding from the chair. With youthful energy she flung herself out the door, allowing it to slam behind her.

Charlotte shook her head. Quieting the screen door seemed out of the question with kids around.

Flipping through a magazine, Charlotte was quickly bored. She had never been one to sit around the house.

"Knock, knock," Hannah called out.

Maybe they needed a revolving door.

"Come in, Hannah." Charlotte straightened the quilt around her and primped her hair a tad.

Heavy sneakers padded across the carpet. "Well, well, well. Look at you." Hannah loomed before her, casserole dish in hand. "Some people will do anything to get out of church."

"Thanks for bringing Emily home, by the way. You can't have been cooking already this morning."

Hannah shrugged and walked the dish into the kitchen. "What else am I gonna do when my friend is down?"

Charlotte heard the opening of the refrigerator door, dishes being moved and scooted about, and the closing door. She loved that she and Hannah had the kind of friendship where they could come into one another's house and just take care of things.

"It's chicken and rice." Hannah stepped back into the family room and sat in the chair Emily had occupied earlier. "I know the kids are going out for lunch, but you could have this for dinner."

"Yum. Thanks."

"Want some hot tea?" Hannah asked.

"Sure."

Hannah went back into the kitchen and clanged around before returning with a tray of tea fixings.

"How did you find the time to make a casserole already?"

"I always keep something on hand for emergencies." She poured tea into a cup for Charlotte and handed it to her.

"You are one in a million. Thanks, Hannah."

"Frank's probably glad of that." Hannah took a drink from her cup. She propped her feet on the coffee table. "Where's Bob?"

"He had a meeting after church. He'll be here soon."

"I'll bet Sam and Emily feel pretty bad about everything," Hannah whispered.

"Yeah. They shouldn't have been scaring poor Christopher and Dylan that way. But it was my own fault I fell. I should have been more careful."

"You taking your calcium?" Hannah swirled the spoon around in her cup.

"Yes." Sometimes Hannah tended to fuss too much. Okay, maybe that was the pot calling the kettle black, but still . . .

"Have you gotten any sponsors for the diabetes walk yet?" Hannah asked.

"A few," Charlotte said. "But now I'm wondering if I'll be able to participate."

"Oh, I sure hope so," Hannah said. "I'd hate to think all this pain we've been building up in our legs was for nothing."

Charlotte laughed and felt a glitch in her back. Right now, she'd settle for leg pain.

EMILY PULLED THE CARAMEL and cream lapghan from her bag. It now draped over her lap and down her legs. Thankfully, it was an easy pattern and would be smaller than an afghan, so she hoped to finish it in time. A fresh breeze swept in through Miss Middleton's window, stirring the dainty sheer and filling the room with warm, sweet air.

Emily had been working on the lapghan every night in her bedroom. Though it was Sunday and she didn't have to work, she was glad Miss Middleton had invited her over for a visit. It would give her time to work on her project.

"My, my, you're coming right along on that," Miss Middleton said, fingering Emily's work. "And doing a very fine job."

Emily appreciated her kind words, but Miss Middleton was edging ninety, so Emily had to wonder just how closely the woman could inspect her work.

"I love doing it. Thanks for teaching me."

Miss Middleton waved her hand and hobbled over to her chair opposite Emily. She reached into the large wicker basket beside her chair and pulled out the yellow baby blanket she was working on. "I enjoy your company, Emily."

She hadn't said much about the Orphan Train in a while, and Emily was hoping she would open up about it again soon.

With a glance at Miss Middleton, Emily took in the weary set of her brow, the stooped shoulders, the slow-working fingers. For the first time since meeting Miss Middleton, it suddenly dawned on Emily that she had never known someone as old as her before. In fact, the more she thought about it, the more she realized she didn't like the idea of growing old. Then she thought of her mother. Her beautiful, deceased mother who didn't have a choice in the matter.

Sometimes life seemed so unfair.

The soft yarn worked through Emily's fingers in a steady rhythm, now that she had the hang of making double crochets. She hoped Grandma and Grandpa would like it.

"I suppose you want to hear more about the Orphan Train?" Miss Middleton said out of the blue.

"If you want to talk about it."

The yarn stilled between her fingers as Miss Middleton seemed to collect her thoughts before speaking. Emily didn't know why this woman had such a hold on her, but she could hardly wait to hear her stories. Ashley didn't seem as interested anymore. Maybe it was because she had to help her mom and just lost interest in Miss Middleton's history. Emily didn't know. She knew only that she couldn't wait from one story to the next.

"Let's see, I'm trying to remember where we left off the last time. I think we had gone to the station and the man had picked Rose to go, but she refused and I didn't force her."

Emily nodded.

Miss Middleton pulled in a long breath and blew it out, scarcely stirring the dust around her.

"We went back to the bridge. Zana didn't look happy to see us. She looked sad. I thought it was because she didn't want us." Her crooked fingers worked the yarn. Her words came out slow and deliberate. "Now I know the truth. She wanted us to have a home. We waited months for the next train to come and went through the whole cleaning-up ritual all over again."

She chuckled. "Probably didn't have a single bath in between." Her slim shoulders shrugged. "That's how we lived back then."

Without saying a word, she rocked a couple of times, stopped and then took another breath—as though it was too hard to rock and talk at the same time.

"All those children, my lands." She shook her head. "I remember it as though it were yesterday." Her eyes glazed. "Poured down rain all morning. I begged Zana to let us stay. It was early spring, and the rain showers were plenty cold." She gave an involuntary shiver. "'Course, the winters were much worse."

Emily got up and placed a nearby shawl around Miss Middleton's shoulders.

"Thank you, dear."

"Did you make that?" Emily asked, pointing to the shawl.

Miss Middleton smiled. "A long time ago, I'm afraid. I don't think my hands could work with the lace the way they used to."

"It's beautiful." Emily sat back down and picked up her yarn and hook.

Miss Middleton rocked a few times and seemed to mentally search for where she had left off on her story. "Rose started coughing. She'd had a cough for quite some time by then. But she was so little to go through all that. I was older—and tougher, I think."

Emily couldn't imagine "Miss Middleton" and "tough" being in the same sentence. She looked as though one stiff wind could blow her into Kansas.

"This time the man chose both of us." Her fingers stopped working the yarn, and she looked at Emily. "Zana had tears in her eyes when she hugged us good-bye. We cried like babies—which, of course, we were."

Her face clouded over, and for a minute, Emily thought the woman might cry. But she didn't.

"With Rose's chubby fist clinging to mine, we boarded that train and never looked back. Miles and miles of track, as far as the eye could see." She shook her head. "Think of it. There were kids everywhere. Rambunctious boys throwing punches and teasing the girls. Wiggles and giggles. Noise, noise, noise." She *tsked, tsked.*

"Station after station came and went. The whistle announced our arrival into each community. Faces were scrubbed clean, clothes smoothed and straightened. The orphans lined up for inspection, just like cattle, while the townsfolk looked us over." She paused a moment.

"We heard some kids went to homes where they were treated like slaves. But Zana had reminded us that, slave or not, at least we'd have a roof over our heads." She shrugged. "So we waited to be chosen and prayed for God's protection."

A spray of golden sunlight suddenly burst through Miss Middleton's picture window, shining brightly on the old woman's features. It was as though in one glance, Emily could see how far and long the woman had traveled this earth.

Miss Middleton blinked. "Oh my. I've prattled on, and

you told me your grandma hurt her back. We'd better discuss this another time so you can go home and check on her."

Emily suspected there was more to it than that, but she agreed. Maybe Miss Middleton wasn't feeling so well.

"Okay." Emily got to her feet.

Miss Middleton seemed to mentally say, *On the count of three,* and shoved herself out of the rocker.

Emily gave her a tender hug. "I'll see you again soon."

"Is your ride here?"

"Not yet, but it's just about time for him to come. I'll just wait outside so I can see him when he pulls up."

"All right, dear. I may just go take a nap then, if you're sure."

"I'm sure."

The balmy breezes of summer ruffled through her hair as Emily stepped outside. Sunlight warmed her as she turned this way and that, trying to get a signal on her cell phone to call her brother. She hoped she could reach him.

Chapter Eighteen

Charlotte noticed the pedometer on Bob's dresser was collecting dust. She doubted he had even used it once since she had bought it for him. It frustrated her no end. This was his health she was trying to save, but he seemed to want no part of it. What could she do?

"What are you doing up? You need to be on the sofa," Bob said with obvious affection when he walked into the bedroom behind her.

"I know. I just needed to get a new magazine from my night table."

"Here, let me help you back to the sofa."

She picked up a cooking magazine from her night table. Then Bob placed his arm around her and allowed her to lean into him while he helped her into the family room. She couldn't mention the pedometer now. She was injured, not stupid.

"Is Emily home yet?" she asked.

"Haven't seen her. Wasn't she at Lydia Middleton's for the afternoon?"

"Well, I thought Sam was supposed to pick her up around three, and it's four-thirty. Maybe I got things wrong."

"You've been asleep a while. With your recent upheaval, could it be you're mistaken?"

"Yeah, you're probably right. Just the same, I think I might call and check on her."

Bob slipped her over the well-worn carpet and eased her onto the sofa. Plumping a pillow behind her and adjusting her heating pad, he said, "I'll get you the phone."

She couldn't figure out why he was being so nice. Hannah's Frank acted like this, yes, but not Bob. Maybe he was sick. Oh dear, she just *had* to go on that diabetes walk.

She called Emily's cell phone, but it went straight to voicemail. Now she understood why the kids were always complaining about the spotty reception around Bedford.

"Bob, could you bring me the church directory? I can't get through to Emily."

She dialed Miss Middleton's phone number and waited for the woman to pick up. On the fifth ring, she finally answered.

"Miss Middleton, hi. This is Charlotte Stevenson. I was calling to see if Emily was still there."

"Why no. She left some time ago." Lydia's voice was soft and sleepy.

Fear struck Charlotte's chest. She told herself to stay calm. Most likely she and Sam had gone out for a while. They could have called, but nothing to worry about—yet.

"Oh, that's fine. She and her brother no doubt went out for a little while. No problem. Just thought I'd see if I could catch her." No need to worry Miss Middleton. The old woman had enough to deal with at her age.

Just as she hung up the phone, she heard the rattle of

Sam's car. Fear flittered away with her sigh. All was right with her world once again.

Faint female laughter lilted through the open door. She wouldn't scold them, but she would remind them that they needed to check in if their plans changed. After all, they both insisted on carrying cell phones, and they could be thoughtful enough to check in when needed.

The screen door slammed, causing Charlotte to cringe—again. Sam was saying something as their footsteps drew near.

"Hey, how ya doin', Grandma?" Sam grinned from ear to ear as though he was having a great day.

"I'm doing all right. Listen, Sam, when your plans change, if you wouldn't mind, it would be very helpful if you—"

Just then Arielle stepped into view, and fear clutched at Charlotte's chest once again.

"Where's Emily?"

Sam's eyes grew wide. He smacked his forehead. "My car stalled and—" He stopped when he saw the look on Charlotte's face. "I'll go get her right now."

"THAT WAS NICE OF YOUR MOM to drop us off here. I was really in the mood for ice cream," Emily said. "I'm surprised she didn't stay. I thought Jenny's Creamery was one of her favorite places."

"It is. But she was going to a friend's house. Besides, she's trying to lose weight," Ashley said.

Emily scrunched her nose. "It seems like most women

are always worrying about their weight." She dug her spoon farther into her hot fudge sundae and scooped out a bite.

"I don't think you need to worry. You worked off enough just walking to my house from Miss Middleton's. Besides, you'll probably be thin like your grandma." Before Ashley could bring the spoon back to her mouth, Emily stopped her cold.

"Grandma!" Emily dropped her spoon.

"What's the matter?"

"I couldn't get a signal on my cell phone when I left Miss Middleton's house, so after I got to your house, I was going to call her. When you mentioned coming here, I forgot." Emily clawed through her jeans pocket to retrieve her cell phone. Numbers punched, she waited. It rang busy.

"Grrrr."

"Are they gone?" Ashley asked.

"It's busy. Don't let me forget to call her, or I'm toast."

"WERE YOU ABLE TO GET MEL?" Bob asked.

Charlotte shook her head. "She's not home." She rubbed her forehead.

Bob put his hand over hers. "Now, Charlotte. You know everything is fine. This is Bedford. People take care of their own here. She's probably with Ashley somewhere."

"But why wouldn't she call me?"

"Who knows? But I'm sure there's a reason. Sometimes teenage girls forget things."

"Menopausal women forget things, Bob. Teenage girls still have young minds. There's no excuse."

The look on his face said he wasn't about to argue.

"And where was Sam when he was supposed to pick her up?" Charlotte said. "Why can't the kids be responsible?" She normally didn't rant like this, especially where the kids were concerned. But her back throbbed, and now her head joined in. It all proved too much.

Just then the phone rang. Charlotte yanked it off the hook.

"Hello?"

"Grandma, I'm sorry I haven't called." Emily's voice immediately flooded her with relief. Then anger.

"Where are you right now?"

"I'm sitting outside at Jenny's Creamery with Ashley."

"Stay right there. Call Sam and let him know where you are so he can come and get you. He was going to Ashley's house to see if he could find you. He can take Ashley back home while he's at it. We'll talk more when you get home." Charlotte hung up the phone.

Bob settled back in the chair. Charlotte wasn't so relaxed. A you'd-better-call-home speech was already forming in her mind.

EMILY AND SAM SLOGGED into the room.

Charlotte exchanged a glance with Bob and then looked at the kids. "You both know how your actions affected this family, so I won't bother to go into that. Suffice it to say that Grandpa and I have a project for you two. For the next couple of days, aside from your usual chores and duties, Emily, you will help me in the garden. I want you to learn family thoughtfulness. You owed us the courtesy of a phone call so we would know where you were instead of letting us get sick with worry."

"But I tried—" Emily's rant was cut short when she took one look at her grandma.

Charlotte turned to Sam, whose jaw was already firm and set.

"Sam, you had a responsibility to pick up your sister, and you failed to do that. You said you had car trouble. Fine. Those things happen. But you also had a phone and could have let us know. The fact remains that you forgot to pick up your sister. It's inexcusable. You will clean the chicken coop."

His eyes grew wide with horror. "The chicken coop?"

Had the situation not been so serious, Charlotte might have laughed. "Yes, the chicken coop." The firm edge of her voice left no room for argument. "Both of you have been acting irresponsibly. First that deal with Christopher and now this."

Though she hated doling out punishments, they had left her no choice. Besides, the chicken coop needed cleaning, and the garden needed tending and with her back, she couldn't do either, so this was a good way to get the jobs done.

"You may be excused," she said.

Heads hung low, shoulders stooped, they turned and, scarcely picking up their feet, shuffled out of the room.

Chapter Nineteen

Pete and Charlotte shoved through the AA Tractor Supply the next morning, the floorboards groaning beneath them as they milled around the store. The room smelled of tractor tires, fan belts and stale coffee.

"Do you know where the carpet cleaner is, Pete?" Charlotte rarely came in here. Bob and Pete, on the other hand, were regular customers and knew their way around. Unfortunately, she couldn't remember the name of the carpet cleaner the ladies at church had raved about last week. Charlotte hoped seeing the bottles on display would help jog her memory for the best product because their carpet was in desperate need of spot removal.

Just then Brad Weber, the owner's grown son, stepped into view carrying a box that read TRACTOR SPROCKETS on the side of it; he plunked it on the counter with a clang and jingle of steel.

Brad was a tall, paunchy sort of guy around Pete's age. His black hair was allowed to roam freely, and a two-day stubble covered his face. Charlotte always thought his carefree ways made him look approachable and he was an easy target for anyone who wanted to shoot the breeze with on a lazy summer's day.

"Hey, Pete, Mrs. Stevenson, how's it going?" Brad rifled through the box, clinking steel against steel, apparently categorizing the sprockets for placement on the shelf.

Charlotte smiled. She'd known Brad since he was a little boy, and he never got used to the idea of calling her by her first name.

"We're doing all right. Just looking around to see if you've gotten anything new since I was in yesterday." Pete grinned.

Brad obviously noticed that Charlotte was moving a little slowly. "You all right?"

Charlotte explained the mishap.

"I'm sorry about your fall, Mrs. Stevenson, but I would have given a shiny nickel to see those two kids running out of the tent that night." He and Pete both laughed. Charlotte chuckled a tad herself.

"I have to admit it was pretty funny—well, until I fell. I'm doing better now though."

In response, Brad launched into the story of his broken ankle after the big football game of his senior year. Charlotte remembered it well. Brad had been the town hero that night. She suspected he had relived that night many times in his mind, and no doubt would replay it many more throughout his lifetime.

"You sure were a good player," Charlotte said, encouraging him.

"Thank you," he said.

Before he could launch into more glory-days memories,

she asked, "Could you tell me where you keep your carpet cleaner?"

"Oh, sure. Let me show you."

Charlotte hobbled behind him over to the carpet cleaner aisle. Once she spotted the cleaner and snatched it from the shelf, she walked back toward the counter and listened as the men talked a little about the farming business, the weather, and their opinions on how the crops would do this year.

"Sorry to hear about Bill's silent partner backing out of their joint venture for that development on the south side of town," Brad said, scooping a section of sprockets into a plastic carrier. "Heard they were buying the Watkins farm." He whistled. "Nice land, and they were paying a pretty penny for it, from what I hear."

Charlotte steadied herself against the counter. Bill's partner backed out? If Bill didn't have problems before, he sure had them now. She had to do something. Fast.

"It's a shame. I know Ralph Morner was banking on building those homes. They don't get their earnest money back either, so they're out a wad of cash. But then I'm sure Bill told you that. Tell him I'm sorry to hear how it all turned out."

Brad had no idea the tsunami he had caused in the pit of Charlotte's stomach. Her world was suddenly off-kilter, and she needed to sit down. Glancing around, she saw no chairs, so she continued to lean against the counter to steady herself. She forced a smile.

"Want some coffee?"

"Sure," they said in unison.

"Okay. Why don't you grab yourselves a mug from the rack while I re-shelve these sprockets." Brad headed toward a back aisle.

The coffee in the machine at the end of the cluttered counter looked like it had been sitting around for a while, but Charlotte didn't really care at the moment.

"You all right, Mom? You look a little pale."

"I'm fine."

Pete shrugged. "It's like I've been saying all along; farmland should be kept for farming. All some people care about is filling their pockets. What were the Watkinses thinking, selling out for a housing development? That farm has been in their family for years."

Charlotte wasn't up for this conversation right now. "Maybe they're having some problems, Pete. Sometimes people have to do things they don't want because of health reasons or other things."

"Maybe." Pete didn't look convinced. "I don't wish ill on them or my brother, for that matter. You know that, Mom. But why can't Bill make money doing something else? I just don't get it."

"Here we go," Brad said as he slipped behind the counter and filled their coffee cups.

"Thanks."

"Anyway, as I was saying, I guess it hurt the guys. Too bad Bill already started on those renovations for the new baby. Have they gotten very far?"

He was digging for information. And they said women were gossips! Charlotte began to wonder if AA Tractor Supply was a local hangout to find out the latest town happenings.

After allowing a respectable amount of time for them to comment, and seeing that they weren't going to, Brad continued. "Well, it's just a shame, that's all."

"I'm not big on buying up farmland anyway, Brad. You know that," Pete said.

"Oh, that's right. I'd forgotten."

Charlotte wondered if he had truly forgotten or just wanted to get a little trouble stirred up between the brothers. He'd done that more than a few times in their younger days. Brad was an okay kid, but sometimes he reminded her of Eddie Haskell on *Leave it to Beaver.*

Pete and Charlotte quickly finished their coffee, paid for the carpet cleaner, and said their good-byes. Clutching the bag next to her and trying not to wince from the tenderness in her back, Charlotte made her way to the door. As Pete held it open for her, they came face to face with Silas Maynard.

"How's it going, Silas?"

"Hey, Pete. Seems we keep running into each other."

Pete grinned and nodded.

They climbed into the truck. "Looks like Silas got some new clothes." The brown bag crackled as Charlotte laid it beside her on the seat.

"He came into some money," Pete said, shoving the truck into gear.

"How nice for him." Charlotte stared at the storefront as they pulled away, her mind racing to find answers for her son.

"WE HAVE TO DO SOMETHING," Charlotte said.

Bob tore his gaze away from the newspaper and looked at her. "What's that?"

"About Bill. We need to help him."

"Why is that?" Bob sighed, folded his newspaper, and laid it on the floor beside his chair.

She told him about their conversation with Brad at the store. Once again, Charlotte leaned against the heating pad behind her back. "We have to do something. He could be in trouble, Bob. We can't let them lose their house."

Bob held up his hand. "Now hold on right there. Nobody has said anything about them losing their home. You're blowing this out of proportion, Char."

"You can't be serious! You've read the paper; you've heard the talk in town. Things are bad. People are having trouble getting loans," she said.

"Charlotte, you know I'm not opposed to helping others when they're in trouble, especially if it's our kids, but we're not really in a position to offer financial help. Aside from that, Bill is a grown man, and this is his business. If he wants us to help, he'll ask us. Until then, I think we need to stay out of it. As I've said, he has a good head on his shoulders."

She opened her mouth to speak, but thought better of it. Bob was right, she knew. If only she didn't feel so . . . helpless.

Chapter Twenty

With the toe of his boot, Sam kicked around a clump of dirt on the playground, glancing up from time to time to watch the kids. What a way to spend his Tuesday afternoon. He'd hardly seen Jake and Paul so far this summer. It was one thing to miss out on hanging with his buds because of flying, but to miss out for this stupid job at the day care bugged him no end.

Wasn't it enough that he'd had to leave California and live on a dumb farm? To add the misery of working at a day-care center with a bunch of hyper kids was too much.

"Mr. Sam, I've gotta go to the bathroom."

Sam looked down into a face crusted with peanut butter and jelly. No matter how you sliced it, kids were gross. He was never going to have any when he got married—if he ever got married.

"You'll have to wait until we get inside. Break time will be over in a minute."

"But I gotta go." The kid stomped his pudgy legs with urgency. The look on his face made Sam nervous. He blew out a deep sigh. "Come with me."

Sam walked over and asked Arielle to watch his group while he took junior to the bathroom. Another teacher was in charge of Arielle's group, so Arielle offered to take the child inside.

He thanked her and watched her walk off. Beautiful and nice. Not too many girls like her around. Especially here on Walton's Mountain. He groaned. He hadn't even known what Walton's Mountain was until he moved here. Not only did he have to watch it on TV, but he also had to live it.

Too bad Sam wouldn't get to know Arielle better. Once graduation was over, he was heading back to San Diego. Home. With or without his mom, it was home. Either that or he'd go looking for his dad. But one thing he knew for certain: He wasn't staying on the farm. He loved his grandparents and appreciated all they had done for them, but farm life was not for him.

A couple of boys found sticks and banged them on the chain-link fence. Girls huddled in groups with their dolls. Some kids chased. Others ran. Teachers wore expressions that said they'd rather be anywhere else. Or maybe Sam was reading into their faces what he felt sure was on his.

Knee-high people everywhere the eye could see.

The play area confined them all like a prison. When he was flying, he could take in the wide-open spaces. Nothing but blue skies. Just him and God.

He blinked. What had made him think about God? Maybe Grandpa's Bible reading was getting to him. He had nothing against God, but figured he was more important to old people. He tolerated his grandparents' "devotional" time, though he didn't know what that had to do with him.

When he had his own place, he'd run things differently. He certainly wouldn't make his kids listen to something just because it was his belief. His kids—if he had any, which he doubted—would be free to believe what they wanted. He wouldn't tarnish them one way or the other. Freedom of speech, and all that.

"Mr. Sam, Logan won't let me have the ball." Xander pulled his chubby arms into a stubborn fold against his chest and squeezed his lips together.

"Logan, you need to share."

"I do share. Xander doesn't. He's a ball hog. My daddy says you're not supposed to be a ball hog."

"What's a ball hog?" Sam asked, amused in spite of himself.

"Daddy says it's someone who keeps the ball and won't share it."

"That's what you did," Xander said, pointing.

"Did not!"

"Did too!"

"I'm telling my daddy," Logan said.

"Go ahead, you big baby," Xander said.

"All right, you two." He was so not having kids.

Arielle dropped off junior from his bathroom break just as the bell rang. The kids jumped into line, knocking each other out of the way and finally settling in. Another deep breath, and Sam led them forward, the father duck leading his ducklings.

He was so glad his friends back home couldn't see this.

EMILY COULD NOT BELIEVE she was stuck working outside as she dug the hoe deeper into the soil of the garden. It was bad enough that she had to do this at all, but with Grandma sitting on a chair watching her, it was too much. She wasn't a baby.

Fortunately, the rainy weather helped keep the soil soft, but her back still hurt. She wondered if it hurt as much as Grandma's.

"Hoe in between those rows of green beans. I don't want to give those weeds a foothold."

Emily clenched her teeth. Taking her anger out with the hoe, she beat the ground till it was practically like sand.

"Be careful you don't hit those plants. They're not all that strong just yet."

If she had her way, she just might wallop those plants to oblivion so she wouldn't have to work in the stupid garden at all. Emily stopped hoeing a minute to catch her breath.

"I know it's hard work," Grandma said, "but there is something so rewarding about growing your own food, living off the land."

Emily wanted to say, "Yeah, whatever," but she held her tongue. The last thing she needed was to be in more trouble.

"Would you like to take a break and get some iced tea?"

At last Grandma had noticed the sweat dripping off her face.

"Yeah."

They both went into the kitchen and grabbed some glasses that they filled with ice and tea. Emily took a long drink. "Thanks." The cold drink made her feel lots better.

"You're welcome." Grandma's face was soft and apologetic. "Listen, Emily—"

"It's all right. You did what you had to do." Emily wasn't sure why she said that, but she thought it a good thing to make the best of the situation. The sooner she got out of this job, the better.

A look of relief swept over Grandma, which made Emily feel a little guilty.

"You know, Emily, your mother used to help me in the garden." A faraway look clouded her grandma's eyes. "She loved having a part in making things grow." Grandma turned to Emily and smiled. "From the earth to the table, she used to say."

Emily took a moment to digest that information. She loved learning new things about her mom. She normally liked to do the things her mom had liked to do. It made her feel closer to her mom somehow. But Emily couldn't see sharing this with her mom. There were just some things she couldn't get into, and she suspected gardening was one of them.

"Guess I'd better get back to work," she said.

"Once you're certain the weeds are dealt with, you can call it a day out there."

"Okay," she said, dragging herself back to the garden. She was so thankful her friends in California couldn't see her now.

CHRISTOPHER PLOPPED onto a chair in the kitchen. "He makes me so mad," he said with a pout.

"Who does?" Charlotte put a sheet of chocolate chip cookies into the oven.

"Dylan."

"Why?"

"He thinks he knows everything." Hair disheveled, fingernails dirty, Christopher slumped farther into the chair.

"Why don't you wash your hands at the sink so you'll be ready when the cookies come out of the oven," Charlotte said with a wink.

That seemed to perk him up. He quickly complied and then sat back down into his seat across from her.

"Now, what seems to be the problem?"

"Dylan thinks he knows everything. He doesn't even have a dog." Christopher shoved his chin into the palm of his hand.

"How do you mean?"

"He keeps telling me how to train Toby. I'm following what the man at the fairgrounds said to do. That sheet you gave me. I showed it to Dylan, but he said I didn't have to follow it. He knows a better way."

Charlotte looked at him in earnest. "I see your concern. Was Dylan mad when he left here?"

"Maybe." Christopher obviously didn't want to commit one way or the other.

"It's not right for him to tell you what to do."

Christopher looked at her with surprise. "Really?"

"Well, no. You know how to do it, after all." She crossed her arms in front of her. "He probably thought he was trying to help, right?"

"Right." The way he said that, she wasn't sure if it was a question or an answer.

"You can always get another friend who will agree with you. Then you can send Dylan packing," Charlotte suggested.

Christopher looked positively horror stricken. "What?"

Charlotte nonchalantly rubbed at a spot on the table. "Well, if he's going to tell you how to do things, just forget the whole thing and find a new friend."

"Oh. I don't know. Sometimes he's a good friend."

"Yeah, but probably not good enough most of the time. I'll bet Toby doesn't like him either."

"Oh, yeah, Toby does like him. She always goes to him instead of me."

Bingo. Charlotte had found the root of the problem.

"*Hmm*. Well, if you want to keep Dylan as your friend, I guess you'll have to lock Toby away from him when he comes over."

Christopher seemed to ponder this idea, which unnerved Charlotte a little, making her wonder if she'd taken this whole psychology thing a little too far.

"I don't think that will work."

Hiding her smile, she said, "You don't?"

Christopher shook his head. "It wouldn't be fair to Toby. She shouldn't be punished just because she likes Dylan too."

"You think?"

Christopher sighed. "I'll just have to buck it up."

She said in her most serious voice, "It would seem the sensible thing to do."

"Yeah."

"Hey, I've got an idea."

Christopher looked up, hope in his eyes.

"What if you work with Toby on her obedience training and have Dylan help you with grooming Toby? That way you both can be a part of it—that is, if you want Dylan to help you."

Christopher's eyes grew wide and sparkly. "That would be great. He likes to brush her too." Christopher jumped up from the table. "Thanks, Grandma." He darted out of the room.

"Wait. What about the cookies?"

"I'll be back," his fading voice called out.

Charlotte wished all of life's problems could be remedied so easily.

Chapter Twenty-One

Her form, light and ethereal, ran through the colorful meadow of wildflowers. A wisp of wind rippled through her golden hair. She laughed. Eyes vibrant. So alive. She turned to Charlotte. "Catch me if you can."

"Denise, don't go." Charlotte reached for her, running, running until her view of her only daughter blurred and finally disappeared.

"Charlotte, wake up. You're having a bad dream."

Charlotte felt a hand clamped onto her shoulder, shaking her gently as she worked her way from the meadow back to consciousness. "What?" A sleepy fog muddled her mind.

"You were dreaming, honey. Talking in your sleep." Bob brushed the hair from her face.

Charlotte rubbed her eyes. "I was?" She thought a moment.

"You said, 'Denise, don't go.'"

Suddenly she remembered. The meadow. Denise running. Charlotte unable to stop her. Then she was gone. Tears surfaced. "Oh, Bob." She leaned into him, and he held her close against his chest.

"I know," he whispered. "I know." The words rumbled in his chest, the steady rhythm of his heart bringing calm to her world.

Once Bob drifted back to sleep, Charlotte decided to get up. She slipped from the covers and quietly put on some clothes. A shroud of darkness covered Heather Creek Farm. She tiptoed down the hallway and into the family room. Her back felt stronger every day.

In the family room, she grabbed the bookkeeping ledger and sat down at the table. If she couldn't sleep, she might as well update the farm books. It would put her ahead of the game before the light dawned. She could hardly believe it was almost the end of June already. Summer would be over before they knew it.

The figures blurred before her, but not because she was tired. She kept seeing Denise in her mind. She didn't know why this was happening all these months later.

Denise was dead.

She tried not to let that thought take over her mind. The word *dead* was so final.

But they had faith. Hope. One day they would see Denise again. And she believed with all her heart, they *would* see her again. Still, there was the here and now, and Denise wasn't in it.

She shook herself. She had to stop the torturing thoughts. Denise was gone, and she had to accept it. The thing was, she thought she had. What was stirring up the memories?

The garden.

Emily working in the garden, looking so much like Denise at that age; that was it. Of course, Charlotte wouldn't stop Emily from working in the garden. They had doled out the punishment, and they would have to see it through. If only Emily didn't look so much like Denise . . .

LATER THAT MORNING, Emily came bounding down the stairs two by two, legs long and lanky, dressed in jeans and a T-shirt.

Charlotte tried not to gasp at the resemblance to her daughter. "You hungry?" she asked.

"Starving." Emily followed her through the hallway, past the framed pictures on the wall and into the kitchen.

"Everyone else has had breakfast already," Charlotte called over her shoulder.

"How come you let me sleep in?"

Charlotte grabbed an oven mitt. "You worked very hard in the garden yesterday, so I figured it wouldn't hurt to let you sleep a little." Charlotte glanced out the window to see Christopher already hard at work with Toby. Sunlight stretched long fingers of golden rays across the yard, wrapping Christopher and Toby in a bright clean glow.

"Thanks, Grandma." Emily grabbed the chilled milk jug from the refrigerator. "Do you mind if I go to Miss Middleton's this morning instead of this afternoon? I'll check the chickens just as soon as I get back."

"How will you get there?"

Emily put the milk jug on the table and then washed her hands at the sink. "I was hoping Sam or Pete would take me. Are they out in the barn?"

"As far as I know. Why the change in time?" The sweet smell of cinnamon lifted when Charlotte pulled the rolls from the oven. She'd had to wait and put them in the oven after Bob had gone to the supply store so he wouldn't be tempted.

"Miss Middleton's been tired in the afternoons lately, so I thought it might be better if I tried to go this morning and see if she's more rested. I mentioned that to her and she agreed."

"That was very thoughtful of you, Emily."

"Thanks."

"I thought you normally went over on Monday and Friday. Why today?"

Emily shrugged. "She had a few extra jobs she wanted me to do."

"Mmmm, those rolls smell great." Emily grabbed two glasses from the cupboard and then hesitated. "You gonna eat any with me?"

The way she said that tugged at Charlotte's heart. There was a hint of Emily wanting her grandmother to join her at the table.

"Absolutely. How could I pass up such a breakfast?" Charlotte drizzled icing over the warm rolls, scooped them onto a serving dish, and placed them on the table.

Charlotte said a prayer over their breakfast, flipped a napkin across her lap, and dug her fork into the warm, sugary treat.

They talked about Emily's summer and how fond she had become of Miss Middleton. They discussed the garden, and Charlotte shared a story about Denise trying to trap a snake there once.

Emily didn't know snakes could get in the garden. Great. That was all she needed.

THE SWEET BREEZE OF SUMMER wafted through the open window in the family room, causing a stir in the drapes.

Bob nudged the foot of his recliner to a close and laid the folded newspaper on the floor beside his chair.

"Want to go into town?" he asked.

Charlotte rested the embroidery in her lap and looked at him. "Sure. What do you want to do there?"

"Oh, I don't know. It's a nice day. Christopher's at Dylan's, Emily's at Miss Middleton's, and Sam's at the day care or helping Pete, whatever. Just seems a good time to walk around. Do you think you're up for it?"

"Sure, I can do a little walking." *A marathon? Not yet. A little walk through town? Yes.* "Just give me a second to grab my purse."

Charlotte felt practically giddy. It wasn't often that Bob meandered through town with her. She loved getting away from the house and the responsibilities. Maybe she should feel ashamed for that, but she didn't. She figured everyone needed space now and then. Some days having kids proved to be harder than she anticipated. Other days, like today, she enjoyed it immensely. Especially having the little snatch of time with Emily at the breakfast table.

Once they had parked the car downtown, Charlotte grabbed her lightweight black sweater. The gentle winds of summer were harmless enough, but since she tended to feel the cold, she had learned to dress accordingly. Most buildings kept their air conditioning at the polar-ice level.

"Hi, Bob, Charlotte." Brenda Schroeder stepped out the door of Brenda's Boutique and stooped for the newspaper. Perched beside the door were two large pottery tubs where clusters of bright impatiens lifted their heads to the sunlight and waved in the afternoon breezes. "Just now getting around to picking this up," she said, lifting the thick rolled paper in her hands. "Fine day for walking."

Dressed in a long yellow shift and matching pumps, Brenda stood and stretched her back. Her plump face reddened with the effort. Bright red lips lifted in a friendly smile.

"It certainly is," Charlotte said.

"How you feeling, Bob? You getting along okay?"

"I'm doing fine," he said, looking surprised.

"That's wonderful. My gal told me you bought a pair of jeans the other day, Charlotte. Are you enjoying them?"

Charlotte smiled and nodded. She hadn't told Bob about them yet.

"I got a new shipment in yesterday. You need to come in and check them out." Brenda winked and gave a neighborly wave before disappearing behind the door.

"New jeans?"

"Emily talked me into them."

"Oh, I see." An ornery glint flickered in his eyes. He reached for her hand, which surprised her.

They walked over to Morley Park and sat down on a weather-beaten wooden bench. Squirrels scurried from one poplar tree to the next. Birds chirped, fluttered, and winged about. Scrappy clouds drifted lazily across the light blue sky.

Walt Freeman, a neighbor and friend, drove up to the light in his black truck. With hair the color of steel wool and just as unruly, he poked his head out the window and yelled, "Hey, neighbors."

Bob and Charlotte waved.

"You doing okay, Bob?"

"I'm doing great. How about you?"

"Good." The light turned green. "You folks take care." He lifted a friendly wave, the engine of his big truck growling with importance as he continued down Main Street.

"Why do people keep asking me how I'm doing?" Bob said to Charlotte.

"Well, I suppose they're checking up on you because of the diabetes." Charlotte took in a long breath and lingered in the moment.

"Lots of people have diabetes. I've had it for a while now and they haven't asked me how I was. Now two people on the same day ask me." He scratched his head.

"What's the matter with that?"

"You think they know something I don't?"

"I'll let you know if I hear anything." She thought this might be a good time to mention the pedometer, but things were going so well, she decided to keep silent.

They started walking again. Passing a jewelry store, Charlotte stopped to admire a necklace in the window—a simple gathering of birthstones separated by dainty crystal beads and spacers, all held together on a sterling silver chain. The label read GRANDMOTHER'S NECKLACE.

"My, isn't that beautiful."

Bob leaned in. "What makes it a grandmother's necklace?"

"See those colored stones?"

"Uh-huh."

"Those are the birthstones for each grandchild."

"Seems kind of fancy to me."

"Yes, I suppose. Still, it's nice." Charlotte's gaze lingered a moment longer on the lovely stones and then they continued walking.

Charlotte reveled in their afternoon walk together and offered a prayer of thanksgiving in her heart.

THE KIDS CLIMBED OVER the playground equipment like bugs on a sandwich. Sam wanted to fly, not babysit. He kept telling himself this job made it all possible, but when he watched them eat peanut butter and jelly sandwiches, it just didn't help all that much.

He'd messed up his flying lesson today. Why was it so hard for him to trust the instruments? Ed said in a heavy fog you can't go by "feel." Sam couldn't count how many times Ed told him to trust the instruments.

It sure was hard to let go of things and trust something or someone else to handle it. Maybe he'd been disappointed one too many times.

"Mr. Sam, I'm bored." Big brown eyes looked up at him from a smudged face. The kid had grass stains on his jeans and a tattered shirt.

"Listen, I'm bored too, okay?"

The little guy shrugged and skipped away.

They were barely at the end of June, and he was already struggling to come up with games for the kids. He'd have to do some more Internet searches.

Sam went along with Mrs. Jackson as she took her class on a nature walk near the school. All nine kids lined up and set out for the trees, following Mrs. Jackson as though she were the Pied Piper. Sam was the last one in line so he could watch for any possible strays.

Partway through their walk, they stopped and rested on a fallen log. Mrs. Jackson gave the names of nearby trees and a few birds that flitted overhead. Sam told them the story of Snow White and the seven dwarfs.

One kid raised his hand. "Mr. Sam, do you think the seven dwarfs live in *these* woods?"

Sam's gaze clamped onto Mrs. Jackson's, who smiled.

"I don't think so, buddy. That's a pretend story, remember?"

The whole row of kids let out a collective sigh of disappointment.

A girl raised her hand. She was covered in so much pink, she reminded him of Pepto-Bismol.

"Yeah, Sarah?"

"I wish I could be Snow White."

The boy beside her nudged her arm. "No, you don't. Snow White ate the poison apple, you doofus."

The boys laughed and squirmed; the girls gasped.

Sarah's bottom lip quivered. "I'm not a doofus."

Mrs. Jackson took over. "Okay, Levi, that's enough. It's time to head back to the classroom for rest time."

The kids groaned in unison.

"I don't want to go back," Levi said, arms crossed in front of him, bottom firmly planted on the log.

Mrs. Jackson raised her brows and gave him a teacherly stare. "Levi, we're going back to the classroom now."

Levi considered this a moment and then dropped his arms in resignation. "Oh, okay."

The children jumped off the log and little feet pattered along the hardened earth as they made the trek back to the school. The receptionist ran out to meet them when they reached the playground.

"Mrs. Jackson, you have an emergency phone call in the office," she said, quite out of breath.

Mrs. Jackson turned to Sam. "Can you take the kids back to the classroom for quiet time?"

"Sure, no problem."

Mrs. Jackson and the receptionist ran back inside. Sam hoped everything would be all right.

The children settled in for quiet time, some resting, some looking at picture books, others coloring. They weren't allowed to talk during rest time. It was a time of sheer heaven for Sam.

He pulled out the airplane book Ed had given him to study and started browsing through it while the kids rested. In the quiet of the room, his eyelids grew heavy.

"Mr. Sam." A kid tugged on Sam's pant leg, startling him to attention.

"You're supposed to be resting." Sam recognized the snap in his voice and immediately felt repentant. It wasn't the kid's fault Sam felt groggy.

"But I need to tell you something."

"Do you have to go to the bathroom?"

"No."

"Then it can wait." Good grief, couldn't these kids give him five minutes of uninterrupted silence? Was that too much to ask? A good run on his skateboard would make him feel better. He'd call Jake and Paul tonight and see if they wanted to get together—oh, wait. He still had to clean the chicken coop.

Could things get any worse?

"But Mr. Sam—"

Sam refocused on the kid. "Are you still here?"

The kid's shoulders slumped, and he headed back toward his cot. Sam blew out a sigh.

"All right, come back here."

The kid brightened and scuttled back to Sam.

"Now, what is it you want?"

"I just wanted to ask where Levi was."

Fear struck Sam's chest like lightning spearing the sky. He looked around the classroom.

Levi was gone.

Chapter Twenty-Two

"That's coming along nicely, Emily." Miss Middleton inspected the lapghan with approval. "You'll be putting the finishing touches on it today."

Emily sat up taller in her seat. She couldn't deny how proud she felt for having crocheted the throw herself for her grandparents. She sure hoped they liked it.

"Thanks for teaching me." She never would have believed she could have an eighty-eight-year-old woman for a friend, but Miss Middleton was cool. And Emily looked forward to their get-togethers. She wondered what excuse she could come up with to visit if Miss Middleton decided not to hire her to clean anymore.

Miss Middleton groaned when she fell back into her recliner rocker. She lifted the baby blanket between her fingers, looped the soft yarn onto her hook, and set to work on her pattern.

Emily was glad she had finished cleaning the house for the day. She was anxious to complete the lapghan. Something about crocheting relaxed her. Her thoughts had already moved on to what project she might start next.

"Let's see, now where was I on the Orphan Train last time you were here?" Miss Middleton wondered.

Emily's rambling thoughts halted to attention. She didn't want to miss a single thread of Miss Middleton's story.

"We pulled into the last station. Rose and I were two of the few children left." She finished a loop and then looked up at Emily. "You see, at every station, I grabbed Rose's hand and held it fiercely, making it clear from the start that we went together or we didn't go at all." She shrugged. "And up to that point, each time we had to trudge our way back up to the steel carrier and keep on rolling."

"But this last stop was different?" The last row of single crochets slipped easily from Emily's fingers onto the hook. Emily didn't want the project to end, and she definitely didn't want Miss Middleton's story to end.

"It sure was." She stopped crocheting and rested her wrinkled hands in her lap. Her gaze brushed past the worn carpet beneath them.

"Eliza and Adam Middleton were there. She was as pretty as anyone I'd ever seen. She stood there, tall and elegant, in her fashionable dress and matching hat, hair pinned to perfection." Miss Middleton clicked her tongue. "Mr. Middleton wore a suit with a razor-sharp crease in his pants. I remember that so well." She shook her head. "I hadn't seen anything so neatly pressed in all my young days that I could remember."

"They took you and Rose," Emily said, feeling happy for her.

"What they saw in us, I'll never know. We were dressed in flour sacks."

"What's that?"

"Bags used for storing flour. It's what poor folks used to make dresses for little girls back then. Remember Luigi's Restaurant? Someone there had made them for us, I suppose." She sighed.

"So what did Mr. and Mrs. Middleton say when they saw you?"

"They stepped so close, I got a whiff of Mama's—Mrs. Middleton's—sweet perfume. I had never smelled anything so delicious in all my born days."

Emily smiled.

"She looked at the two of us and lifted a kind smile. Then she turned to me and said, 'You come together?'

"I nodded at her, but my spirits dropped. I figured she wouldn't take us once she learned that."

"What happened next?" Emily's crochet now rested on her lap.

"The sweetest sparkle shone in her eyes. She reached out her hand for Papa—Mr. Middleton—and he stepped closer, taking her hand into his. There was something so protecting, so secure about him. He smiled tenderly; kindness shone from his eyes. He looked me square in the face and said, 'We wouldn't have it any other way.'"

Emily's heart warmed.

"And that was that." She sagged back into her chair. "They took us home and raised us as their own." Her smile faded. "'Course, we didn't have Rose for long. When she died, it broke all of our hearts. But they loved me all their days, and there was nothing I wouldn't do for them. I knew Zana would have been pleased with them."

Emily thought about that. Then she thought how glad she was she didn't have to wear flour sacks. She couldn't imagine anything more humiliating. How did Miss Middleton bear it all? Emily also realized her grandma and grandpa were like the Middletons, taking in Emily and her brothers and loving them when they didn't have to.

"It's cool that Mr. and Mrs. Middleton took you in. You were lucky." Emily picked up her yarn again.

"Blessed. As are you." Miss Middleton pointed at her. "There are no better people in Bedford than your grandparents. Godly, loving people. You're blessed to have them as family."

Emily merely nodded but said nothing. She loved her grandparents, and she was grateful for them, but she couldn't help wishing things were back like they used to be. Back when her mom was alive, when they could go to the beach on a sunny afternoon—back when she didn't have to feed smelly chickens.

Speaking of chickens, it was time for her to get back and take care of them. Then she and Ashley were going for their walk. The walkathon was this weekend, and she wanted to be ready.

AFTER TELLING THE DIRECTOR that Levi was missing, Sam ran back to the woods to search for the little boy. Mrs. Jackson had rushed home earlier. Her ten-year-old son had fallen out of a tree and broken his arm, so she wasn't aware of the missing child. The director sent someone to cover the classroom and sent other workers to help Sam search the woods, while she called the sheriff's office.

Sam couldn't remember seeing Levi once they were inside the room. It was possible he could have scurried back to the woods when they were on the playground and the receptionist ran out to meet them.

Sam ran through the maze of trees till his lungs burned and screamed for air. Summer winds ruffled tree branches, whispering and taunting him, causing his fears to multiply. Short gulps of air kept him going. He whipped past trees and shrubs, calling Levi's name over and over. Not a single clue rode in the wind.

He thought of Christopher, the days after their mom died. His brother had looked so scared and alone. Sam felt every inch the protector, as though all the weight of their family rested on him. At first he resented his grandparents for "coming to the rescue." He had thought he was old enough to handle things and keep the family together in California. Now that he was looking for a lost child, he realized how stupid he had been.

"Levi. It's Mr. Sam. Where are you?" Sam stampeded across the hardened soil strewn with old leaves and twigs. Tree limbs blocked his way; he lifted and tugged at branches to get past them, the fear of a lost child pushing him onward.

"We need to get back to the day care, Levi. Come on. I'll play you a game of checkers. I'll bet I can beat you too. Are you up for it, big guy?" He could only imagine how scared that kid was right now.

Some protector he had turned out to be.

His eyes stung—whether from the search or the worry, he didn't know. Stopping a moment, he rubbed them. The woods grew eerily quiet. No snap of twigs beneath his boots. No wind blowing through trees. No rustle of chipmunks or ground squirrels. He couldn't even hear the other people searching for Levi. Not a sound stirred anywhere.

The silence was deafening.

"GRANDMA, TOBY JUST WON'T OBEY. It's not working. I can't do this." Christopher plopped down on the kitchen chair and smacked his palm against his forehead.

Charlotte could see this was quite serious. He was obviously having a midafternoon meltdown. She wiped her hands with a dishcloth and settled beside him at the table.

"It can't be all that bad, can it?" Sometimes it seemed she had just settled one problem, when another one surfaced. Thankfully, the farm seemed to be holding its own these days. Goodness knew she couldn't handle one more thing with these kids home for the summer.

He looked up at her with lackluster eyes that said he'd had enough. The show was over.

"I understand how you feel. I had a dog once when I was a kid, and I tried to teach him some tricks too. I wanted him to sit and bark for a treat. Tried everything to get that dog to do it. When it seemed he finally had it down, I gathered my family around to show them. Dumb dog wouldn't do it. I tried to coax him to perform for the family, but he just sat there until one by one, the family members left the room. When everyone was gone but me, he sat back on his haunches and barked." She laughed with the memory.

Christopher looked at her as though he couldn't believe failure had touched his grandmother's life.

"What did you do?" he asked.

"My mother said she didn't raise any quitters. I had to keep at it until I could get our dog to perform the trick for the family. I did. And he did. We had quite a celebration when he finally performed for everyone."

"At least he finally did it," Christopher said.

"But it was only after I kept at it. If Toby messes up because she's distracted it's one thing. If she doesn't perform because you haven't done your job, that's another matter. When you do your job and do it well, the rewards will come."

For a moment, Christopher sat in silence and studied his fingers. Charlotte wasn't at all sure her little speech had encouraged him in the least. But finally he looked up at her with fresh determination in his eyes and said, "I'll do it."

She smiled after him. Once he went back outside, Charlotte grabbed her straw hat and ventured outside to the garden. With a sweeping look at her treasured plot of ground, she decided things were shaping up nicely. More tiny green plants had poked through the kneaded sod, standing firm with potential, rewarding Charlotte's and Emily's hard work. Each morning, Emily hoed the soil between the rows of beans, carrots, tomatoes, and squash. Charlotte smiled. She knew Emily didn't enjoy the work all that much, but Charlotte hoped her granddaughter would eventually learn to appreciate it. Time would tell.

Charlotte bent over, pulled a weed, and then straightened her stiff back. There was something about tilling the fields and providing for her family that made her feel a kinship with the woman of the Bible, the one described in Proverbs 31 who worked hard to provide for her family.

She turned and pushed up her hat to survey the never-ending sky. The sun had scrubbed the sky clean before starting its afternoon descent.

Gathering her gardening tools, she decided the summer seemed to be shaping up well after all. It took her a bit to get used to life with the kids home all the time, but they had finally settled into a routine that appeared to work for them. While her mind rambled, she put her tools away and settled on the front porch.

Sam certainly didn't enjoy his work in the chicken coop, but then it wasn't supposed to be pleasant. It was a punishment. She hoped that boy would learn responsibility. He would be out on his own one day soon, and she hoped he'd be ready. Her own boys had been more settled at that age—or so she thought. Mental cobwebs had formed over the years, clouding her memories, so she couldn't be sure.

A car engine hummed its approach, causing Charlotte to look up and see Bill. By the look on his face when he climbed out of the car, she wondered if the day was taking a nosedive.

"Good afternoon," she said pleasantly. "What brings you here today?"

He let out a long sigh. "Another meeting."

Her motherly radar was up. He needed some TLC, no doubt about it. "How about you lead the way to the kitchen and I'll get you something to drink."

"Thanks."

His shoulders drooped and his feet lagged with every

step. Charlotte lifted a quick prayer for wisdom. Once she had brought Bill a cold glass of lemonade, she mulled over how to approach what was bothering him. Surely he would mention the problem with his partner.

He glanced around the yard. "This place always calms me."

There was the open door. She'd step through it while she had the chance. "Oh? Rough meeting?"

He raked his fingers through his hair. "It's not the meeting." He seemed to be about to open up and then seemed to think better of it. He shrugged.

Charlotte sipped her lemonade, wondering what to say next. She would wait. Give him a moment to calm down, drink in the comfort of the farm before she said anything.

"Anna wants to do so much to the house for the baby. I just have too much going on to deal with that right now."

Charlotte knew it was much more than that, but she held her tongue. If he wanted her to know their financial business, he'd say so.

"Have you talked to her?"

"I've tried to. She just doesn't get it. All she can think about is the baby and moving this wall, tearing out that carpet . . ." His voice rose with every word. ". . . painting this or that. It never ends. She's never satisfied. Money, always spending money."

Surprised eyes met hers. He hadn't meant to say that. She could see it on his face.

"Bill, there's more going on here than you're saying, isn't there?"

He blew out a long breath and then stared at the calluses

on his fingers. "One of our partners backed out of the development deal."

There. He'd said it.

"Oh."

"I don't know what we're going to do." He pushed back from the table and started to pace.

"Can't you get someone else?" She wanted to be able to step up and help him, but Bob was right. She couldn't interfere—especially, when he didn't ask for help.

"Not just anybody has that kind of money."

"That's true. But people get through hard times, Bill. So you might have to tighten your belts for a while, but you'll get through it. You'll manage better than you think."

He stopped and looked her full in the face. "Tell Anna that."

"I know Anna likes nice things, Bill, but if you don't have the money, you just don't have the money. She'll soon learn how to make do."

He slumped back in his chair. "I guess you're right." He looked as though the fight had gone out of him. "Not much I can do about it anyway."

She didn't know if he was resigning himself to the situation or was just too weary to care.

"I know this sounds trite, son, but have you prayed about it?"

"I've done little else."

"Then you know you'll get through it. We're never alone, remember?"

He took a deep breath and then blew it out. "I remember." His breathing slowly returned to normal.

She reached over and squeezed his hand. "We'll be praying for you."

"Thanks, Mom. I need it." He hesitated. "Is Dad around?"

"He and Pete went to the hardware store. They're always finding something that they need to get. I think it's just an excuse to get away and talk with the guys. You could go join them."

He shook his head. "Haven't got the time. I've got to get back to town."

Charlotte couldn't help feeling there was so much more he wanted to say.

"Thanks for the lemonade, Mom."

She tried to calm the concern that fringed her heart. "Things will turn out all right, Bill. You'll see."

He turned to her with a smile. "Yeah, I'm sure you're right." He bent over and dropped a kiss on her head. "Love you." With that he walked off—a little brighter, a little taller, but still in a bit of a slump—and got in his car.

A prayer was on her lips before he pulled out of the driveway.

Chapter Twenty-Three

"Grandma, this is Sam."

The shaky sound of his voice sent a shiver through Charlotte. "What's wrong?"

"One of the kids from the day care is missing. I was in charge of his class when we realized he was gone."

Her hand flew to her mouth in an effort to muffle the gasp. Fear sparked and burned across her chest like wildfire. A million admonitions swirled in her head, but now was not the time. He needed her support.

Before she could respond, he stumbled on with what had happened and how they were all searching and the police had been called in—everything. The more he talked, the more a sickening acid burned its way from her stomach to her throat.

"We'll come over there."

"No, no. Please, Grandma. I just wanted to let you know what was going on before you heard it from someone else." The childlike vulnerability in his voice caused a squeeze in her chest.

"I will pray, Sam. Call us the minute you hear something."

"Okay." Defeat lined the word. "Thanks, Grandma." The phone went silent.

Charlotte slipped off the sofa and onto bended knees. In the quiet of the family room, she pleaded for the child's safety and for Sam's peace. The longer she prayed, the more the fear in her own chest eased. By the time she had finished, she had wiped the tears from her eyes and remembered anew that God was in control and he would get them through this.

SAM SCOURED THE WOODS until his legs hurt. Slivers of sunlight poked through treetops, but they didn't dispel the gloom that nearly choked off his air supply. "Levi," he called out time and again until his voice felt scratchy and raw.

What would he do if they didn't find this kid? He was responsible. If anything happened to that little boy, he would never forgive himself. He should have recounted the kids once they returned to the classroom.

He spotted a log and stumbled down onto it. Tears burned his eyes. He wasn't one for crying. That was for sissies. A lump swelled in his throat, and he swallowed hard.

"Please, God, help us find him." The balls of his hands blotted the tears, refusing to allow more to fall. He would find Levi. He had to.

Shoving himself off the log, he continued his search. In the distance, others called out Levi's name. Finally he stepped into the clearing and saw Arielle. The look in her eyes, one of deep pity, shamed him. If only he could start the day over; he would do anything to turn back the hands of time.

In a tender gesture, she reached for his arm. "We'd better go back to the day care and see if he's turned up."

He knew she was right, but it scared him to think of leaving the woods while Levi might still be there. After checking the day care, he'd come back to the woods. He would not give up, would not sleep, until Levi was found.

Their footfall on the path was the only sound between them as they made their trek back to the school. No words could make him feel better. Nothing could help ease his guilt, his fear. To make matters worse, when they got there, a police car pulled up to the premises. Two uniformed officers climbed out of the car.

If they didn't find Levi, would he go to jail? He couldn't blame them if they shoved him in a cell and threw away the key.

Arielle, no doubt sensing his agony, grabbed his arm till he turned and looked straight into her unblinking eyes. "It's going to be all right, Sam."

He didn't trust himself to respond. He merely nodded, and they walked on. By the time they reached the police officers, the director and a couple of the teachers had crowded around them, answering questions about the missing student.

"Do the parents know yet?" one of the officers asked.

The director said, "Yes, they're on their way."

Hot bile climbed Sam's throat. He'd have to face the parents. Have to let them know that he was the one who had lost their son.

Just as the police officer turned to Sam for questioning, a voice called to them, causing everyone to turn around. "Is this the kid you're looking for?" Albert, the maintenance man, stood in the doorway. Five-year-old Levi stood beside him, rumpled, droopy, and sleepy-eyed, his mouth forming into an enormous yawn.

An overwhelming wave of relief swept over Sam. He'd never been so happy to see a little kid in all his life. His head dropped forward. "Thanks," he whispered.

Everyone was full of questions, coming at the sleepy-eyed child like Hollywood paparazzi, and by the time they got the entire story, it appeared that Levi had taken another boy's toy and hid out in the supply closet to play with it. While he was in there, he got tired and fell asleep. Albert woke him up when he went into the closet to pull out a broom.

Once the frenzy died down, Sam tried to regain his equilibrium. He knew the discipline would be coming. No doubt he would lose yet another job—which was sure to upset his grandpa. He also knew he deserved everything they would dish out. He would take it. All of it. What the day care handed him and what Grandpa and Grandma handed him. In fact, he would feel better once they gave it to him good.

HER GRANDMA WAS ON THE TELEPHONE, so Emily went outside to check on the garden. Not that she cared, but knowing her mom had enjoyed gardening made Emily want to do a good job. Still, she didn't want her grandma to see her. No need to make her think she actually enjoyed the work. Her grandma might make her keep at it or something.

Emily plucked some weeds here and there. Funny how they seemed to grow faster than the plants. The sun warmed her back as she walked along, inspecting everything.

"Well, look at you," she said, bending over to get a closer look at some new growth on a green-bean plant. A tiny thrill shimmied through her, surprising her. How silly; it was just a leaf. No big deal. A couple of rows down, she saw another new leaf.

Her thoughts drifted to pioneer women. Life had to be hard back then. Her mom's words of "from the earth to the table" came back to her. She guessed that might be satisfying—if there were no grocery store around.

The more she strolled through the garden rows, the more it amazed her to see the tiny plants sprouting through the soil and reaching toward the warmth of the sun. Even she had to admit that was kind of cool.

"They found him." Her grandma's voice caused Emily to turn around.

"The little boy? They found him?"

Holding her hand to her chest, Grandma nodded.

"That's great news." Emily brushed the dirt from her hands. She was really learning about this prayer thing. She had offered a prayer of her own when she learned about the missing child. Could it be that God had heard her too? "I'm sure Sam's relieved."

"He certainly is. I could hear it in his voice."

Emily stared at the ground. "Poor Sam. That had to be hard."

"He's been through a lot. I'm just thankful it all turned out all right."

"Yeah, me too."

"Your garden is looking good," Grandma said.

My garden?

"You have a knack for it. Just like your mom."

Another shiver, a pleasant one that Emily couldn't deny. "Thanks."

Grandma smiled. "Well, just wanted to give you the good news. There's lemonade in the fridge when you're ready for a break." Grandma turned and walked back to the house.

Emily bent over and pulled the last remaining weeds. Tiny insects scurried across the lumpy soil, giving her the willies, but she found a soft spot inside herself for the baby leaves, and that feeling pushed her to keep going. They depended on her.

She spotted a bloom on a tomato plant. "Wow, that's cool." Her fingers brushed lightly against the new leaves on the plant. Of course, she couldn't take the credit. Grandma had planted everything and had done most of the work up to now. But she wondered if her efforts in the past couple of days had anything to do with the new growth. That idea made her feel sort of good.

Picking up the hoe, she lightly worked the ground between the rows. A fly buzzed around her, and she swatted it away. Emily imagined her mom hoeing the garden as a teenager. Standing there, Emily could almost sense her mother working alongside her. Silly, she knew, but the thought comforted her.

It was funny that her mom hadn't talked about Grandma and Grandpa much. When Emily had asked her about them, she usually said it was too hard to get there for a visit. Yet, even as a young kid, Emily wondered if there was a problem between them.

Why did parents have so much trouble understanding teenagers? Her mom had been different, of course. Emily remembered great times with her. They had gone together shopping and then out for ice cream. Sometimes they went out for mochas. Her mom had taken the boys special places too.

"I miss you, Mom," she whispered while turning clods of dirt.

After hoeing, she picked up the water hose, hauled it over to the garden, and watered it. The one thing she had to admit she liked about the garden was the uninterrupted thinking time it offered. She could work the soil, watch over and protect the plants, and at the same time allow her mind to wander, working through frustrations while working her arms with the hoe.

"Since you didn't come in, I decided to bring this out to you." Grandma held a glass of lemonade in her hand.

Emily put the hose back in place and walked over to her grandma. "That looks great. Thanks." The cold drink tasted so good.

"I brought something else." Grandma handed her a picture.

Emily took it and looked at the photo. It was her mom as a teenager. Standing in the garden, her mother smiled, leaning her head against the hoe she had propped beside her. She was dressed in cute shorts, a matching top, and sneakers. Her hair was pulled up in a perky ponytail. It was uncanny how much Emily could see herself in her mom.

"Wow, we do look alike."

Grandma grinned. "Like I said. She would be proud of you, you know. It would thrill her to see you working in the garden." Grandma chuckled. "She hated bugs though. It took her awhile to work through that."

"Really? I hate them too," Emily confessed.

"They have sprays for the critters. But unfortunately, they're part of a garden's life. It really gets fun when the veggies start growing. When you see the results of your hard labor, it makes it all worthwhile."

So far that "fun" thing wasn't happening for her, but seeing the plants grow held the tiniest sliver of cool, to her way of thinking.

"Your mom even helped me can quarts of green beans and stewed tomatoes. You don't have to do that, but maybe you'd like to learn?"

That was exactly why Emily didn't want to show any enthusiasm whatsoever. It always led to more work. She shrugged.

Grandma smiled. "Well, we have time to think about that. In the meantime, you've done a good job today. Now you might want to go wash up. Ashley called. She'll likely have some plans for the two of you." Grandma smiled.

That surprised and delighted Emily. "Thanks, Grandma."

Emily went back to the house, thinking how she enjoyed hearing stories about her mom. The love she and her grandma shared for her mother seemed to bring the two of them together in unexpected ways. Suddenly, it became very important that Grandma and Grandpa like the lapghan she had made them for their anniversary.

WITH GREAT COURAGE, Sam shuffled over to the grateful couple embracing their son, Levi. He took a deep breath and gulped silently, praying he could get through this.

"Mr. and Mrs. Stryker?" His voice cracked, making him sound like a kid in puberty.

They turned.

"I'm so sorry for, well, for everything."

A look of compassion crossed Levi's mother's face, her arms still protectively around her son. "I'm just thankful he's all right."

"Yes, ma'am," Sam said. "Me too."

"I hope you've learned a lesson or two from this," her husband said, the look on his face not quite so compassionate.

Sam couldn't blame him. "Yes, sir." He turned to go when Mrs. Stryker's hand stopped him.

"It wasn't your fault, you know. It could have happened on anybody's watch." She shrugged. "Still, next time it might be a good idea to take frequent headcounts."

He swallowed hard and nodded.

One boulder out of the way. Now he shuffled over to the director, prepared to gather his things and bring his daycare career to an end. He should be happy about that, but he wasn't. He felt like a failure, and not only that, he realized he cared about these kids more than he had thought.

"Mrs. Wilkens?"

Her soft features were drawn tight. One day made her appear ten years older. She turned to him.

"Sam. We'll talk tomorrow. It's been a long afternoon for all of us."

"Yes, ma'am." He wondered why she didn't just get this ugliness over with. Why prolong it? He shuffled out of the room feeling every inch the failure but oh, so thankful that Levi was all right.

Chapter Twenty-Four

Though Levi was safe and sound, the first morning light brought little comfort to Sam. He had hardly slept a wink and was tired beyond his years. He was glad it was Thursday. One more day and then he'd have the weekend to catch up on sleep.

"You doing all right today, Sam?" Bob asked just after breakfast.

"I've been better."

"Before you leave, I want to talk to you," Bob said, pointing toward the door. "Let's sit on the porch."

Whatever his grandpa dished out, Sam knew he deserved it. He just wished he didn't have to face it already this morning.

They no sooner sat down on the porch than Grandpa began. "I know you've been through a lot. And your grandmother and I have been giving it some thought. I don't have to tell you the responsibility involved with watching over children."

Sam didn't like where this was going.

"Just as I don't need to remind you of the responsibility of flying an airplane. I don't mind you working at the airport, but I want you to put the lessons on hold for now. We'll discuss it again next year if you're still interested."

"Yes, sir." Sam didn't have the fight in him to argue. Though disappointment flooded through him, he understood his grandpa's concerns.

"You'll get through this. We all go through growing times. This is yours. Just make the most of it. That's the important thing. Learn from it and grow. Then it will be worth it."

Sam nodded, fighting against the knot in his throat.

"Well, that's all I wanted to say. You'd better get to the airport." Without another word, his grandpa got up and went into the house.

Once Sam arrived at the airport, he met Ed in the office. "Can I talk to you a second?" He wanted to speak his piece before he was tempted to go up in the plane.

"Sure. I need to tell the maintenance guy something; then I'll be back in the office."

"Thanks." Sam walked to Ed's office and slumped into the chair across from his desk. The room was sparsely furnished. Concrete floors, uncomfortable steel chairs, white walls. Unkempt, like a guy's room. Even the coffee was nothing to brag about—or so he had heard. He hadn't yet developed a taste for it. He'd tried some at a coffeehouse once since that was all the rage, but he couldn't get into it.

This place was nothing that would lure someone to linger, yet men came out here all the time to talk flying and just watch the planes go in and out. It seemed a sport all its own.

He was fidgeting with the corners of a flight magazine when Ed entered the room and slid into his chair.

"Okay, so what can I do for you? Don't tell me you're going to quit on me?"

"No, no, nothing like that." Sam took a deep breath and quickly explained what had happened at the day care.

"I see." Ed folded his hands in front of him and laid them on the desk. "So why are you telling me this, Sam?"

"Well, it's like this. I love flying, and I appreciate all you've been teaching me. But I'm going to have to quit my lessons for now."

"Oh?" Ed listened attentively.

Sam looked at his hands. "Because of everything that happened with the boy getting lost at the day care on my watch, my grandparents say I can't take flying lessons anymore." He looked up. "To be honest, I think they're right. But I can still work for you, if you want me, and we can talk about starting up lessons next year."

"I see." Ed rubbed his jaw. "Well, of course, I want you to stick around." He thought a moment. "In fact, I think it's a good thing, Sam. You'll get to know more and more about the airport, the business of flying, all that. You'll have a better handle on things before you get behind the instrument panel again. You could have a real future in it."

Sam brightened, thankful that Ed didn't think him a total loser. "Thanks."

"And as far as the whole flying thing, it won't hurt you to go up with me as simply a passenger once in a while—providing your grandparents approve."

Hope shot through Sam.

They settled upon a reasonable salary, though Sam would have been happy to help out voluntarily.

"Things are kind of slow today. I want you to go back home, rest a while before you have to go into the day care today. Take a little time off today and tomorrow."

Sam started to protest.

Ed held up his hand. "Don't argue with me. Things aren't that busy, and you've got those airplanes shining. Give yourself a break and take the time. I'll see you back here bright and early on Monday morning." Ed rose from his chair. "You're a good kid, Sam. Don't be too hard on yourself. Everyone makes mistakes. I'll bet it's one you never make again."

Sam nodded. He was sure of that. He stood and watched Ed walk out of the office. Then Sam headed toward his car.

One hurdle down, one to go.

"HOW COME YOU'RE NOT WORKING at the airport right now?" Emily asked. She adjusted her seat belt.

"Things were slow, so Ed let me come home early."

"That was nice. You going in to the day care this afternoon?"

"Yeah. They told me to come in a little later today."

"You worried?"

He shrugged. "It's my own fault. Guess I have to own up to it."

She'd never seen her brother acting so, well, grown up about things. "I'm sorry, Sam." Sometimes he drove her nuts, but she didn't like seeing him hurt this way. She wanted to make things better for him. "And I'm sorry you're stuck with cleaning the chicken coop."

He groaned. "Thanks for the reminder, monkey." He reached over and rumpled her hair.

"Hey, cut it out." She straightened her hair, and he laughed. That was Sam, always trying to cut the tension. "Have you gotten much done on the coop?"

"Haven't had time," Sam said. "Every time I tried to get out there to work, something pulled me away from it." He maneuvered the car in a right turn. "By the way, I thought you were going to hang out with Ashley today."

"Yeah, later. Ashley gets off from her work at the restaurant early this afternoon, so I asked Miss Middleton if I could come over for a visit while waiting on Ashley. I just wanted to check on her."

"That's nice." Sam drove the car to the curb in front of Miss Middleton's house. "Just remember, whatever you do, don't walk anywhere without letting Grandma know. She's picking you up, right?"

"Right. Thanks, Sam." She climbed out and turned to shut the door. Leaning in through the window, she said, "Good luck. At the day care, I mean."

He smiled. "Thanks, sis."

She watched him drive off and then made her way to Miss Middleton's door. She planned to go to the store and see if she could find some more crochet patterns. Ashley had told her about some cool patterns for flowers that they could put on the pockets of their jeans. Maybe she'd ask Miss Middleton if she knew how to make them. She might even be able to find some free patterns on the Internet. She'd be sure to check that out tonight when she got home.

At the front door, she knocked. No one answered. She

thought a moment. Miss Middleton had told her to come today, hadn't she? Yes, Emily decided, she had that right.

Another knock. Still no answer. Emily listened for movement, but heard nothing. Miss Middleton might be in the back of the house. She looked around to make sure no one was watching, and then lifted the welcome mat to retrieve the key Miss Middleton left under it for emergencies such as this.

Opening the door, she called out again. "Miss Middleton? It's Emily. I'm here to clean, if you still want me to."

Silence.

She stepped through the hallway and headed toward the living room. When she walked into the room, the sight caused fear to knot in her throat. There sat Miss Middleton crumpled in her rocking chair, her head drooped, a crochet hook between the fingers of her motionless hand.

Chapter Twenty-Five

Miss Middleton's neighbor had taken Emily to the hospital and Charlotte met her there. "Are you all right, Em?" Charlotte greeted her granddaughter with open arms in the sterile hallway of Bedford Medical Center. Behind them the elevator pinged the arrival of more visitors.

Thin arms wound about Charlotte's neck. Wet tears dampened her shoulders. Charlotte held her granddaughter close and tried to calm her trembling. She had no idea Emily's feelings for Miss Middleton went so deep.

A nasally voice over the intercom told a doctor to report to triage. Emily finally pulled away, revealing red, puffy eyes.

"I'm scared for her, Grandma."

Charlotte handed her a tissue to mop up the fresh tears. "I know, honey. But we haven't heard from the doctor yet. Let's not borrow trouble."

They left the sharp scents of antiseptic and ammonia behind as they walked into the waiting room, where fresh hot coffee streamed into a carafe.

They slid into the green, vinyl chairs and passed a couple of hours talking, stretching, reading magazines, and sighing. Finally, a man dressed in a white jacket with a stethoscope dangling from his neck stepped into view. "Family of Lydia Middleton," he called out.

Charlotte was surprised to see someone other than Dr. Carr, but suspected he was on vacation.

She and Emily stood up and went to meet the doctor.

"We're her friends. Miss Middleton has no living family," Charlotte said.

"Oh, I see. I'm Dr. Sloane. And you are?"

"Charlotte Stevenson. This is my granddaughter, Emily Slater. She works for Miss Middleton."

He flipped through the brown chart in his hand and shook his head. "I'm sorry, but she hasn't listed you as someone with access to her medical care. With the confidentiality laws in place, I'm unable to give you information on her condition."

Emily grabbed her grandma's arm and squeezed it lightly.

"Can't you tell us anything?" Charlotte pleaded.

"I'm afraid not." He turned to go.

"Is it life-threatening? Can you tell us that?"

He pondered her question. "You can go in and talk to her." The light tone of his voice and gentle expression in his eyes suggested perhaps things weren't as bleak as they feared.

"Thank you, Doctor."

He gave a curt nod and padded down the tiled hallway, which had been waxed to a glossy shine.

"I think she'll be all right, Emily."

Emily swallowed hard, but said nothing. They passed the nurses' station. One uniformed woman sat at a computer, inputting something from a chart. Another nurse talked on the phone to a patient's family member. Others slipped in and out of rooms checking vitals, dispensing medicine, adjusting IVs.

Charlotte and Emily stepped into Miss Middleton's room. Their friend lay pale and wrinkled beneath the stark white sheets. A speck of life flickered in her eyes when she saw them. A smile peeked from the corners of her mouth. An IV needle had punctured her arm, administering life-giving fluids. An abundance of medical tape held it in place. On the opposite side of her bed a heart monitor flashed lines and graphs upon a screen. Drips and bleeps whispered in the silence.

Her eyes blinked. "They tell me I'm gonna live," she said in a breathy voice, raising her hand toward Charlotte. A glint of orneriness shone in her cloudy eyes.

"We're glad to hear it," Charlotte said, walking over and lifting Lydia's hand into her own. She stroked it gently. "Do they know what's wrong?"

Miss Middleton nodded. "They think it was dehydration. Guess they're gonna make me drink more water." She shrugged. "I've never been much of a drinker." Another smile.

Emily's shoulders sagged with relief. She tenderly patted Miss Middleton's other hand. "I'm so glad you're all right."

"Looks like you won't get out of that cleaning job for a while."

Emily smiled. "I don't care about that. I just want you to be okay."

They talked a short while longer and then left Miss Middleton to get her rest.

"Sure you don't want me to take you to Ashley's now?" Charlotte asked.

"No thanks. I just want to go home."

Once they arrived home, Emily was unusually quiet; Charlotte's heart ached for her.

"Could I take Princess for a ride?"

Charlotte looked at her. "Sure, honey."

Emily turned to go.

"Em?"

"Yeah."

"You going to be okay?"

"Yeah." She just hoped she could say the same for Miss Middleton.

THANKFUL FOR THE REPRIEVE, Emily saddled and mounted Princess and headed down toward the creek. The afternoon sun beat down on her.

"Giddyup," Emily called, giving Princess a gentle nudge in her side. The filly kicked into a quick gallop. The wind dried the tears on her cheeks as Emily lifted her face heavenward, praying for Miss Middleton.

"I've just found a new friend, a special friend. Please don't take her too." She wanted to be respectful, but she was angry and scared, and in her mind, God was behind it all.

"Why do you take people away from us? We need them—I need them." She knew that sounded as though everything was all about her. She didn't mean it that way. Not really. Emily just felt so tired of being lonely, of hurting in the deep places of her heart.

The only sound she heard was the horse's hoofbeats beating rock hard against the ground. Hard. Just like life—so hard. She pushed Princess onward.

More tears flowed out of her than she thought possible. She and Princess covered miles of trails before her anger and tears were spent. She slowed her filly to a restful trot, speaking soothing words and promising a treat when they got back to the farm.

By the time she returned, Emily still didn't have the answers. She didn't know why her mom had to die, and she didn't know how long Miss Middleton would be with her. But she did know that for the first time in her life, she had truly prayed from the depths of her heart. And she believed God not only heard her, but was also there for her.

THE AFTERNOON AT THE DAY CARE had turned out better than Sam had thought it would. He had a meeting with the director and Levi's parents. They were much more understanding than he deserved. The director gave him a good talking to and let him get back to work. It appeared he would have kitchen duty for a couple of weeks, but at least he still had a job. That boggled his mind. He had been sure she would fire him. It was a lesson he'd learned well; that much he knew.

Now, as dusk settled over the farm, he was paying his just dues to society—well, to his grandparents, anyway. When he opened the door to the chicken coop, the stench almost knocked him over. He closed it, took a deep gulp of fresh air, and tried again.

To think his life had come to this.

He sprayed the roosts, walls, and nests for mites, and then padded the nests with straw. Disgruntled chickens protested with fowl language.

He had no room to complain. He deserved every bit of their squawking. His grandma was right. He had been irresponsible. The way he had handled Emily and then Levi was lame. He hadn't meant to mess up, but the truth was hanging out there, exposed and naked, for all to see.

No one else was more frustrated with him than he was with himself. How could he have been so stupid as to forget his sister, and even worse, not notice that a kid was missing? He should have kept count.

A cranky rooster made his attitude known, charging and pecking at Sam. "Oh, yeah? Get in line, buddy." Sam poked the broom at the rooster, which didn't so much as ruffle a feather on the testy bird. "You'd better back off, or we'll be finding you on our dinner plates."

That did the trick.

Hens puffed their feathers to twice their size as Sam stuffed the nests with more straw. The squawking, the scratching, the bits of oats and corn scrunching beneath his feet . . . Sam just wanted to run out of there and take a hot shower. He made great, long strokes across the floor with his broom.

The odor stung his nose and made his eyes water. This was punishment in its most horrific form, a memory he wouldn't forget soon enough.

In fact, he had no doubt this smell would haunt him for years to come.

THE BACK DOOR OPENED and closed. Sam soon appeared at the family room entrance. Everyone looked up. Christopher made a face as though Sam smelled, well, *fowl*. Before Charlotte could say anything, Emily nudged her little brother.

Sam ignored Christopher and looked at his grandparents. "I got a good start on the chicken coop. Now I'm going to take a shower."

There was no denying the audible sigh of relief that came from Christopher's side of the room.

"All right," Bob said.

Sam walked away. Charlotte and Bob shared a glance. Then Bob went back to his newspaper, and Charlotte returned to her embroidery.

Whipping her needle in and out of the material, Charlotte lifted a silent prayer for Sam. He'd been through so much lately. Maybe she should have told him to forget about the chicken coop.

She'd never liked being the heavy when it came to parenting, but as a farmer's wife, she'd grown used to it. Farmers were out in the field most daylight hours, leaving the wives to deal with much of the discipline—at least that had been the routine in their case. That's why she had felt like such a failure when Denise left home. It seemed to be all her fault. No matter what anyone said, she felt that way.

EMILY'S CLOSET DOORS SQUAWKED with protest as she opened them to look at the lapghan again, admiring the earthy tones of brown and tan, worked in a simple pattern.

She thought it would look nice draped across their sofa. Her first crochet project had turned out pretty cool, if she did say so herself. With a sigh of contentment, she closed the doors and plopped onto her bed.

She could have sewn something for her grandparents, but she wanted to do something different, unexpected. They would never expect a lapghan, for sure. That thought made her smile. She loved surprises. Who didn't? She hoped Sunday would be a good day for them. They deserved it.

True, sometimes they drove her crazy, but it wasn't exactly their fault that they had three kids to deal with now.

Her thoughts steered toward her mom. She glanced at her picture on the nightstand. Maybe with time her mom's image would become more and more vague, but Emily figured if Miss Middleton could remember all those things about her past, Emily could remember her mom. Perhaps she'd learn a thing or two about scrapbooking and make some pages with the pictures she had of her mom. One thing she knew: As long as they had stories and pictures, she and her brothers—and her grandparents—would keep her mom's memory alive.

She tugged her pillow free from beneath the covers and slid onto the floor, pulling the pillow close to her heart.

She hoped Miss Middleton would be all right. Ashley teased her about Miss Middleton becoming her new best friend, and Emily smiled with the thought. She had grown to like the old woman. There was something very different about her. Without Miss Middleton even saying so, Emily felt that her friend understood her like few did. After all, she'd had to move to a strange place, just like Emily. Only,

Miss Middleton wasn't even related to the people who took her in.

Miss Middleton had talked about the scent of homemade bread baking in the oven of her new home. How her mother's evenings were spent working on hand-stitched quilts that would one day adorn Miss Middleton's own bed, along with soft feather pillows.

Emily glanced around her room. Hadn't her grandma and grandpa made their home just as comfortable for Emily and her brothers? Grandma cooked like no one she'd ever known. She made the best desserts around—well, Grandma and her friend Hannah.

Miss Middleton had lost her sister, so she understood Emily's "down days" too. At least Emily still had her brothers.

She hugged her knees to her chest. Though she still missed her mom, she was becoming more thankful every day for her grandparents and their new life on the farm.

She lifted a silent prayer of thanks for Miss Middleton, that everything would be all right. Emily just wasn't up to losing anyone else in her life.

Chapter Twenty-Six

After dinner, everyone migrated toward the front porch. Christopher went out in the yard to wrestle with Toby.

"What did you say Dana was doing tonight, Pete?" Charlotte asked.

He scratched his jaw. "Aw, she's helping a neighbor make desserts for something or other."

Charlotte noted the disappointment on his face. "Not exactly the way you want to spend a Friday night."

"Yeah."

"At least it's nice out tonight," Emily said. "Glad it's not raining."

Charlotte chuckled. "Nebraska summers are a little different than California I guess?"

"Boy, I'll say," Sam joined in.

"They sure are." Emily's gaze took on a far-off look.

"Do you miss it terribly, kids?" The words had barely escaped her mouth before Charlotte wished she could take them back. She didn't want to lead her grandkids down a gloomy trail.

"Sometimes," Emily said wistfully. "But I'm getting kind of used to farm life." Charlotte and Bob shared a glance of thankfulness. Then they looked at Sam, who just shrugged.

"Hey, Grandma and Grandpa, watch this!" Christopher called out.

Everyone turned to him.

He walked Toby closer to the porch so they could hear his commands.

"This is called the drop-on-recall exercise," Christopher said in a very official voice.

He ordered Toby to sit; then Christopher walked to the opposite side, a distance away from Toby. After a moment, he said, "Toby, come."

Toby went running toward Christopher at a brisk trot. When Christopher gave the signal, Toby dropped into a lying-down position.

Everyone took a collective breath.

Christopher moved away and once again commanded, "Come."

Toby broke into a brisk trot, heading straight for Christopher. Charlotte could almost hear the brakes squeak when Toby came to a harsh stop just in front of her grandson. At the sight of another signal, Toby immediately assumed the heel position.

Everyone on the porch broke out in uproarious applause. Once the clapping died down, Bob was the first to speak.

"If I hadn't seen it myself, I never would have believed it."

Charlotte laughed and shook her head. "It's like I always said, there is potential hiding in that dog."

"Yes, and if Christopher hadn't worked like a dog himself, Toby would have kept it hidden," Pete said.

Charlotte glanced at Christopher, who was all rosy-cheeked and proud.

"You did an awesome job, little brother," Emily said.

"You sure did," Sam said.

"Well, you all can stay out here if you want to, but I'm going in to watch a little TV," Bob said, rising from his seat.

"Party pooper," Charlotte said.

Bob just nodded.

Once he went inside, Charlotte looked at the kids and whispered, "We all set for the walk-a-thon tomorrow?"

The kids grinned and nodded.

"You're bringing Grandpa over to the finish line, right Uncle Pete?" Sam asked.

Pete leaned in. "Yep. Got it all planned out. I'm keeping him busy for a while in the barn; then I'll take him over to the tractor supply to talk with the guys a little, and then off to a leisurely lunch. That should put us there right about finish time." He gave a crisp nod of his head and leaned back in his chair.

"Great. Sounds like we're all set," Charlotte said.

The kids gave eager nods.

"Oh, I forgot to tell you, Grandma. I called Miss Middleton. She said they're releasing her either tomorrow afternoon or Sunday. I offered to stay with her—I figured you'd let me," Emily quickly added. "But she said they told her she'd be fine alone. And since she has helpful neighbors, she thought she would be fine too. I'm so thankful."

"That's wonderful news."

"Yeah."

"So you gonna work for her all summer or what?" Pete asked.

"I hope so."

"Good money, huh?" he pressed.

"It's not about the money. She's my friend." She got up and walked into the house, leaving everyone behind her speechless.

"Did I say something wrong?" Pete asked.

"No, not at all. She's just very fond of Miss Middleton," Charlotte said, staring after her mysterious granddaughter.

CHARLOTTE ADJUSTED the sweatband on her forehead; the kids had made it for her to wear for the diabetes walk. They obviously believed one couldn't walk without it. She had her doubts.

She could feel her energy wearing down. It was Saturday, after all. This major walk after a full week was a lot to endure. Not only that but the morning had been filled with taking care of the critters, milking the cows, feeding the livestock, not to mention cooking for the family.

Charlotte rounded the bend toward the last mile of their six-mile walk, thankful the end was in sight. She was also thankful her back had behaved and she could join in the adventure.

"You kids do not have to stay with me," Charlotte said, huffing and puffing with every step. She prayed for enough breath to get her through to the end of the walk.

"We wanted Grandpa to see us cross the finish line together," Emily said. Ashley walked beside her and nodded in agreement.

"Yeah, plus we wanted to make sure you finished," Sam teased.

"I'll make it just fine, thank you." Charlotte tried to quiet her great gulps of air.

People gathered on front lawns, waving and cheering the walkers and runners onward. The event seemed to bring out a spirit of community with the townsfolk. Charlotte had to admit there was something very inspiring about it all. Even if she was on her last breath.

They came upon a refreshment station where water had been set out for the walkers. "I need to stop here," Charlotte said as she retrieved a bottle. Sam and Emily followed suit.

"You gonna be all right, Grandma?" Sam asked, a worry line furrowing his brow.

"I'll be fine. It's just a little farther than I'm used to. I've been working up to this, but I haven't walked this far before. Still, my back is holding up fine, so that's good." She wasn't about to mention that her heart was pounding like a bongo drum and her legs felt like lead. A mile to go and then she just might soak in a hot tub till Christmas.

Emily wiped the sweat from her brow and took a long swig from her water bottle. "Ready to get back at it?"

Charlotte nodded.

"Do you think Hannah and Frank are ever gonna catch up with us?" Emily asked, looking back for them.

"They'll come along. I think their goal wasn't to go fast but just to finish." Charlotte wanted to add that that was her goal too, but she decided against it. The kids wanted to walk with her. They didn't realize they were pushing her faster than she wanted to go. She wanted to make a memory with them. She just hoped it wasn't her last memory!

"Sam, did you call Uncle Pete yet?" Charlotte was gaining momentum.

"Yeah. He's on his way."

"Wonder what he told Grandpa," Emily said.

"I'm sure Pete came up with something." Charlotte twisted the cap back on her water bottle.

"Let's just hope Christopher didn't spoil anything. Sometimes he can be a blabbermouth," Emily said.

Charlotte shot her a look that said to be kind, but she didn't have the air capacity to give her granddaughter a talking to just now.

"I'm glad Christopher didn't try this walk. We'd have been hearing 'Are we there yet?' for the last five miles," Sam said.

Charlotte laughed. "You're probably right."

Sam and Emily chatted as they continued on their way while Charlotte kept her sights on the goal. Maybe by doing this, Bob would see how important his health was to all of them. She hoped, with their efforts, he would see the need to push himself a little more, not only for his own health, but out of his love for them.

Soon—though not soon enough to suit Charlotte—they rounded the bend to the last stretch of their journey. With tired and aching muscles, Charlotte pushed forward, praying all the while she had the strength to make it.

"There they are!" Emily said, pointing toward Pete's truck, which had just rolled up to the parking lot.

"Grandpa looks confused," Sam said with a laugh.

Charlotte had to admit he did indeed. She doubted if he even knew the town was having the diabetes walk today.

Other walkers crossed the finish line, got their cards stamped, and met greeters on the other side. Pete, Bob, and

Christopher all walked up to the sidelines just as Charlotte, Emily, and Sam inched within a couple of yards of the finish line. The moment they crossed, Pete whooped, hollered, and gave a whistle call loud enough to shake the corn from its husks.

They got their cards stamped, and then walked over to a smiling Bob. When they reached him, Charlotte could see he was deeply touched.

"You did this for me?" Bob asked in a near-whisper.

"We love you, Grandpa." Emily gave him a slight hug and then looked him full in the face. "We want you to be around for a long time."

Charlotte's heart clenched. Bob nodded.

"Yeah, Grandpa," Sam said, giving Bob a pat on the back.

The kids walked away, chattering with Christopher while the grown-ups looked on.

"You should feel all warm and fuzzy right about now," Pete said with a chuckle.

"I did until you said that." Bob and Charlotte laughed.

"I'll meet you back at the truck," Pete said.

Charlotte's heart finally returned to its normal rhythm now that her protesting legs had come to a much-needed standstill. Bob looked into her eyes. "I can't believe you did this for me. You just got over a bad back."

Charlotte shrugged. "The things we do for love, and all that." She smiled up to him.

"Forty-six years of it, right?"

She let out a contented sigh. He remembered. "Forty-six years."

"A quiet dinner out all right this year?"

"A quiet dinner out would be perfect," she said, meaning it. The big celebrations didn't matter to them. As long as they had each other, that was enough. She leaned into him and let him help her back to the truck.

AFTER CHURCH and a special anniversary lunch in Harding, compliments of the kids and grandkids, the family took their usual places out on the front porch.

Anna said to Bill, loud enough for all to hear, "Are you going to tell them?"

"Tell us what?" Bob asked.

Bill smiled. "I didn't want to interrupt your anniversary celebration with our news, but I'm about to burst."

Charlotte smiled and turned to Bob. "Didn't I tell you he looked extra happy today?"

Bob grinned and looked at Bill. "That she did."

"Well, as always, you were right, Mom. You know how stressed we were when the partner backed out of the housing development deal. I really wasn't sure we would find a way out."

"*You* were stressed," Anna corrected. "I knew it would work itself out."

Anna just refused to believe anything that didn't fit with her plans.

"Well, okay, *I* was upset. With our partner backing out, we were left in a bad way, to say the least." He turned to his brother. "Now, hold steady, Pete, but, well, we've found a new partner."

"Oh, here we go," Pete said with forced drama as he dropped back against his chair.

Bob ignored his younger son. "Can I ask who is it?"

"Silas Maynard."

Charlotte nearly choked on her tea. Her gaze flew to Pete, who kept his eyes fixed on the cherry tree that would soon feed the neighborhood bird population.

Pete had told her that Silas had come into money. Was it possible that Pete had mentioned the deal to Silas? It was a long shot, knowing how strongly he felt about preserving farmland, but still, she wondered.

"Cut me some slack, little brother. I needed this deal."

"Yeah, yeah, whatever." Pete lifted the hint of a teasing grin to soften his words, but everyone knew exactly how he felt about the matter.

Congratulations and warm hugs abounded.

"I can't tell you how relieved I am," Charlotte said.

"You and me both," Bill said with a chuckle.

"I never worried for a moment," Anna said, dabbing her brow with a tissue.

Everyone laughed. Anna looked perplexed and then joined in the fun.

"Sounds like just the party we're looking for," Hannah said with a smile as she and Frank strolled up the walk.

"Welcome, friends," Charlotte said.

"We figured what kind of neighbors would we be if we didn't come over and wish our best friends a happy anniversary," Frank said.

"And we thank you," Bob said with unusual cheerfulness. "Pull up a chair and sit with us a while."

Frank and Hannah had just settled in, and the porch group had barely solved the problems of the way they run farms today when Charlotte heard the screen door, spotted the grin on Christopher's face, and turned to see what was going on.

Out came Anna and Emily carrying a large sheet cake frosted with roses and scrawled with anniversary wishes while everyone sang "Happy Anniversary" to Bob and Charlotte. After the song, Charlotte took a moment to get her emotions in check.

"You kids shouldn't have done this. The meal was more than enough celebration."

"I should say so," Bob added, patting his ample belly.

Emily grinned. "You can blame Hannah," Emily said. "She was in on this. And she did most of the work. I only helped her with the decorating."

Charlotte looked at Hannah, who merely shrugged. "What are friends for?"

"Well, what are we waiting for? Let's dig into some of that cake," Bob said, already pushing himself up from his chair.

"No, Grandpa. You stay put. We're going to serve you out here," Emily said.

Charlotte wanted to remind Bob about his diabetes, but decided this wasn't the time. It couldn't hurt him to have just a little piece once in awhile. If only she could limit him to that.

Anna and Emily took the cake back into the house, and Dana joined them. In no time at all, the trio returned with dessert dishes filled with white cake and frosting along with ice-filled glasses and a pitcher of tea.

While everyone enjoyed their desserts, Emily walked over to Charlotte and Bob.

"Grandma, Grandpa, I have something for you."

The chatter instantly died down and everyone turned to her.

"This isn't perfect by any means, but Miss Middleton taught me how to crochet, so I made you something for your anniversary." Emily handed them a large silver bag.

"Thank you, Emily," Charlotte said, looking at her granddaughter with surprise. She knew Emily liked to sew, but she couldn't imagine what she might have created for them. Pulling the tissue out of the bag, Charlotte looked inside and gasped. Very carefully, as though it were the most fragile of gifts, Charlotte lifted out the beautiful earth-toned lapghan.

"It is absolutely gorgeous, Emily," Charlotte said with pure delight. She looked over at a beaming Emily and gave her a hard squeeze.

"It's mighty fine, Em. Mighty fine." Bob gave her a hug too.

"I can't believe you're a beginner and you made something so lovely, so soon," Charlotte said, admiring the design.

The others on the porch agreed.

"I've been wanting to learn how to crochet or knit, Emily. Will you teach me?" Dana asked.

"Sure. I still have a lot to learn, though. I only had to know a couple of stitches to crochet the lapghan. It was just a matter of working the same stitches over and over. I had fun doing it." She looked at her grandparents. "The trick was keeping it a secret when you kept coming in and cleaning my room."

Everyone chuckled.

"That's sure to keep us warm," Bob said.

"Oh, Emily, before I forget, Miss Middleton called the church this morning and left a message to thank everyone for praying for her. She's doing great and is back at home," Hannah said.

Emily's eyes sparkled. "That's awesome."

"She also said to tell you she's looking forward to you visiting her next week."

Emily grinned. "Thanks for telling me."

Christopher shuffled his feet. "I don't have any money. I was gonna save Toby's trick for you as a surprise." He looked down at his shoes, "But I couldn't wait."

The adults exchanged grins. "It was a very fine gift, Christopher. We are thrilled that you are sticking with Toby and not giving up on her."

"Thanks, Grandma."

Bob nodded in agreement.

Sam offered to wash and gas Charlotte's car and Bob's truck over the next month as his gift to them.

"Well, I'm absolutely speechless that you kids went to all this trouble. Really. Thank you so much," Charlotte said. Then she turned to Bob. "And it just so happens I have a little something for you. I'll be right back."

She went inside to pick up the wrapped DVDs she had bought him of *The Real McCoys*. She didn't care in the least if Bob hadn't gotten her anything. It was gift enough that she had his love. This anniversary had been special from start to finish. And because of the thought behind the kids' meaningful gifts, it was one she would always remember.

He ripped off the wrapping like a little kid and stared at the DVD titles with wide-eyed wonder. "*The Real McCoys*! How did you—? Where did you—?" He jumped up from his chair and swept Charlotte off her feet so fast she was sure they'd both keel over right then and there on the spot.

The kids laughed.

Bob shook the DVDs toward them. "Do you have any idea how much I loved this show as a kid?"

The shakes of their heads assured him they did not. Charlotte watched with amusement and a heart bursting all over again with love for this man.

"I had no idea you could get these on DVD," he said as he examined the back cover.

"Hard to believe they could put anything that old on DVD, isn't it?" Pete teased.

"You'll get there one of these days, young man," Charlotte said with her nose in the air.

Once the fun had died down, Bob turned to Charlotte. "There's only one thing left to do. You probably thought I'd forgotten, but I didn't. I have something for you too." Bob reached into his pocket, dug out a small package, and handed it to her.

She couldn't imagine what he might have gotten her that was so small. Tearing open the wrap, she saw a black velvet box. She tenderly opened the box and caught her breath. There, perched in the slit of the cushion, sat the grandmother's necklace she had spotted in town. A sterling silver chain was dotted with colorful stones for every one of her grandchildren's birthdays. Tears pooled in her eyes and slipped down her cheeks. Bob had never been so frivolous, and it touched her deeply that he would do this for her.

"Bob, it's beautiful. But you shouldn't have spent so much money." She threw her arms around him right in front of the kids, and he hugged her right back.

Everyone on the porch cheered.

"I love you," he whispered into her ear.

An overwhelming sense of love and gratitude curled through her.

"We'll add the next stone once Bill and Anna's baby gets here," Bob said.

After passing around the necklace for all to see, Bob placed it around Charlotte's neck. Her cheeks warmed from the excitement of it all.

Bob settled beside her on the porch swing, strong and steady. The brush of his arm against hers still made her sigh with thankfulness that they had this time together. With a sweeping glance toward her family, she was reminded anew of her many blessings.

Bill's girls and Christopher raced into the yard with Toby. Emily walked toward the barn with her cell phone glued to her ear. Sam sat alone, his thoughts appearing to take him to faraway places. Pete and Dana sat side by side on the steps, holding hands and sharing secrets.

Afternoon light shimmered in the summer sky, and all seemed right with Charlotte's world. For now. And that was enough. All she could ever do was take things one day at a time and trust God with every step.

LATER THAT EVENING, Charlotte caught Pete alone in the kitchen, snitching another sliver of cake.

"Something tells me you aren't as tough as you pretend," she said.

He turned to her, cake crumbs around his mouth. "I don't know what you're talking about." He brushed the crumbs from his face.

"Silas, the silent partner?" She raised an eyebrow.

Pete tried to feign innocence, but she wasn't buying it.

"Okay, we'll play it your way," she said. He was never good at fibbing. Charlotte walked over and gave her son a light kiss on the cheek. "You are a blessing, Pete. In case you ever wonder, we're very proud of you. See you in the morning." Charlotte turned and walked out with a smile on her face.

Charlotte and Bob had just retired to their bedroom when a knock sounded on the door. Charlotte went over to answer it.

The kids stood in the doorway. Bob walked over to them.

"Good night, Grandma and Grandpa." Sam, Emily, and Christopher reached in and gave them hugs.

Another round of "Thank you for the gifts," and sweet sentiments flowed between them. Then the kids walked a few steps down the hall, turned, and in unison said, "Gnily."

Charlotte felt Bob lean into her. The term obviously took him by surprise.

"Gnily, kids," she said.

"Gnily." Bob's voice was barely audible.

Once Charlotte closed their bedroom door, Bob looked at her, eyes watery. "Well, that one got to me," he said.

Charlotte patted his arm. "Me too."

He took a deep breath and walked over to his dresser. "Did you have a good anniversary, Charlotte?"

She turned to him. "The best." She fingered the chain and stones draping her neck. "And I absolutely love this necklace, Bob."

He smiled. "I'm glad. I hoped you would. You know I

can't wait to watch *The Real McCoys*. I never thought I'd get to relive those memories."

Charlotte carefully removed her necklace and returned it to its box. Then she unscrewed the lid of her cold cream jar. With short, snappy strokes, she rubbed the cream onto her face, and then wiped off the excess. "Emily did a great job on that lapghan."

"Yeah, she did." Bob emptied the contents of his pockets onto his dresser.

"All the kids were so thoughtful."

"Yeah."

Walking over to her side of the bed, she saw Bob unclip the pedometer from his belt and put it on top of his dresser. A gasp stuck in her throat. He turned around and shrugged.

"I figure if everyone else is going to go to all that trouble to keep me healthy, I'd better take some responsibility myself. After all, I can't expect the kids to be responsible if I'm not." He glanced down at the pedometer. "I've only worn it for a couple of hours, so there's not much on here." He gave a shy grin. "I'll have more tomorrow."

Charlotte walked up to him and placed her hands on his chest. "Have I told you, Bob Stevenson, that I love you?"

His eyes grazed the ceiling, "Maybe once or twice." He looked back at her and pulled her close. "I hope we get at least fifty more years together."

She snuggled her head against his shoulder. "Me too, Bob," she whispered. "Me too."

About the Author

Diann Hunt is the author of three novellas and fourteen novels. Her books have finaled in the Holt Medallion and American Christian Fiction Writers Book of the Year contests. Her novel *RV There Yet?* was a 2006 Women of Faith pick, and in 2007 her novel *Hot Tropics & Cold Feet* won the ACFW Book of the Year Award for the Lit category. Diann lives in Indiana with her husband of thirty-four years, where together they spoil their grandchildren ad nauseam.

Someone Cares

Guideposts knows there are hundreds of people who have greeting card ministries, just like Miss Middleton in *On the Right Path*. That's why we created *Someone Cares*, a unique greeting card program that delivers beautiful and inspirational cards right to your home. Each card features gorgeous artwork, an uplifting message, a carefully chosen Scripture verse, and a moving story that encourages you—and the person you send it to! Each shipment includes selections for all occasions, from birthday and anniversary cards to get well and thank-you cards. Greeting cards are the perfect way to remind the special people in your life how much you care!

To find out more about *Someone Cares*, call (800) 932-2145, or write to: Guideposts Customer Service, P.O. Box 5815, Harlan, Iowa 51593.

A Note from the Editors

We hope you enjoy Home to Heather Creek, created by Guideposts Books and Inspirational Media. In all of our books, magazines and outreach efforts, we aim to deliver inspiration and encouragement, help you grow in your faith, and celebrate God's love in every aspect of your daily life.

Thank you for making a difference with your purchase of this book, which helps fund our many outreach programs to the military, prisons, hospitals, nursing homes and schools. To learn more, visit GuidepostsFoundation.org.

We also maintain many useful and uplifting online resources. Visit Guideposts.org to read true stories of hope and inspiration, access Our Prayer network, sign up for free newsletters, join our Facebook community, and subscribe to our stimulating blogs.

To order your favorite Guideposts publication, go to ShopGuideposts.org, call (800) 932-2145 or write to Guideposts, PO Box 5815, Harlan, Iowa 51593.